Evergreen

Evergreen

DEVIN GREENLEE

This book is a work of fiction. Names, characters, places, and incidents are the product of the author's imagination or are used fictitiously. Any resemblance to actual events, locales, or persons, living or dead, is coincidental.

Entangled Publishing, LLC
644 Shrewsbury Commons Ave., STE 181
Shrewsbury, PA 17361
rights@entangledpublishing.com

Entangled Teen is an imprint of Entangled Publishing, LLC.

Visit our website at www.entangledpublishing.com.

Edited by Jen Bouvier
Cover design LJ Anderson, Mayhem Cover Creations
Cover images by Vizerskaya/Gettyimages, Leo Lintang/Gettyimages
Interior design by Toni Kerr

ISBN 978-1-64937-537-7
Ebook ISBN 978-1-64937-514-8

Manufactured in the United States of America

First Edition January 2024

10 9 8 7 6 5 4 3 2 1

entangled teen
an imprint of Entangled Publishing LLC

To my sister and my aunt—seasons come and go,
but love remains.

At Entangled, we want our readers to be well-informed. If you would like to know if this book contains any elements that might be of concern for you, please check the back of the book for details.

Chapter One

"So you'll probably need to get up a few hours earlier than normal," my mom rattles off as her strong hands move mindlessly through the water, suds running off tonight's dinner dishes. "I left an order sheet on the counter. I had a last-minute call for a wedding before we closed up tonight, and it needs to be filled by noon."

I take the pots and plates she hands me one by one, drying them off and trying not to think of another backbreaking day in the garden plots. "Oh good. Another blushing bride."

"Two blushing brides, actually," she corrects me. She purses her mouth out of the corner of my eye. "Please don't be upset."

"I'm not," I say, trying to reassure her. It's not successful. But "upset" isn't the right word for how I'm feeling. It's more like "defeated." Every day is the same. Wake up, coffee, work. Work a little more, work some more after that, and then keep working until the day is through. Come home, dinner with my mom, fall asleep. The next day?

Do it all again. It's been this way since I turned thirteen. Four. Long. Years. I guess that's nothing compared to the millennia I have ahead of me.

She turns off the water and looks up at me. My height's never stopped her from leveling with me. "I know you. Better than anyone. You're upset."

I hate it when she's right. I never show much emotion—and sarcasm is my neutral place—but somehow she has this X-ray vision that lets her see what's actually in my head. It's beyond annoying.

She sighs and puts her hand over mine, gently pressing it against the wooden counter. Our sun-worn hands are the exact same shade of golden tan. "Quill, if something's bothering you, you know you can talk to me about it." She shakes her head gently, and her mass of red curls ripples at the tops of her shoulders.

That's the thing—I have talked to her about it. A thousand and a half times, but the answer never changes. I want something more than working in my family's garden—albeit a magical one—day after day. Magic isn't all it's cracked up to be. It's kind of boring, to be honest—working around mystical plants all day. The novelty wears off.

I know the deal—it's a rite of passage. Every dryad's done it—my grandmothers, then my mother, then Laurel, and now it's my turn. If you can take care of it, you prove that you can take care of yourself. Fail, and… I don't actually know. No one's ever failed before. I suppose to my mom it means I'll never be strong enough to be away from the family.

The difference between me and my family before me, though, is that they all had powers. Mine haven't come in yet and may never come, though that's not something we ever really talk about. I think it's because my mom honestly doesn't know what to say, other than to be encouraging and insist my powers will come one day. But this might be one of the few things my mother doesn't actually know for certain. As much knowledge as she's gained over her hundreds of years on Earth, I'm the first male dryad ever born, and of a half-human, half-dryad relationship at that. I try not to think about how confusing it all is.

"I'm just tired, Mom," I say, shrugging and putting down the last plate on the rack. "I'm tired, I'm sore, and when I close my eyes, I swear the sheep turn into flowers. The family business has officially taken over my life."

She smirks and nods knowingly. "I remember those days. I was in your shoes once, and I had this exact conversation with your grandmother. It gets better. It's only temporary." She looks so young, I almost forget the ridiculous number of years older than me she is. The sentiment doesn't help.

I groan and flop onto one of the three tan sofas in the living room, soft and made for napping. The whole room is designed to feel warm and cozy. Four pots of Devil's Ivy, tendrils hanging from every inch of the ceiling. Two wooden bookshelves, filled to the brim with books of plants and potion recipes. Chocolate-brown walls framing the tall windows. So familiar and comfortable, but lately the walls of this apartment feel like they're closing in on me.

"Can't we just say I was a roaring success and you can send me to school now? You can even pick which one. It can be a boarding school. In Siberia. Indoor plumbing optional, I don't care." We've had the agreement forever, only without a set date: once I turn thirteen, I prove myself through my work in the garden, and I gain entry to the outside world and all it entails, including school. Now it's the beginning of what would be my senior year and, knowing it's my last chance, all I feel is pressure.

All I've known is the inside of the building my mother bought when she relocated me and my older sister, Laurel, to the small, sleepy town of Castleview. It was the perfect setup for a family of dryads trying to garden under the radar: the day-to-day flower shop on the ground floor, and the boundless magical garden our family tends to for eternity tucked behind a door in our private apartment, all under one roof and hidden from the public eye. She sectioned off the rest of the building into other units, even giving one to my sister. I'm supposed to get my own one day.

Magical creatures are completely hidden from the world, for our safety and for humans'. But every once in a while, one or two bend the rules. My mom, as careful as she is, has spent her life helping people. It's something that brings her joy, and she's tried to instill that in her children. She's done so much good and brought so much joy, and she has every intention of keeping that up—which is the main reason she hasn't just hidden us away in the forest somewhere.

I stare at my mother expectantly for an answer, but all she does is nod with patience and that same love in her forest-green eyes that she always has when she looks at me. "Tempting. But seeing as how you're already so pleasant here, I can't imagine you'd be much of a people person in a place like that."

"You'll never know unless you give me the chance," I say hopefully, with an honest smile on my face.

She lets out a small laugh and puts her hands on her hips, the russet dress draped over her curves swishing along the ground. "They'd beg for a list of my demands and ask what they did to offend me."

"Okay fine, no school. Let's start small. The mall?"

"There aren't any malls in town, love," she says, shaking her head.

No matter what I say, there's always a reason for her to say no. It never changes. I lose my patience as my face goes flat. "Fine, then. Walmart."

She sighs again, sympathy filling her heart-shaped face. "Sweetheart, it's on my mind. I promise. Not yet, though. There's so much I need to teach you, and I need to socialize you and… If you give it—"

"A little more time. I know, I know." I turn away from the counter and head to my room.

"I love you!" she calls down the hall after me.

"You too," I say quietly before closing my door.

I don't know what I expected. I mash it all down and do my best not to be too upset. Feelings are overrated, anyway.

Maybe rinsing will make me feel better—get my mind away from things. Walking into my room and stripping away my clothes, I can't help but still feel frustrated about the conversation with my mom. She never budges.

My shower hisses as I turn it on, and I stop to look at myself in the mirror. All this hard labor's transformed me over the last few years—my skin has a golden glow and my lean muscles have kept up with all my growth spurts.

I don't know what my mom's so worried about.

I look like any other normal teenage boy. Well, I guess there's one exception.

My eyes may be the exact shade of a rainforest, but my hair matches them exactly—leaf green. I mean, it's not totally weird… Ugh, who am I kidding? No wonder she doesn't think I'll fit in.

I'm never getting out of here.

Chapter Two

Boom.

The thunder outside rips the summer sky open, while the wind struggles to tear the rusty fire escape off the side of my building. To most people it would be a nightmare, but the sounds are doing nothing but enhancing my best dreams. That fire escape is my favorite place in the world—my only connection to the outside when no one's around. Just hearing it is a comfort.

It's the perfect lullaby—that moment before the rain blesses everything it touches. The scent of the storm creeps into my room, paired with the strobes of lightning and thunder in the distance that still manage to make my room shake. It puts me at ease, except something is starting to feel…wrong.

There's a presence. It doesn't belong—and it wants something.

I do my best to block out both the world and the feeling, but my window slams shut and my eyes fly open.

A shadow is outside, looking in.

My blood runs cold as my lungs suck in a startled breath, and I'm frozen for a split second before I can decide what to do next. Do I run? Or do I fight?

I jump out of bed in the dim light and scoop up a weapon from against my nightstand—a rose branch as thick as a baseball bat, thorns still attached.

I never thought I'd have to use it, and I never wanted to. Whoever it is throws their hands up and backs away, almost falling off the edge of the scaffolding outside. I push the tall window open and step out into the electrically charged night.

"What are you doing here?" I shout at the figure, gripping the club on my shoulder. Honestly, it takes everything in me to stop my voice from shaking, but I'm still able to make the words come out sharp. I grip the handle as tight as I can. I hope I look more threatening than I feel.

"I live here!" The figure pulls down the hoodie he's wearing underneath his blue and yellow letterman jacket and puts his hands back up. His dark red hair flies in the wind as he takes two steps backward.

"Liar," I shoot back. "We've been the only ones here since we moved in!" *Sixteen years ago*, I add silently. Seriously? First he breaks in, and then he's careless enough to feed me a lie?

He freezes in place and I get a good look at him, and he's...my age and with fear in his eyes. He's a few inches taller and definitely more built than I am—he could easily overpower me if he wanted to, but then again, he isn't the one with a botanical mace.

I wring it in my palms again to steady myself, but the irritation is making it easy to stand my ground. He's trespassing in a place that's sacred to me.

"I swear, we just moved in," he says, pointing at the window along the wall and barely a few feet away from mine. It's coming from the empty—or so I thought—apartment next door. A dim light glows from inside, mixing with the surrounding darkness. The sky roars again above us, bolts of lightning flooding us with flashes of white. They highlight the freckles on his cheeks.

My eyes narrow; I'm not buying his story. Sure, it looks believable and he could be telling the truth, but there's no way my mom wouldn't have told me she rented out the empty unit to someone. That's a big deal.

For what it's worth, though, he seems more scared of me than I am of him.

I let my bat slide off my shoulder and thunk onto the metal beneath my feet. "Then what the hell were you doing outside my window?"

Chapter Three

A car speeds off through the alleyway below us, but my eyes stay on him. He puts his hands in his pockets. "I came out to get some air and saw it was open. I thought I'd be neighborly and shut it before the rain starts." He looks me up and down, a small grin crossing his face. All fear in his eyes is replaced with… What the hell is he looking at?

Wait.

I know exactly what he's looking at.

"Were you honestly gonna attack me in your underwear?" he asks as his thick eyebrows rise, tottering slightly. "At least let me buy you dinner first."

My face grows hot, but I force my voice to go cold. "No, but I can think of at least one place you can shove this bat, thorns and all."

The smile falls off his mouth and he rights himself, staring at me with a grimace. "Sorry, my bad. I do like your hair, though. Very…green." Suddenly he takes a huge breath in and sneezes, covering his mouth with his elbow.

I've had enough of this. I scoff and turn back to my room.

If I'm lucky I can get back to sleep quickly, but a sharp pain shoots through my foot as soon as I take my first step. I jump back and pull my foot up, lifting a rusty nail embedded deep inside the tissue.

"Son of a..." I say through gritted teeth, trying not to let loose a string of curses.

"Are you okay?" he asks, moving toward me.

I hold out my arm to stop him. I'm beyond frustrated at this point and would like to forget this ever happened. Right now I'd at least settle for only a few hours of uninterrupted sleep.

"Just stay on your fucking side," I snap. Blood trickles across my foot as I hobble back through my windowsill.

"I'm Liam," he yells after me. "Who are you?"

"Someone who likes his space," I shout without looking back at him. Hopefully he gets the hint. I yank the window shut behind me and twist the lock closed. The rose branch bat goes back to its dusty home.

I plop on my bed and wrench my foot up onto my knee.

Yup—straight through. Damn it.

This isn't the first time I've had an injury like this—punctures in my hand, slices on my legs and feet. Luckily dryads heal quickly, especially with a bit of botanical help.

I grab a clean-ish T-shirt from my floor and ready it before I slide the nail out, wincing. I may not be human, but it hurts all the same.

The little piece of metal clinks as it drops on my nightstand before I wrap the shirt around my foot. How do you get blood out of clothes again? Water? Vinegar? Bleach?

My best hope is one of my mom's potions can help

sterilize the wound and take away a little bit of the pain. We rarely get hurt—even rarer that we get sick—but this *is* a rare occasion. I throw on some clothes and limp down the dark hallway to the closet, mentally running through each vial she has in stock.

Red for headaches, green for nausea, white for burns, blue for sleep… She doesn't believe in Neosporin because she can do better, but for the life of me, I can't remember what her version is. I turn the corner, but I freeze as my skin prickles.

The door to the garden is open.

Chapter Four

Whatever fear I was feeling at the sight of someone outside my window? That terror is absolutely nothing compared to the thought of someone getting in here.

A massive forest stretches out through the frame—one I know like the back of my hand and one that's followed my family from house to house for generations.

Day or night, the magically enlarged ceiling and walls are obscured with clouds of deep blue and violet. Twinkling white lights beam through like spotlights, acting as tiny suns.

It's calling me inside—an escape from the real world where everything is okay. It wants me to drink from its streams and lie in its meadows, dissolving my cares and worries. The most peaceful place I know, but with this door open, I'm anything but at peace right now.

Someone was in here.

And I'd put money on who it was.

• • •

I rush through the threshold and shut the door behind me, limping along the cobblestone path that splits off to the different areas of the garden. My eyes fly across everything along the edge of the path.

I need to see what he did, broke, stole… Damn it.

This is so bad.

If I saw him on his way out, there's no telling what sort of damage he could have done in such a short time, but there's only one area that could be irreparable.

A whole new level of panic dawns on me before I beeline for the back.

There are plants in here that are beyond fragile and valuable—they're one of a kind and can't survive outside these walls. We rely on them, just like they rely on us. If one of them dies, we weaken. Some things can't be undone.

It's the longest two minutes of my life as I pass the orchard, rainbows of ever-ripe fruit lining the path. The sweet scents mix with the warm humid air, begging me to stop and take a bite. I can't slow down now.

I hang a right at the pond housing our fields of lotuses, pink and white and green painting the reflection as the blooms overflow on the banks. They look so calm, which somehow only heightens my tension. *How did he even know it was here? And how the hell did he get past me without waking me up?*

Left at the towering waterfall, crystal water shattering into mist on the rocks below.

The tiny droplets cling to my skin for a few more minutes down the path, absorbed by the time I take another few steps.

My mom is gonna fly off the handle if I can't cover this up. She's going to blame me. Humans are the last creatures allowed in here—they can't help but ruin everything they touch.

Our giant vegetable patch makes my next left, pumpkins the size of pickups obscuring my vision from what's around the bend. My head swings wildly from left to right and back again as I look for damage, for something amiss. So far so good, but who knows what I might find? Who knows what'll happen if he did something horrible to our paradise?

One more right turn down the rows and rows of herbs, high enough to swallow a horse up to its shoulders. Their mixture of scents assaults my nostrils, but my nose burning is the least of my problems.

I slip through the small paths between each species, finally arriving at the edge of the garden—hidden away as far as you can go.

My eyes glide around our rarest flowers and trees, all inside a grove created by my mother's magic. Tiny patches of light beam down from the stars above, serving as spotlights for each plot. Everything looks as it should, except for a dainty person with long, braided blond hair in front of a glass conservatory.

I let out a deep breath I've been holding for who knows how long at this point.

My heartbeat leaves my ears as a welcome relief seeps into my limbs.

"When did you get home?" I call, still walking on my heel as I get near her.

No intruders.

No thieves.

Just my sister, Laurel, forgetting to close the door.

She turns to me, fair-skinned and with her floor-length white gown rippling beneath her. She looks as stunning as ever, but she isn't as glad to see me as I am her. "Yesterday.

Quill, when was the last time you were in here?"

Weird question. I'm not quite sure I like where this is going. "I haven't been since this afternoon. Why?"

Her slight arm reaches out, pointing a finger at the lock on the conservatory—mangled and broken open in the most brutal way possible.

Shit. I definitely don't like where this is going.

"When did you find this?" I ask her, moving closer and running my hand over it.

It's not a normal lock—it's been shut with nearby vines resembling steel cables. A human couldn't get through these without blunt force. I couldn't even get through these without breaking them—my mom's the only one who could do it in a clean fashion. The worry is back with a vengeance.

"Maybe a half hour ago. I came back with some new seeds and thought Mom would have the fresh plot ready for me. The garden door was open and the lock to the conservatory was like this."

I shake my head and look at her. "Why didn't you wake me?"

She crosses her arms. "I thought whoever did this might still be inside the garden. I couldn't find anyone, though."

I clench my teeth and carefully consider telling her about what I just went through. I sigh. Might as well. "There was someone on my fire escape who woke me up. Our new neighbor."

Her eyebrows raise. "You think a human did this?"

There's no sugarcoating this, as unlikely as it may seem, so I try to be as serious as I can. "I don't know, but I woke up to him shutting my window."

Her emerald eyes go wide and her voice grows worried.

"Do you know what's behind these vines, Quill?"

Maybe serious wasn't the way to go. Maybe it isn't too late to downplay this? "I—no, I don't. But it can't be much worse than anything else we keep in here, can it?" She's probably overreacting. I may let all my clothes pile up in mountains on my bedroom floor, but the garden? Painstakingly studied and tended to, nonstop, for years. I've basically memorized every leaf and blade of grass. Mom never mentions what lives behind the conservatory door, and honestly, I've never really thought to ask. It was just one small area of the garden I never had to account for in my daily upkeep.

At least...I thought I didn't, up until now.

"It's probably the most prized and dangerous thing in this garden," Laurel says, eyes closed.

Knowing her, she's going through all the ways she thinks the world is going to end. Yes, this is bad. But I know her. I love her, even if she's dramatic. "Come on, Laurel. It can't be that bad."

Her eyebrows raise as she pauses. "How did you hurt your foot?"

I look down at it and tilt it to the side. It's gross—I'm starting to leave a trail. "Ugh. Sending that asshole back to his house."

Laurel nods. "Looks like you need a demonstration. Come on, then."

I follow her inside. A dull red glow hangs in the air inside as we walk through the threshold of the small conservatory inside the garden—almost like walking into a dream. Ominous, but calming. On the far side sits a single pedestal holding up another glass case—housing the most beautiful flower I've ever seen. Thin, curly crimson petals swaying back and forth within its confines. I step closer and note the bloodred berries growing where old blooms had once been.

"That's it?" I'm mesmerized, but still, unimpressed. I was expecting Charles Manson by the way she made it sound.

"The Azazel plant. Go get that kit in the corner," she says, pointing to a small wooden box near the door.

I grab it, return to set it on the pedestal, and see her remove the glass dome. The flower turns toward her, flowing, begging for her to get closer. It's unsettling. Sure, I see my mom and sister move plants all the time with a flick of their fingers, but this is the first time I've seen one move on its own. Laurel, however, is unsurprised. She plucks a single berry and returns the top.

I narrow my eyes. "So that's the big secret? A berry?"

"Not so easy." She grabs a small knife and scrapes off the black dots on the outside of the berry before draping a cloth over a vial and tying it off. She then pulls out a mortar and pestle from the box and crushes the bulb, draining the red juice from inside. "Step one—and the most important one—you can never use any seeds. Are we clear?"

"No seeds," I say. "Got it." Am I curious? Yes. But this is most likely another type of magic I don't have a grasp on, so I take it with a grain of salt.

"Good." She removes the cloth, returns the box of supplies to the corner, and ushers me outside the conservatory. "Step two." She walks around the corner and points down to a stalk the size of green onion, only stark black and white. "Do you know what that is?"

She's probably pulling some prank on me. "Phantom Root? You mean that actually does something?"

"It dulls magical effects, and in this case, makes consuming the berry safe. Mom said there are nasty side effects if you don't. She never told me what, but I'd rather not find out."

I nod. *Go figure.* Apparently, after all these years, there's stuff about the garden I don't even know.

"You should try to learn more about the plants back here," she says, basically reading my mind, as usual. "Potions aren't the only things that can come in handy in a pinch."

"Noted," I say, hurrying her along. "So what about the Phantom Root?"

"Hold this," she says, handing me the vial.

She uproots one Phantom, holds it flat above the mouth of the glass, and breaks it in half. Clear juice runs from either side and fills the container. She buries the empty stock in the garden, grabs the vial, and pulls a cork from her pocket. She shakes it for ten seconds, the liquid quickly turning magenta. She holds it out to me. "There you have it. A potion that can cure anything."

I roll the glass around in my fingers. "So…what do you want me to do with it?"

"Drink it."

I freeze and look her dead in the eye. "Seriously?"

"Seriously. Just a sip should do."

I sigh. *Why not?* "Bottoms up," I tell her with a deep breath and take a quick swig.

Sweet and tangy—*pineapple? Raspberry?* It's unlike any fruit I've ever tasted. Warmth grows in my stomach and spreads through my limbs, paired with a gentle tingling. I point and flex my foot, rolling it around, waiting for some hint of pain. But it's as good as new.

"How does it feel?" she asks.

"Better than ever," I say, paying way less attention to her at this point than my mystery injury. I take off the shirt and check it out—not even a pinprick left.

"Keep the rest for later. And not a single word of this to Mom," she says, eyes wide.

"I was about to say the same thing." This is all way above my pay grade. "So you think he broke in and tried to steal this? Is any of it missing?"

"The conservatory is the only thing that's damaged, so yeah. Whoever it was clearly had a plan. But it doesn't look like they took any of it. At least not this time," Laurel says as she closes the doors and flourishes her hand over the lock. The thick silver vines regrow and restore the mechanism, warping and sealing it tight.

I'm still not convinced they found something better along the way. Diamonds from the Midas Vine would have been way more useful for a human. Or Lotus Blooms for making suggestions? Perfect for makeshift mind control.

"Luckily any sprigs wouldn't survive outside the garden," she continues. "I swear I heard footsteps when I got here." She shakes her head. "If only I'd gotten here sooner. You honestly think it was him?"

"I'm pretty sure. I don't know who else it could have been. I've been home all day." I pause, remembering the sharp screech of wheels on pavement. "I did see a car speeding off, though, when I was talking to that guy."

She shakes her head and crosses her arms. "Pretty sure doesn't cut it. I mean, anything he took would die within a few hours without the garden's magic. But find out, be completely sure, and I'll help you handle it."

"What did you have in mind?"

"We'll figure something out," Laurel sighs and shakes her head. "But he could come back and do worse. If the garden is in danger, so is our magic."

"Yeah, tell me something I don't know."

She nods. "I came in here to plant some seeds, but I think I've had enough excitement for tonight. You'd better find out what's going on before Mom catches on. I mean, unless you want to be stuck in this house forever. She'll board it up with you still in it."

Operative word: you. *I* need to figure out what's going on. The worst part is I know every word she's saying is right. My stomach soaks up a thick dread as I think about my future—or lack thereof—if this all goes badly. I've spent seventeen long years away from people, but that's nothing compared to a thousand more.

Chapter Five

I wipe the sweat on my forehead with my forearm, or at least whatever my skin doesn't absorb right away. The magic may make the garden the perfect climate for the plants, but I still could use some air conditioning.

A dip in the stream might be nice, but I'm dead on my feet. My body is aching and my bed is calling. I've been working in the garden tirelessly all morning. It's exhausting, and I can feel it in my bones. The thought of a thief in my family's garden kept me up most of the night. All night, actually. Worry is a foreign feeling when your life is generally boring, which makes it worse when it takes hold. Suddenly I'd give anything for my biggest problem to be errant roots or skin sticky with pollen. The only thing I could do to keep myself from panicking was getting a head start on today's flower orders. And maybe I can keep my mom distracted if I'm extra on top of things.

But even as I think it, I know there will be no distracting her if something was stolen that puts us in jeopardy. Destroy a dryad's garden, you destroy their magic. And their ancestors. And their immortality.

So, no big deal, really.

I pick up my shirt from a nearby rock and dry off as much as possible before slipping it back on. The last of the morning's flower order barely fits in my wagon as I retrace my steps through the forest and back into our apartment.

One trip at a time, I take the stairwell next to my mom's room down to the back of her shop, which takes up the ground floor of our building. It ends at the back entrance of the walk-in cooler.

I pass her shelves of potions and concoctions—rows and rows of blue and red and yellow flasks, green and purple pastes, and white and orange powders. It's a kaleidoscope of natural cures for whatever you may need. No one can mix potions like my mom.

I set down my last armful of blooms on the cold stainless steel table, sorting them by pickup time in buckets arranged on the opposite wall.

Her soft voice travels through the wall, talking to a customer in the front of the shop. "Right, but the wedding planner told me…"

"I don't care what the wedding planner said, I'm telling you now that I need daisies."

"Daisies are beautiful, but they cause a huge amount of allergies. Covering the entire venue in them might make your guests…"

"I didn't ask your opinion, I came to make a purchase. Is that a problem?"

My eyes go wide as I stand alone in the back. Holy fuck, who talks to working people like that?

My mom's voice doesn't skip a beat. "Well, we already

have all the freesias you needed in the cooler…"

"Then send them back. Exchange them. Burn them. It doesn't matter what you do because that's not what I want anymore."

I press my hands to either side of my face and try not to scream. This is the order I've been working on all morning. I could strangle this woman right now. I could have slept in.

My mother is silent, most likely pacifying her with a few nods and a calm smile. "When do you need them by?"

The woman scoffs. "The wedding is still tomorrow, so what do you think?"

"Then we'll see you this afternoon."

I wait a few more seconds before I hear the bell on the front door jingle. "You can come out now," my mom calls. She can always tell when someone's around.

I slide the door open and poke my head out. "Yikes. Long day at the office?"

She turns toward the door with a warm smile reaching all the way up to her green eyes. My green eyes. "Another day in paradise," she says. "Don't stand in there all day. Come out before you catch a cold."

I chuckle as I walk through the threshold—I've been sick only once in my life, and it wasn't from some chilly air. I slide the door shut behind me and my eyes scan the room. I don't come into the front very often. The shop feels as homey as our house—wooden floor, wooden shelves, and glass cases lining the walls.

Not particularly tidy, but that's what gives it its soft appeal. Makes people comfortable here. Vines hang from the ceiling as a woodsy scent drifts through the air. If nature were more organized, a normal person would think the shop sprouted from the ground on its own.

"What was her problem?" I ask, sliding the glass shut behind me.

"Just a bride with the ideal wedding in mind," she says calmly, turning back to her ledger as she scribbles next to the register. "Nothing I haven't seen before."

I scoff and hop up to sit on the counter beside her. I'm already taller than her to begin with, but I tower over her up here. "She seemed kind of like an ass—"

"Language," she corrects me softly, holding out one finger without looking at me. Her wild red curls give a slight bounce. "She's only stressed, is all. I could sense a cramp or two, also."

"Doesn't give her the excuse to talk to you like that."

She looks at me with a patient gaze, a small smirk morphing on her full lips. "Most people are inherently good if you give them a chance."

I let my head fall back and stare at the ceiling. "Says the woman who keeps me as far away from them as possible," I say under my breath.

I know my mouth works faster than my brain sometimes, but even if I am bitter, that was harsh. As soon as the words leave my tongue, I regret them. And so do the plants in the shop—the leaves and petals lining the walls begin to droop and wilt.

Guilt runs through my spine for hurting the person who cares most about me. One of the few times I regret my quick mouth.

She sighs and puts her pen down, the loose sleeves of her shirt resting on the counter. "You know it's not safe for you to be on your own yet."

I close my eyes, wishing I could take back the words. "I know. I'm sorry, I'm just so tired."

"Didn't you get any sleep last night?" She walks over to

me and puts her hands on either side of my face, examining my eyes and skin.

Shit.

She's catching on already. I need to tell a half-truth. "No, the storm kept me up." I should stop there, but this may be the best chance to learn more. "And a few strange noises from next door. Did you rent it out?"

"I did, actually. A nice man with a nice son. Mr. Watson and his son, Liam," she says as she keeps inspecting. "They were probably only settling in. I'll have a talk with him."

"I mean, I could do it," I say quickly. The last thing I need is for her to find out he broke in last night. The further I keep her away from what happened last night, the closer I am to getting away from the garden.

Her curls bounce as she shakes her head, putting her hands on her hips. "Sweetheart, you know the rules."

"It's fine. I doubt he'll remember me anyway." I hop down from the counter to face her. She brushes back my hair, twisting a few locks in her fingers while giving me a knowing look. I'm cautiously hopeful this is another chance to change her mind. "I told you," I continue. "More and more people are picking wild hair colors. Everyone will just think I'm *edgy.*"

"Oh, you've got some edges all right," she says with a chuckle. She ruffles my hair and kisses my forehead. "My beautiful boy. Go back upstairs and take a nap. You could probably pop by the garden and grab some valerian root. It'll send you right off."

"Thanks, Mom." I see the plants perk up again as I turn to go inside the cooler again.

"Speaking of," she calls behind me. "Why didn't you grab some last night to begin with?"

I look at her with a blank face. Another half-truth. "I could have eaten the entire bushel and the storm still would have woken me up."

She grins. "Let's not test that theory."

I slip through the shop door and trudge up the two flights of stairs into the apartment. I shut the door behind me, thankful for two things—rest and a single last name. My fingers slip my phone out of my pocket and get to work searching for a Liam Watson.

After my share of middle-aged men from around the country, at last I find one article worth looking at: *Castleview High School Goes to State.*

"Got you," I say, pleased with myself.

I click on the link and immediately a swim team is looking back at me, his smiling face and wet red hair right in the center. Obviously he's a good student to be on a team, obviously he works well with others, and obviously he can pass a drug test. Who knows what he does when he's not in front of a camera or coach?

I need to know more, but I'm too exhausted to keep searching right now.

I save the thought for later and shuffle into my bathroom. The hot water in the shower blasts as I strip my dirty clothes off onto the floor. I can barely keep my eyes open, my limbs feel weak, and my skin feels tight and greasy. Disgusting.

As the streams careen across my skin, my mind drifts back to Liam.

He seems like a typical jock type—arrogant.

I don't even know him and he's already irritating me.

It's weird because my mom is generally a good judge of character. She said he was a nice boy. Maybe she's right, and maybe I'm wrong. It's not like I have much experience with people. But he was literally lurking right outside my window, for nature's sake. If she is wrong, it frustrates me that he of all people could slip past her radar.

I shut off the water and watch as the errant droplets sink into my pores—no towel needed. I guess I was thirstier than I thought. I forgot my water bottle this morning, but I'm already feeling worlds better.

The sunbeams shine through my tall windows, illuminating the canopy of leaves coating my ceiling. Trees growing along the walls, twisting into geometric patterns, and holding up my hundreds of books and knickknacks. Perks of my mom's magic—homegrown furniture.

I drop my dirty clothes back on the floor where I found them so early this morning, yank on some clean ones from my dresser, and collapse into my bed.

I bury myself in the pit of fabric, if only for a few hours.

Chapter Six

"Time to wake up," a chipper voice chimes out.

"Nooooooooo," I grumble, burying myself deeper into my bedding.

The hinges creak, and Laurel coaxes my door open. "Aren't you supposed to be productive?"

I scoff. "I'm still on summer vacation."

"You're homeschooled," she says with a laugh. I don't need to see her to know she's closing in on me.

"Even more of a reason for a vacation," I say, nodding slowly. I would give anything for more sleep right now. Maybe a fair share of sarcasm will tip her off that I'm irritated and get her to go away.

Turns out I'm wrong. The delicate weight of her body sinks into the side of the mattress. "Come on, Mom told me to come down and help. She said you looked terrible this morning. I think we both know why."

I roll my eyes, despite knowing she can't see them. "Be my guest."

"Alone? And get my new dress dirty? I don't think so."

Typical Laurel. Twenty-two and with her own apartment, but still acts sixteen when it comes to her looks.

"Couldn't she have made me a pick-me-up potion?"

"Couldn't you have made yourself a pick-me-up potion?"

I let out a dark laugh. "You know I probably would have ended up offing myself."

She pauses and puts her hand on the lump of blankets bunched over my shoulder. "Oh come on, Quill, don't be like that. You're getting better. You'll get the hang of it."

"Says the dryad prodigy." Seriously though, I'd like to feel defeated alone. I can't do magic. I can't make potions. I can't even keep strangers out of a secret garden hidden inside a locked second-floor apartment.

"The prodigy who wants to spend time with her little brother after a long trip away from home."

I throw the covers off me and scowl. "Fine."

"Attaboy." Her perfect teeth morph into a perfect smile as the sun glows on her perfectly straight gold hair. I'd hate her if I didn't love her so much. "On a more serious note, how goes the search into the guy next door?"

"Apparently he wears a Speedo on the weekends."

She sighs. "Somehow I don't think that's helpful. You might need to get more up close and personal."

I pause, trying to figure out if she's being serious or not. "You know Mom's rule about me talking to humans."

"Desperate times, Quill. It might scare him off if I do it. He knows you already." She simply shrugs.

I groan and fall back down. "Fine."

"I'll let you get dressed," she says and pats the bed twice. "Meet you in the garden in five. We have work to do."

• • •

What she actually means is me. *I* have work to do. She's there to pry.

I match Laurel's pace as we walk into the woods along the cobblestone, my sister flitting from one side of the path to the other to smell the flowers. The blooms burst open as soon as she comes near, begging her to be closer.

I resist the urge to roll my eyes. Show-off.

She smiles and exhales, turning her face up to the swirling ceiling, mimicking a vast galaxy. "I'll never get over how beautiful this place is."

"Only because you can take a break from it. Where were you off to this time?"

"India. You wouldn't *believe* the jungles there. And the cities! And the *food*! My mouth is watering just thinking about it."

"Yeah, yeah, don't rub it in," I say as we turn the corner at the sunflowers, easily the size of tires on a semitruck. My stomach grumbles and my mouth waters at the thought of a nice meal. I make a note to come back and chop one down for dinner tonight.

"Don't get me wrong," she says, holding out one manicured finger. "It was hard tracking down what we needed. It wasn't all fun and games."

"Oh, to see what you've seen," I say, maybe with a little too much sarcasm. "Any gentleman fans this time?"

"Who said they had to be gentlemen?" she says with a wink and a gentle flip of her hair. "And maybe. But you know the rules—goals first."

Her life, her choice. But as far as I'm concerned? I've never had a friend, much less a crush. All I have is work. Then again, is devoting your life to a garden much better?

She reaches into the top of her dress and pulls out a small baggie of seeds.

I sigh. "This family. A bunch of workaholics."

She stops, sighs, and puts her hand on my shoulder. "Quill, it's not work. It's our legacy."

"Joy. A lifetime of hoeing." Her eyes narrow as she shoots me a scowl. "I was talking about me and the garden."

She rolls her eyes and shakes her head. "Gifts or not, you're just as important. You know that. You've got to stay close only until it's safe."

And there it is. "So you *have* been talking to Mom."

She keeps going. "Quill, I know you're itching to get out into the world. It'll happen. I promise."

"Yeah, except no one knows when. You were growing roses in your room by the time you were two. Your hair finished turning when you were six."

"You're the first male dryad ever born. Things are bound to be…different."

"By different, you mean I'm a dryad dud." It's true. It would be cool to have powers, but I've accepted it.

"I never said that. I said *different*."

"Laurel, I'm a helpless creature with a scalp the color of broccoli. Except for a few things, I'm basically human. I wish she would just let me be normal." I try not to sound defeated, but I can't help but feel it.

I love the way I look, even if it worries my mom. I wonder what it would be like if she let up. Could I go to school? Would I fit in? Maybe find something I'm good at that doesn't involve dirt? Have friends?

"Trust her. Deep down you know she's right. Besides, look how I turned out."

That doesn't inspire much hope. I decide silence is the best option.

We walk deeper into the woods than I normally go, stranger and more obnoxious looking plants surrounding the path. It's not often I stray past the common species you would see in everyday gardening. Laurel keeps humming her favorite tunes as her steps echo, but my curiosity grows.

"So tell me more about this new addition," I say. "Must have been pretty important for you to go halfway around the globe."

Excitement grows in her eyes and voice. "Rumors were it was deep in the heart of the forest. A nice village boy insisted he show me the way, but we both know I can clear a path faster than anyone."

"I'll tell you what he wanted a clear path to," I say under my breath. A thick purple tree branch smacks me in the back of my head and I stumble forward. I look over at my sister as I rub the spot it popped, but all she's doing is walking straight forward, checking out the integrity of her nails.

"It's incredibly rare," she continues. "Couples who seek it rarely find it. Not all love is true—at least the kind the plant can sense."

"How did you even learn about it?"

"Legend goes a prince and his bride were presented the blossom on the night of their engagement. He expected it to produce a beautiful, glowing flower. But when nothing happened, the prince was furious. He ordered it to be burned. The princess insisted they keep such a rare plant, suggesting it hadn't fully grown. She had it brought back to her room.

"Later that night she got ready for bed, alone as usual, until her bodyguards came to check on her. As soon as they walked in, a flower with the look of white flame unfolded. She sent it away immediately.

"The next morning, the princess and one of her most trusted guards were gone. The flower was right—she never loved the prince. She had already found a soulmate."

"So what happened after that? Did they get away?"

Laurel chuckles. "Oh, absolutely not. The prince hunted them down and publicly executed them before finding a new wife. Lived unhappily ever after until he was captured, tortured, and overthrown. Not the greatest end to the story—probably why it isn't told often. The moral is true love never lies." At last we arrive at the empty plot that looks eerily similar to where we started. "Here we are."

We end at the same rare section we were in last night. I take a quick look over at the conservatory—good as new. You'd never know it was damaged.

She looks at the plants around the empty patch, twirling a lock of her hair, face deep in thought as she nods in approval. "Mom planned this pretty well. Right next to the Dragon's Hide. The Ardor Blossom does like it extra warm."

"Just make sure it's not too close," I say. "The leaves might singe it, and I'd like to avoid a wildfire."

Laurel rolls her eyes. "It's not my first time here, you know."

She gently shakes the bag, emptying the seeds into her opposite palm. She tucks the bag back into her pocket, shuts her eyes, and closes her hands as if the seeds will fly away.

I've seen her and Mom use their powers like this before, but I'm ready for her to show off a bit. Daisies are easy. The rare ones need a more delicate touch.

She gently drops to a polite kneel, brings her clamped hands to her mouth, and blows into the space between. A golden glow sparkles around her fingers before she opens the cup of her hands to reveal a liquid the color of the sun. She tips her fingers toward the soil and pours it out.

It twists and curls along the patch of dirt, dancing along the earth. It begins to slow down and she stands. The light from the tendrils it created burns brighter—hot white—until they flash, leaving a full-grown plant in its wake.

Plain. Lime green. Matte. Sickly looking, devoid of any flowers.

On one hand, it's hard to watch. I'd be lying if I said I wasn't jealous of my sister's gifts. On the other hand, it gives me such pride to be part of such a powerful family. Every time they do something like this, it fills me with awe. The flower on the other hand? Not so much.

"Um… Kind of disappointing."

Laurel sighs. "It'll always be disappointing. I doubt we'll ever see it bloom in here, but I'm sure Mom has plans for it."

I look at the plant and can't help but relate to it. Trapped in this garden, expected to turn into something you'll never be.

Sweet nature, here I am, comparing my life to a clump of leaves and vines. I've been doing this for too long. I have *got* to get away from this garden—no matter what it takes.

Chapter Seven

Midnight.

I haven't gotten around to confronting Liam yet and figuring out whether he was the garden thief, but he's still on my mind. How could he not be? Especially when sounds from a war movie are pumping into my room from next door—choppers, gunshots, and explosions. I'm praying everyone in the movie blows up quickly so he'll go to bed.

I toss and turn as I did the night before. I've already taken two valerian roots.

Is my body calm? Yes.

Is my brain? Anything but.

Before I know it, I find myself grinding my teeth in irritation as the muscles in my neck follow suit. I keep trying to crack my vertebrae, but the pop won't happen no matter what angle I take. *Ugh*.

I think of the look on my mom's face when I told her I wanted to speak to Liam. Definitely surprised I wanted to venture out into the building, but mostly disapproving.

I'm glad she didn't catch on that I was hiding something. She'd absolutely overreact.

I wish she'd ease up. I get that she's worried about exposure to humans, but I don't see what that has to do with me. I don't have any powers. I'm basically human, so shouldn't she just let me act like one?

I'm sick of being treated like I'm fragile. Like I'm less-than, or a project. I accepted I'm not like other dryads a long time ago. I wish my mom and sister could do the same.

My bed rocks with another explosion from next door. The leaves above me shuffle, a few drifting down through the moonlight streaming in through my windows. The shadows dance along the wall as they fall on my chest one by one.

"For the love of nature," I say as I chuck my pillow across the room and force myself to my feet. Mom's disapproval or not, I think it's time.

I pull my shirt over my head, yank up my shorts, and stomp through my house.

My mom is so lucky to fade out once the sun goes down. As calm as she always is, I'm sure all this noise would get on even her last nerve.

I throw my front door open and walk the whole ten necessary steps down the beige hallway. I don't go out here often—only upstairs to visit Laurel—but my irritation numbs my anxiety at the idea of seeing Liam again, face-to-face. Especially if he was the one who broke into the garden.

I bang my fist on the door three times. The war noises inside abruptly cut out, followed by heavy steps getting louder. I tap my foot on the thin carpet, wondering what's going to come out of my mouth this time. Sometimes I speak before I realize what I'm saying. Hopefully this time

I won't regret it.

The locks click, the chain slides, and the doorknob turns. Liam appears—wearing a tight white tank top and notably short gym shorts. He smiles at the sight of me, crosses his arms, and leans against the doorframe. Smug as ever. Only with fewer clothes.

"It's you again." The way his sculpted arms push up his chest is…distracting.

For some reason I'm stunned to see him wearing so little. My posture stiffens and my breath catches as a rush of adrenaline courses through my body. Luckily I've been practicing a poker face for seventeen years and I manage to catch my bearings after a second or two. "No ridiculous letterman jacket tonight?"

"You looked so comfortable last night, I stole your idea. Hope you don't mind." New scents are rolling off of him, too… Bergamot. Cassia.

A fluttering starts in my stomach, but I try to remember he's ruining a decent night's sleep. I narrow my eyes. "You could dress up in a prom gown for all I care. As long as you do it quietly. Some of us have to work in the morning."

"Oh? Where do you work?" As his head tips, his dark red hair falls to the side, right against his cheekbone.

Why does my throat feel tight? I clear it, followed by a quick, "None of your business." My eyes flit to the apartment behind him—completely dark, but I wonder if anyone else is in there with him. I don't want to give too much away to someone I can't even see.

He lifts one arm to prop up against the doorframe and puts the other on his hip. A thin trail of hair connects the bottom of his shirt and the top of his shorts, but my focus stays up at all costs. I clench my jaw and try to ignore how my palms are sweating.

"Oh come on, just a hint?" His face scrunches again like it did on the balcony and he lets out an enormous sneeze. Does he have a cold or something?

I stand there, quiet. Hints of tangerine and tomato leaf add to the mix in the air around us. I have so many questions I need to ask, but why are my words failing me?

"Let me guess." He sniffles, his eyes starting at the top of my head. "Punky appearance..." They go lower with an eyebrow raise. "In shape..." Lower still. "And rough hands and feet. Not to mention the top-notch people skills." His eyes come back to mine with a small smirk on his mouth. "Something with your hands? Behind the scenes? As far away from people as possible?"

I cross my arms and take a deep breath. There's that arrogance I was expecting from him. "If we're playing this game, you must be some all-star jock who's never worked a day in his life. Tell me, can you even spell your name? I'll give you a hint—I think it starts with an *L*."

To my surprise, he lets out a belly laugh. "You're a quick one, gotta give it to you."

I clench my hands for a split second, but relax them again. I'm honestly doing my best to not react right now. Is he still bothering me? Yes, but...less so. "I'm usually quicker when I get some sleep. Seriously. I'm exhausted, and you're the one I'm blaming."

"Don't worry, movie's almost done." He leans forward, notes of rose and pepper joining in. "My offer still stands if you want to see the rest."

I freeze, unsure what to do next. This is exactly what Laurel suggested—get a closer look. Except I didn't expect it to be this easy.

I narrow my eyes and give him a quick nod. "Fine."

"Really?" he asks, eyebrows going up in surprise. "Okay

then." He sidesteps to the edge of the doorframe and ushers me inside. "So what's your name? Since apparently I'm inviting a stranger into my house."

"Quill." I nod with the most pleasant smile I can muster. I'm more interested in what's inside. Maybe I can find evidence while I'm here.

It has to be him. I don't know how, but he has to know what we are. I have no doubt there was something in the garden he wanted—he wouldn't be the first human to steal from a dryad. And after they get what they want? They usually try to destroy the evidence. Burn it all down. Literally.

"Cool name. Nice to meet you, Quill." He walks past me into a kitchen identical to mine, except without the earthy charm. He flips open a thin cardboard box and lifts a greasy slice of pizza. "Want some? Best in town."

The putrid odor of sizzled fat and cheese makes my stomach and face clench in disgust. "No thanks. Vegan."

He lowers the slice and grimaces. "Well…the crust is pretty good?"

"I'll take your word for it." I cross my arms and walk around the living room, glancing at any possible clues. Clumps of berries in the shapes of gems? Purple flowers that smell like vanilla? None of my hunches are checking out. Nothing stolen from the garden, but who's to say they aren't hidden.

Not a whole lot out, now that I'm really looking—only boxes full of junk. Empty bookshelves. No photos, knickknacks, or even houseplants. "So where did you move from?"

"Just across town. My dad wanted to downsize." He takes another bite of his disgusting dinner.

I pause and listen throughout the apartment. Either

his dad's asleep or we're the only ones here. Judging by how loud that TV was, I'm guessing it's the second one.

"Where are your parents?" I ask.

He swallows and picks up a can of Coke. "Just me and my dad. He's out most nights for business."

I nod, still walking around as inconspicuously as I can. I know I shouldn't push too hard, but I'm listening as intently as I can to what he says—or doesn't say. Maybe I can catch him in a lie later. "What does he do?"

"Medical stuff," Liam says with a shrug. "It's boring."

Medical stuff. I'm sure humans would pay a fortune for a magical cure-all like the Azazel plant. "It's funny, you're the first people my mom's ever rented to. How did your dad convince her?"

"My dad's actually been coming to her a lot for remedies since I was little. He's a real homeopath. Your mom offered to help him a long time ago if we ever needed it, and I guess he felt like it was time to reach out."

Bingo. That explains how Liam would know about the garden. It must be him. I can't believe my mom didn't see this coming.

I have to get out of here. Now.

"You know, on second thought," I say, walking toward the door. "I'd better get back home."

A look of confusion crosses his face. "You sure? You just got here."

"Yeah, I work early," I say dismissively. "Besides, I'm sure you have a bunch of other people from the swim team you could call."

He pauses. "How did you know I was on the swim team?"

"Uh," I say, heart skipping a beat. I try coming up with a lie as quickly as I can. "Your letterman. I thought I saw something on it."

"Oh yeah. That." He shakes his head with a light smile.

Phew. He bought it.

"Surprisingly, no one wants to come out this far," he continues with a slight bitterness. "I guess twenty minutes is too long of a drive."

"I guess good luck changing their minds," I say, turning the knob. "Do me a favor and try to keep it down."

A grin crosses his face. "What's the magic word?"

I roll my eyes and look back at him. "Don't be a dick?"

He chuckles. "'Please' usually works, but fine. Only because you asked so nicely," he says with a wink.

I feign a chuckle and back my way out.

"See you soon," he calls after me, holding the door open as I walk down the hallway.

"Not if I can help it," I say under my breath.

I slam the door behind me, sweep back into my room, and collapse into my mound of pillows, adrenaline pumping.

The first thing I need to do in the morning is let Laurel know I was right.

Then we need to make a plan.

Chapter Eight

I pull out my phone and immediately text my sister. My heart is still pounding from my conversation with Liam, and I know deep down that I can't do this alone.

Me: I'm 97.6% sure he's the one who broke in

Laurel: What makes you say that?

Me: I went over there tonight. He's too suspicious. We need to do something

Laurel: Whoa, slow down. Do you have any proof?

Ugh, of course she's worried about proof. Isn't my gut good enough? Can't she just trust me on this one?

Me: Come on. He moves in and then the garden gets broken into. You don't think that's enough?

Laurel: It's fishy, but we need to know for sure before we do anything

I look at her text, shaking my head. I'm surprised she's being so cautious, considering what happened.

Me: Well that brings me to my next question. What do we do?

I really need to know if she has any idea, because I'm

at a complete loss. Telling my mom isn't an option, so we need to handle this ourselves.

She starts typing but stops. And then types again, but the bubble disappears. Finally, a text comes through.

Laurel: I think we could use a memory potion

Me: It sounds like he's known about us for a while. How far back does it go?

Laurel: Depends on how strong we make it

I roll my eyes and type back.

Me: Depends on how strong YOU make it. You know my potion-making skills are null and void. I'd turn his brain into a two-year-old's if I did it

Laurel: All the more reason we need to be absolutely sure. I've never made one so it's risky

I clench my jaw and type back, fingers tapping with extra force.

Me: I don't see the problem. I say we just do it and don't take the chance

Laurel: And I say no. Keep digging. Let me know when you have something concrete

Ugh. I slam my phone face down on the bed. I don't agree with her whatsoever, but I don't have another choice. All I can do is follow her gut.

From that point on, I accept that it has to be business as usual. Hopefully we have no more intruders, no more danger, and nothing standing in the way of my freedom. Then I can finish this test of being the main gardener, everyone's happy, and I can finally get out of here.

I stare at the purple lights glowing from behind the canopy above me, letting my eyes flutter closed and leaving nothing but a calm violet glow on my face. One minute becomes two. Two become five. Five become ten. All I hear is complete silence.

I close my eyes but I'm back to tossing and turning. Liam's words won't leave my mind.

The way his eyes crinkle when he smiles, the way his laugh echoed down the hallway, the light fuzz on his chest muscles… My stomach flutters once again and suddenly I'm ultra awake. *Ugh. Quill. Get a grip.*

It's a serenely clear summer night, and all I can hear are the tiniest sounds coming from the alleyway. But I can't get comfortable. I bury myself under my fortress of pillows—two under my head, one on top, one clutched to my chest, and one squeezed between my thighs. Dark, soft, safe…

The fire escape outside rattles under the weight of footsteps.

My eyes crack open.

My window creaks shut, closing with a small thud.

I risk a glance toward the window. Exactly like the other night, there's a shadow on the fire escape right outside my window. Fear strangles me as cold sweat covers me and my breath catches.

The figure stops to look at me, and it's…waving?

You've got to be kidding me.

I throw off the covers, swivel, and haul myself to my feet, growling in frustration. I stomp toward the glass and snatch up a dirty shirt and pair of shorts to cover up. With a quick push, I wrench the window open.

"What the *hell* do you think you're *doing*?"

Liam smiles at me. "Just being neighborly."

"Listen to me," I say through gritted teeth, pointing at him and walking toward him. "I've had it. I'm done with all of it." He's taking steps backward on the creaking walkway, but I'm cornering him. "Take a fucking hint. Stay. Out. Of. My. House."

He stops in his tracks and his face twists in confusion. "What are you talking about? I've never been inside your house."

"Bullshit." I'm so angry that my limbs are shaking. It's almost hard to keep my balance, but my vision is zeroed on to him. "I know you crawled through my window the other night and you tried to do it again now."

"Wait, you think I broke in?"

"Yeah, and you make a really shitty thief." It's taking all of my self-control to not scream at him.

He holds up his hands. "Quill, I hate to break it to you, but I'm not a criminal and your house reeks of flowers. I'm allergic. Honestly, I was closing your window because the smell keeps getting into mine. Except I didn't want to be rude the first time I met you."

I stop moving and narrow my eyes as my thoughts freeze. That's one thing I never expected. "You're allergic to flowers?"

"Horribly. My eyes were burning out of my skull. You would've heard me coughing and sneezing way before I could make it out of your room."

I pause. It doesn't make sense. The tension in my chest relaxes. "But if it wasn't you, who was—"

Suddenly the fire escape jolts, and my hands clutch the railing as it breaks off of the brick wall. An instantaneous jolt of panic rushes through my body as I grip the bar, holding on for dear life. Holy fuck, this cannot be happening right now. My feet slip from beneath me, falling to one knee as the metal digs into my leg. Pain shoots through my shin.

After all these years of wear and tear, this much weight

finally made it give way. The whole walkway swings to the side, throwing me to my knees. I scramble to get my balance, but my fear is making me flail.

I roll and slide to the edge where I climbed out of my room, holding on to anything I can get my hands on. I'm thinking as fast as I can for a way to save myself, but I can't process fast enough to make a plan. I'm just reacting as quickly as I can, breath catching in my throat. I get my grip on the metal right as I'm about to fall off the second story. The scaffolding halts, leaving me dangling above the ground.

"Quill! Are you okay?" Liam shouts. I can't see him, but I hear his footsteps edging toward me.

"I'm gonna fall!" My breath is rasping and I'm desperately looking for some way, any way, to get back up. Please dear nature, this can't be how it ends. I'm twenty feet off the ground with nothing but hard concrete below me. *Holy shit, I'm gonna fall and break my neck.*

He appears above me and reaches down. "Grab my hand!"

My sweaty hands are slipping. If I let go right now, I don't know if I can hang on. I don't even know if he's strong enough to pull me back up. My pulse is racing and my muscles are losing strength more and more by the second. I will fall if I don't at least try to reach for him. As soon as I let go to take hold of him, the bar holding me up breaks. He manages to catch my arm just in time.

"Hold on to me!" Liam says, gripping my hand as tight as he can.

My skin is stretching as it presses against his. His muscles feel like they're doing everything they can to pull me up, but he's shaking. I don't think he can do it. He's trying to save me, and it's gonna end up pulling us both over the edge.

I'm not worried for myself anymore—I'm worried for him. It doesn't last long, though. More screeching and cracking metal rings through the night. The railing he's clinging to comes unhinged, and we go flying toward the pavement, panels of steel tumbling after.

I hit the concrete feet first, a sharp pain flooding my right foot as I pitch forward. I fall on my stomach as Liam follows right after—my body breaking his fall—but the metal poles and plates finish up the free fall by pummeling us from above.

We lie there, steeped in shock and pain before catching our breaths. His body rolls off mine with a groan.

"Are you okay?" he asks, strained.

"I don't know." I turn over and look down, bloody gashes on my legs and my ankle already turning purple. *Fuck*. Hopefully he's not as battered as I am. "What about you?" I ask.

"I think so," he says. Relief washes over me as soon as the words leave his mouth, but my eyes jump to him to check. There's a slice on the side of his forehead, blood trickling down his neck and staining his shirt. He sits up and looks me over. "You don't look so good."

"Pretty sure I look better than you do." My throat tightens to see him covered in red and still trying to make jokes. It hurts to see him as beat up as he is.

He pushes himself to stand and looks down at me. "I have a first aid kit inside. Let's get you upstairs." He reaches his hand out. I grab it and try to pull myself up, accidentally putting weight on my bad foot. With a yelp I fall back down. I swear, I can feel my heartbeat in my ankle and it hurts more with every pulse.

"Do you need me to call 911?" he asks, holding me still.

I shake my head fervently. "No, don't. My mom would fly off the handle."

"I think she might already panic about your messed-up foot," he says. "If not that, she'll definitely have something to say about the pile of scrap metal that used to be her fire escape."

I close my eyes and clench my jaw, trying to suppress the pain. "Just take me inside. Please."

"If you say so." He bends down and fits his arms around my legs and back.

"What are you doing?" I ask, keeping a close eye on where he's putting his hands.

"Don't worry about it." With one quick motion, he scoops me up. If I didn't feel so awful, I'd say this wouldn't be so…bad.

"You're awfully nonchalant about this," I say through my wincing teeth and motioning to my leg. The second foot injury he's responsible for, and now he's carrying me. I'm starting to wonder if this was somehow his plan all along.

"I've seen worse," he says with a shrug and a confident assurance. "You're not even crying."

Ugh. My eyes go steely as I look him dead in the eye. "I don't cry."

"It's okay to have feelings, y'know," he says, quickly letting me go for a second and opening the door. He quickly picks me back up. "You should try it sometime."

I roll my eyes. "I have feelings, thanks. I'm hard to read."

"Looks like I'll have to learn," he says as we get to the stairs.

That's not something I expected him to say. My stomach does another flutter that's kept happening since

I met him.

We manage to get inside the door and up to the second floor, but as he goes toward his apartment, I realize there isn't much he'll be able to do. "Can you take me up to the third floor? My sister can help me."

"So your whole family lives in this building?"

I stare at him with a deadpan face. "You really want to discuss that right now?"

He cringes. "Right. Are you sure?"

"Positive." I nod and try to be as reassuring as possible.

He sighs. "If you say so."

We climb one more floor and go down the hallway to her door. He angles me down to stand on my good foot and turns to knock, but I stop him.

"I've got it," I say. "You can probably head back."

"I'm not leaving you alone."

He looks way worse than I do, and I know he needs to take care of himself. I soften my face and try to exude as much calm as I can. "Trust me. Please. I'll be fine."

"Okay then."

I prop myself up on her doorframe as he turns to go back down the stairwell.

"And Liam," I call after him. He turns to look me in the eye. "Thank you."

"You're welcome. Can I come by to check on you later?"

Again, I…didn't expect that. I blink a couple times before I can find the words. "Not the best idea. Go get yourself cleaned up." He nods once and disappears at the end of the hall with a small wave.

I watch him go. Honestly, in another situation, I might've said yes.

• • •

"Quill! What happened?" Laurel rushes out in her silver silk pajamas, hair braided into a tight bun, and angles herself under my arm and helps me hop inside.

"I fell," I say plainly. "I think something's wrong with my ankle."

She pokes her head out of her doorway and checks to make sure no one is around. With a flourish of her arm, the vines from her houseplants lengthen at an alarming rate. They snake toward me, sweep me off my feet, and cradle me.

Lifting me through the doorway, they fly me through her living room as they set me down on her gold couch.

"What do you mean you fell?" she asks as she sits on her coffee table to get a better look at me.

Half-truth. "That Liam kid showed up outside my window again. I went out to tell him to go back home," I say.

"I've been telling Mom to get that death trap looked at for years," she says.

Looks like she believed me—one fewer thing to worry about.

She pokes and prods for a few moments before letting out a worried sigh. "This is a terrible sprain," she says. "It's already almost black in most places, and the cuts are deep. I'm not sure what to do."

Damn it. This is worse than I thought. "There's nothing you can do?"

"I mean…I can think of one thing. Where's that potion I made for you?"

"Under my mattress," I say. "But are you sure I should use it again?"

"Did you have anything better in mind?"

I press my lips together, resigned to use our last resort.

"Good point. But hurry. Mom can't find out."

"Okay, I'll just go in through the shop. I'll be right back."

I lay in pain for the next fifteen minutes, foot pulsing and cuts staining her couch red. I try to focus on what's around me to stay calm.

Four white paper lamps hanging from the ceiling. Three potted palms, leaves as big as elephant ears. Two gold stools in front of the bar. One floor-to-ceiling mirror with marquee lights around the edges.

I take a deep breath in and out, noting the cream filigree wallpaper all around the room. My anxiety quells, but my irritation still hasn't settled.

Fucking Liam. This wouldn't have happened without him being so pushy. But at the same time… I hope he's okay. I doubt that first aid kit could do much for him.

My stomach twists at the thought of a deep slice on his face.

Laurel comes back through the door, closes it behind her, and paces up to me holding a bright pink vial.

"Ready?" she asks as I take it in my fingers.

I uncork it. I guzzle down the rest of the bottle as a warm sensation fills my limbs. The wounds on my leg begin to undo themselves, the dark blotches on my foot fading into my normal golden tan. It's like nothing ever happened.

"For the record," she says as she stands. "You need a better place to hide things. I'm grateful I didn't find anything worse under that bed."

"Oh no, that's all in the nightstand," I say, feigning innocence.

She scoffs. "You're disgusting."

"I'm a guy," I point out. Now that the pain from my ankle isn't overpowering every other sense, I remember what I need to tell Laurel. "By the way. I don't think the thief was Liam after all. Turns out he's allergic to flowers." The thought that Liam wasn't behind the garden break-in gives me more relief than I'd like to admit.

But if it wasn't him, then who?

Laurel rubs her eyes, her face weary. "Okay, so no memory potion needed, then. But now we're back to square one." She shakes her head in frustration. "Let's talk about this tomorrow after we've both had some sleep. I'll come check on you. Gonna take me hours to get all of this blood out…"

I cringe. "Sorry… I can help you tomorrow after Mom goes to work."

"Don't worry about it. Good night."

"Night, sis. Thanks again."

Laurel follows me out and closes the door behind me as I head toward the stairs.

One step at a time, Liam keeps crossing my mind. I was lucky to have my family's magic, but he's going to have to live with this night every time he looks in the mirror for the rest of his life. Unless…

No, I can't. It's too risky. He's a human, and he can't be trusted with magic.

But…he tried to save me. He carried me inside without a second thought. And he took me at my word when I asked him to leave me. Maybe he's earned magical intervention.

I walk up to my front door and take one last glance at his down the hall. I take a deep breath.

Fuck it.

Chapter Nine

My mouth is dry as I hurry into the garden. Down the path, through the woods, and to the deepest corners of our paradise.

I keep cracking my knuckles to quell the worry, but it's not particularly helping. At last, I arrive at the conservatory, stopping in front of the iridescent patch of clovers outside the door—Rainbow Roots. I bend down, pluck one, and press it to the lock. It morphs into a glass key.

What am I doing? I keep going.

With a click of the lock, the vines unravel from the door and allow me entry. The same red glow hovers around the room as I go inside. Clenching my jaw, I pace to the pedestal with the glass case—the menacing flower still housed inside. The petals and tendrils dance, sensing something near.

Is this actually a good idea? It has to be.

I grab the small wooden box near the door, set it on the pedestal, and remove the dome.

The flower twists and faces me, inviting me in. I close

my eyes briefly, remembering the steps of how Laurel made the potion the other day.

Then I go to work.

I clench my hands before I pluck a single berry and return the top. Cloth over a vial, I tie it off and use the mortar and pestle to crush the bulb. Red juice splatters as I pour it inside. I'm careful—no seeds.

How am I going to explain this to him?

Fingers unsteady, I remove the cloth, return the box of supplies to the corner, and walk outside to the black-and-white stalks near the edge of the conservatory.

I uproot one Phantom, hold it flat above the mouth of the glass, and break it in half. Clear juice runs from either side and fills the container. I bury the empty stock in the garden exactly like Laurel did, cork the vial, and shake it for ten seconds. Magenta.

I'm doing this. I have to.

A turn of the key again and the conservatory wraps itself tightly in the vines once more. With deep breaths, I jog back through the forest. I make a quick stop at my mom's potion cabinet and grab a few pads of gauze and a roll of medical tape. Before I know it, I'm out in the hallway in front of Liam's door.

Last chance to change my mind. But I won't.

Knock, knock, knock.

Within a few seconds, Liam appears from behind the door.

I grimace at the sight of him: the wound on his forehead is pretty ghastly. As bad as it is, though, I'm thankful it's not worse.

"Quill?" He looks down at my leg. "How are you walking?"

I'm risking everything—all of our secrets. I could be putting us all in danger. But one of my mom's most common refrains keeps ringing in my head—*most humans are good if you give them a chance.* "Can you keep a secret?"

He pauses for a second. "I guess so."

I set my jaw and look him seriously in the eye. "I need you to swear you can. I can get in a lot of trouble for doing this."

He remains still, but his eyes meet mine. He nods. "I swear."

I take a deep breath and uncork my mom's anesthetic. "Come here."

Taking a step closer, he tilts his head down. I pour a little of it on the gauze and dab it on the cut. He winces and sucks in air through his teeth, but he relaxes and blows out a long breath within a second.

"Sorry," I say sympathetically. "It stings at first."

"It's fine," he says. "It feels better now."

I nod and cover the cut with another pad of fresh gauze, ripping off a couple of strips of tape with my teeth. I tape it to his forehead, reach into my pocket, and hold out the pink bottle. "Drink this."

His face twists in confusion. "Is it—"

I shake my head and cut him off. The less he knows, the better. There's a fine line between serious and reassuring, but I wish I could reassure myself. "Just do it."

His hand reaches out and closes around it, his skin grazing mine.

My heart jumps, but he breaks the contact quickly. He holds the vial between his fingers and takes a deep breath.

"Okay." He uncorks the bottle and gulps the potion. And I pray I didn't fuck up the recipe.

He closes his eyes and sighs. "That stuff's pretty delicious," he says, eyes widening. "What's it for?"

"It'll help you heal faster," I say with a shrug. Not a lie. "No big deal." Against better judgment, I reach out and run my fingertips along the bandages, going a little past them to his temple. His skin is soft and warm and makes my heart skip another beat. I can't help but gulp, and I think he notices. "Does that hurt?" I ask.

Liam looks into my eyes and shakes his head with a grin. "No."

"You can't tell anyone I did this for you. Understand?"

"Why not?" he asks, genuinely confused.

I grab the bottle out of his hand and stuff it in my pocket. "My mom would kill me. That stuff's a family secret. Seriously, not a soul. Do you understand?"

"I…yeah. I promise."

My lips stretch into a small smile, at ease to see him better than he was. "We're even."

"If you say so." He chuckles.

I turn to head back home, but I stop and look over my shoulder. "Maybe you're not so bad."

"Friends?" He laughs with one eyebrow cocked.

I shake my head. There's a chance I've been wrong about him, but I'm not ready to let him know. "Don't push it."

Chapter Ten

The soft grass caresses the back of my neck and arms, gentle blades between my toes as my knees point to the cosmos above me.

I'm satisfied here—my loose limbs against the earth as my chest rises and falls easily. The only things blocking my view are the branches of the dracaena in this part of the woods.

Most people would think they're only trees, but these are special. Gnarled and twisted, but it's that unsettling contortion I find beautiful. Their trunks are the size of the apartment outside, while their lives are older than the myths told about their kind.

The shop is finally closed. I lie in the one place I know will make me calm—the most ancient part of the garden. Not only because I'm still shaken from last night, although that's part of it. More so because I'm craving peace and this is where I know I'll find it. It's a ritual for me whenever I need to put things in perspective.

I honestly thought I had Liam nailed down as the

person who broke into the garden, that he was up to something and shouldn't be trusted. But after last night? The way he took care of me? The way he was truly shocked when I healed him? Not to mention his flower allergy.

I was wrong. Not that being wrong irritates me—I'm more…intrigued by him than anything else. There's something more about him. Something unexpected and special.

I don't regret giving him that potion, but it's just another thing for me to worry about if my mom ever finds out. She'd overreact. She'd be furious. She'd pack us up and whisk us away to some town no one's ever heard of that may or may not have electricity.

As a magical creature, exposure is one of her greatest fears—which is weird, considering how she sometimes breaks the rules by giving out the occasional remedy to the townsfolk. Humans often attack what they don't understand, and if our secret gets out, we're vulnerable. And so is everything inside our garden.

I remember her telling me stories of a human who broke in when my grandmother was my age, almost a thousand years ago. Some foolish mortal trying to get rich quick. He ended up mistaking something poisonous for something valuable and killed his entire family.

It's arguable we protect them from themselves by keeping dangerous things under lock and key, but that's not how the townsfolk saw it. "Dryad" was soon replaced with "witch," and pitchforks and torches were quick to follow. My great-grandmother packed up the garden and her daughter, and they ran for their lives.

And nature knows my mom wouldn't just look for a new neighborhood. She'd search for an eighth fucking continent if she found out I even whispered the word "magic" to Liam.

My throat tightens and my palms begin to sweat, but I focus on my breathing. Try not to think about it. Only the here and now. If I can figure out who broke into the garden and fix the problem before my mom finds out, nothing bad will happen. I can handle this.

I close my eyes and feel myself drifting away, almost into nothingness. Melting to become one with everything around me. Sometimes I wish I could change the weather in here as my mom can. There's nothing like the sound of a sweet breeze among the leaves.

And somehow, like clockwork, the wind begins to whistle—the leaves on the trees fan a gentle breeze on my skin. I open my eyes and see my mother.

"I thought I'd find you here," she says, smiling with her hands on her hips.

I grin back at her. "You know me well."

She sighs and eases her full-figured body down next to me, sitting with her legs crossed. "Being here is a bit of a religious experience, don't you think?"

I nod. I can always count on her to get me. "I've always wondered what they've been through. The things they've seen. The millennia they've overcome."

"More than we'll ever know," she says, looking at the largest of the trees with soft eyes. She takes a deep breath in and turns her gaze to me. "You've been stressed the last couple of days. Anything on your mind?"

"Not stressed. Super tired." At the moment, that's true.

"Are you sure? Something about you…something inside you. It's different."

I sigh. "Mom, do you think I'll ever be ready to be out on my own? I know I'm not as perfect as Laurel, but…I don't know. Sometimes I wish I could just be normal."

She reaches out and laces her fingers with mine. "Sweetheart, normal is overrated. Your time to be on your own will come."

I look down and pause. She keeps saying that, convinced I'll get my powers one day, but there's a heaviness in my stomach that makes me doubt it. When she's not around, I can accept I'll never be magical. Yet somehow, when she's in front of me, the look on her face always makes me think otherwise. "But when?" I still ask, hopefully.

"I don't know. You're one of a kind, so it's hard to tell. But it's my job as your mother to protect you. You won't fault me for being absolutely sure, will you?"

I put my other hand on top of hers and rub it with the side of my thumb. Her skin is soft, despite all the work she does with them.

"Are you sure that's all that's been bothering you?" she asks as she knits her brows.

I'm still wondering why she let Liam move in, but I don't want to open that subject. Not yet, anyway. "Yeah, that's it," I lie with a small smile. I don't think it makes it all the way up to my eyes, but I hope it does. I'm a little numb, is all. A lot's happened in the last couple of days and I'm trying to process. I absentmindedly twirl the blades of grass with my free hand.

She looks up at the tree above us, massive boughs holding as strong as the day I was born. "If I could only see a sliver of the things they've seen… It puts things in perspective. Even for an old woman like me."

"Five hundred, but you still don't look a day over thirty-five," I say.

She puts her hand on her chest and gasps. "Four hundred and ninety-eight, and don't you forget it," she says with a wink.

I chuckle and squeeze her hand one more time. She's not exactly an open book, kinda like me, but she can make you feel better just by sharing the room with you.

"One more thing," she says as she makes her way to standing. "What happened to the fire escape?"

"Whole thing fell off in the middle of the night," I say, pulling from the numbness to stay calm and make it believable. "I guess it got too heavy. That steel must have gotten pretty rusty after all these years."

She pauses and narrows her eyes. "Thank goodness you weren't on it. I know how you like to go outside when no one's around."

"Pretty lucky." I'm doing my best to not be suspicious, so I keep moving forward casually. "Any idea when it might get fixed?"

"I made a few calls today to find a contractor." She sighs. "Work should start soon. I'm sorry, I know that was one of your favorite spots."

"Don't worry about it, I haven't been using it lately." Okay, *that* was a lie.

"Better head in for dinner," she says, dusting off her hands and wiping them on her apron. "I'll fix a plate for you when you get inside… Take your time." She motions around at the dozens of steadfast Goddesses of the garden. "And don't forget to tell your grandmothers good night."

She walks away as my eyes travel from one ancestor to another, each one her own massive tree. They'll be here, watching over us for eternity—the garden now caring for its earliest keepers. All of the miracles they must have performed in their lifetimes, and all of the ways they must have changed the world over eons…

Dryads never leave us. Once they age their entire lifetimes, they morph into these sacred trees and spend the rest of eternity here in this part of the garden. They watch over us, care for us, and share their magic with us. The more our garden grows, so do our powers. Their power is our power, and our people are as old as nature itself. It'll continue to grow forever.

Maybe my mom is right. Maybe I'm rushing too fast to grow up.

Shouldn't I be happy with the life I have? I mean, I have everything I need, don't I?

But then there are these feelings I've been having ever since Liam showed up outside my window. I've been *feeling* more intensely in general.

Irritation. Anger. But after last night, concern and gratefulness, too. Plus whatever the fuck that tingling is when he gets too close.

I sit for a few more moments, take a deep breath, and make my way to my feet. I crack my neck, but as I twist my head, a sprig of dried brown leaves catches the corner of my eye—right near the path. I squint. Nothing in here should be remotely that color.

I walk up and crouch, gently tracing the stems with my fingertips.

This shouldn't be happening. I reach out carefully, afraid to touch it. As I press the stem of what used to be a rose between my fingers, it dissolves into dust. I gasp and yank my hand away.

Worry creeps into my chest, but I mash it down. What the hell is going on with this place lately?

Chapter Eleven

Later that night, after my mom goes to bed, one thought floats to the top of my mind: Liam.

Is he okay?

Is he weirded out?

Is he going to tell anyone?

Has he been thinking about me, too?

The curiosity itches at me as I finish wiping our dinner plates clean from my family's version of lasagna. I could sit here all night and wonder. Then again, since I've gone this far… What's the harm in finding out? There's always the chance his mind could have run all day long, warping what happened. I should probably calm him down in case he's spiraling.

I turn off the water, close my eyes, and take in the sounds of the apartment.

I focus so hard, all that shows up is my own gentle heartbeat inside my ears. I look over my shoulder into the dark hallway and take gentle steps across the hardwood floor to my mom's room, pressing my ear against the door.

Still—silence. The coast is clear.

I steady my breath, and hopefully my heartbeat, as I stalk back through my kitchen and dark living room to go out into the hall and one door over.

I snatch my mom's house key off the shelf and wipe off the dust. She always comes and goes through the shop.

Why am I so nervous? Especially after last night. It makes no sense. It can't get much worse. I stop in front of his door and look at the ceiling.

I'm frozen. *C'mon Quill, do it.* On the count of three. Yeah, that's it. *One.* I look forward. *Two.* I crack my knuckles. *Three.*

Knock, knock, knock.

Fuck. I guess there's no going back now.

I wait for a few seconds, biting my lip, but there's no answer. Maybe this was a bad idea. There's no way I'm doing it again, and this was a sign.

I take a few steps back to my house, but a lock unlatches behind me and a door opens.

"I've been waiting for you all day."

The words send a shiver up my spine and into my chest. I didn't think I could get more nervous than I already was.

"Sorry," I say, turning around to him. "I know it's late."

The gauze is still on his forehead, untouched. He probably hasn't figured it out yet. He puts his hand to his heart, pressing against a ratty cutoff tee. "Oh my God, did you just apologize? To *me*?"

I roll my eyes. "It must have slipped out." The nerves slide off and are quickly replaced with annoyance. Here I am, trying to be nice, and he takes a jab at me. I don't understand how someone so irritating can be so… attractive? Ew. I can't believe that crossed my mind.

He chuckles, leaning against the doorframe. "I'm

giving you a hard time. Glad you stopped by."

I put my hands in my pockets. "Only wanted to see how you were doing."

"Better than ever, thanks to you. How about you? Did your mom say anything about the fire escape?"

"Kinda." I scratch the back of my head, looking away, but I can't stop my eyes from staying away from his for too long. My stomach flutters the second they come back to his face, so I do my best to steady my breath. There are those fucking nerves again. "I glossed over the part where we were both on it when it fell."

"Yeah, I'm sure she would have gone off about it," he says with a nod.

"You have no idea."

"So…does this mean you trust me now?" he asks with a slight grin.

I tilt my head back and forth. "I mean, I don't *not* trust you. I just don't know you very well."

"Then how about we get to know each other?" He cocks his head, squinting lush eyelashes that invite me to look into his eyes. Dark blue, and I can't help but try to file through all the garden's flowers in my head to find an exact match. Forget-Me-Nots? Too light. Hydrangeas? Too purple.

"You in there?" he asks, furrowing his eyebrows.

"Yeah, sorry," I say, shaking myself out of it. I'll have to keep an eye out for the right shade when I'm working tomorrow. "What did you have in mind?"

"Talking? Like normal people?" He flashes a smile. Bright white teeth and the slightest bit crooked. An imperfection that looks even better on him.

"Oh, okay." I'd be lying if I said I wasn't dazzled. "When?"

"Now?" His thick eyebrows rise.

"Like right now?"

"Is that a problem?"

I think my mom is sleeping. She should be out for the rest of the night. I know I'm not supposed to talk to humans, but…it's a little late for that. "Yeah, I guess that would be fine."

"My place or yours—"

"Yours," I cut him off. The thought of an intruder crosses my mind again. I'm pretty sure he's innocent, but let's not chance it.

He lets out a soft laugh and pushes the door open with his bare arm. "Come on in, then."

Chapter Twelve

Liam's door shuts behind me, and my eyes adjust to the soft blue glow from the TV bathing his living room. Things look more put together than they did last time I was snooping. Minimal furniture, though, and all very sleek and modern and metallic—the opposite of my house. Wait, is it all…leather? Gross.

"Can I get you something to drink?" he asks.

"Water?" I give him a small, awkward smile.

"No problem." He takes a few hesitant steps, eyeing me. "You're free to sit down, you know."

Shit. I guess I look as awkward as I feel. "Thanks."

I see a blanket and pillow balled up on one end of the couch and figure it's safe to sit myself down on the bare end. The feeling of dead animal beneath me weirds me out, but I push the thought down as much as I can.

Patchouli. Sandalwood. Black currant. That same scent is in the air from the last time I was here, and it's frustrating me that I can't place it. "Do you have some kind of air freshener going or something? I keep smelling all these plants, but I don't see any."

"That's probably my cologne," he says. The faucet squeaks behind me as a cup fills. "Gift for my birthday. It's Lacoste. Do you like it?"

"There are worse things in the world." I'm not about to admit I'm more than a little obsessed with it. It's sweet and fresh and so complex.

A few footsteps approach from behind the couch and he appears again, handing me a glass. "Here you go."

"Thanks." I chug the whole thing before he can get back under the blanket.

He freezes. "Want another?"

"Uh…" This whole hanging out with a human thing isn't going very smoothly. Heat floods the sides of my face and burns at my ears while sweat prickles on my palms. "I'm good." I quickly set the empty glass on the silver coffee table in front of me.

He chuckles and gets comfortable. "If you say so."

Maybe if I change the subject, I'll be less… Embarrassed? My eyes flit around in the dark apartment, an exact mirror image of mine. That's the kitchen, which means his room is down the hall, and his dad's room… "Is your dad here?"

"Nope, only me," he says, eyes not leaving the subtitles on the TV screen.

Weird. "Still?" He was alone last time, too. I'm starting to wonder if his dad even exists.

Liam shrugs, curling up tighter into the couch cushions. "Yeah, he's out of town on business a lot. It's why your mom let us move in. My dad worries about me being safe when he's gone."

The distant stare. The flatness in his voice. It clearly upsets him, but comforting people isn't exactly my strong suit. I cross my arms, propping my feet on the coffee table. "You haven't been here for more than a week and you already fell off the side of a building. So things are definitely going pretty well."

He laughs, puts his arm against the back of the couch, and rests his cheek on the palm of his hand. "And somehow you fixed everything afterward, so yeah, looks like it was a good choice after all."

"Lucky you," I say with a grin, mimicking him with my arm.

"So you've lived here your whole life?"

I freeze and narrow my eyes. "Who told you that?"

"You did. The first night when you tried to club me to death."

"Ah, yes. That." I nod and relax again. False alarm. "Surprised you remember."

"Hard to forget," he says, giving a push to my shoulder with his free hand.

The nerve endings tingle from where he touched me. My stomach flutters and the back of my neck gets hot. I kind of hate the feeling, but I want him to do it again. Still, I do my best to ignore it. "But yeah. Just me and my mom now. My older sister lives upstairs."

"That's cool that she's still close. What about your dad?"

I grimace and curl myself into a ball on the cushion. "My parents broke up when I was little. My mom bought this building after that and it's been us ever since. What about you? Any siblings?"

His fingers rake through his messy hair. "Nope, only child. Always wanted one, though."

"Not all it's cracked up to be, especially when they're the prodigy." I freeze and close my eyes. "Sorry, that came out more bitter than I meant it to."

"No, it's all good. I've always been the pride and joy, so trust me when I say it's not always great on the other side."

"What about your mom?"

"Ah. Yeah, here's where it gets awkward," he says. "She died a couple of years ago."

A shock runs through me. I know I didn't mean to put my foot in my mouth, but *fuck*. "I—I am so sorry."

"Yeah, that's the part that makes people act weird." He hunches toward the table to grab his glass of soda. The bubbles shake loose as soon as he picks it up and a light fizzy hiss whispers through the air as he brings it to his mouth. He swallows and continues. "Everyone always feels so bad for bringing it up. But really, thank you. We're still getting through it."

I clench my teeth, desperately clinging to any other subject that comes to mind, except nothing is working as a good transition. I had no idea I'm terrible at having conversations. The last thing I want to do is ask what happened.

"Now you're probably wondering what happened, and don't worry, you're not the first," he says. My heart breaks for him. He's been through this a lot. "Aneurysm. Very sudden. No warning, but no pain. It's probably one of the best ways to go."

"Still, I'm sorry." There's a tightness in my throat and a heaviness in my words. I honestly can't imagine what he's gone through. I don't know what I'd do if I lost my mom. I may have misjudged him this entire time.

"It's all good." He sighs and swirls his drink before taking one more swig. "Anyway, on to lighter subjects. Where do you work?"

I feel myself tense. I clear my throat, wishing I had another glass of water to chug, at least to stall for a decent answer. I end up settling for a shrug. "For my mom. In the back of the flower shop downstairs."

"Oh yeah? What do you do?"

I need to make it sound boring so he stops asking. And, since it actually is boring, that shouldn't be hard. "Stocking, cutting, and so on. I mostly work in her garden."

He nods. "That's cool. Where is it?"

Damn it. I led him straight to that one. "Oh, not too far from here," I say without putting too much emphasis on it. I wish my voice didn't rise like that. This is dangerous territory and I need to change the subject fast. "So what's school like?"

He grins and sets his glass back down with a thunk. "What do you mean 'what's school like?'"

"I'm homeschooled? I thought that was obvious."

"Seriously? I'm jealous. It's boring. You're so lucky you don't have to go."

"I'm actually dying to go," I say, taken aback.

"Don't get me wrong, there are great parts"—he backpedals —"like, I love swimming. More than anything, actually. But school itself is the same thing with the same people every day."

"Don't be offended if I don't take your word for it," I say with a smile. "It would be nice to get out of here."

See the town. Do things normal teenagers get to do… as nervous as the thought makes me. What would it even be like?

All my mom tells me is how dangerous it is. But I know my time will come, as long as I keep playing my part and doing what's asked of me. As frustrating as it is right now, my mom can't keep me in there forever.

Liam clears his throat and gives me a quizzical look, pulling me out of my thoughts.

“Sorry,” I say. “I just work a lot. House, garden, flower shop. Same thing, same people, every day.”

“Grass is greener, says the gardener.”

“Yeah, and I would know,” I say, omitting the bitterness. “Anyway, I should be getting home. In case she wakes up, y’know.” I know she won’t, but it’s my first time breaking the rules this seriously. I push myself up off the couch and stretch my arms above my head.

“It’s too bad the fire escape went down,” he says as he pulls the blanket off and makes his way to standing.

“Yeah, I always liked it out there.”

“I’m only disappointed I don’t have a shortcut to come see you anymore.” He rubs his shoulder with his free hand.

I can’t help but notice a few freckles on either arm, veins like roots under his smooth skin. I don’t know why, but I have this urge to reach out and run my fingers along them.

I quickly push the thought away, shaking my head and giving a short laugh. “Guess you’re gonna have to wait for me.”

“I mean, I could just slip into your DMs,” he says with a wink.

I pause and squint, looking him in the eye. “What did you say?”

He grimaces. “Sorry, I didn’t mean for it to sound like that.”

I honestly don’t have a clue why he’s apologizing. “No, it’s that I have no idea what you’re talking about.”

“DMs? Like social media?”

Oh, those human things. “I don’t have any of that.” I turn to walk toward the front door.

“FacePost? InstaSnap? Anything?” he asks behind me.

I shake my head and shrug. He might as well be

speaking another language.

"What teenager doesn't have social media?"

"Uh, I just told you. Me." Why is he so surprised? "How many times do I have to keep saying I'm not normal before you believe me?" I unlock the door and twist the knob.

"You do have a cell phone, right?"

I chuckle. "Yes, I do have one of those."

"Great, hold on." He flips the lights on and riffles through papers on the table by the door. He grabs a Sharpie and grabs my hand, moving to write something on my palm.

I yank it away. "Sorry, I'm allergic. Do you have a piece of paper or something?" The last thing I need is him seeing the ink disappear into my skin. Or worse, to lose his number.

"Oh, sorry. Sure." He grabs a takeout menu and scribbles a few digits on it. His writing is way better than mine. Thank nature I can read it. He folds it and hands it to me. "So what other quirks do you have?"

I have to be careful how I answer this. Vague is probably the best way to go. "I don't know, depends on what you mean by 'quirks.'"

"You haven't been to public school and you don't have a digital footprint. Don't you have any friends?"

"I have my family. We're super close."

He laughs. "Not the same."

"If you say so, I guess." Maybe my mom was right. I never realized how different from humans I might be.

"I mean, I could be your *friend.*" He takes a step closer to me, close enough to see the slightest bit of sweat on his forehead. *Is he nervous?* His ocean blue eyes bore straight into mine, his soft lips curling into a smile as he leans in. "If you want."

His gaze is intense, forcing me to look down. My pulse quickens. Does he actually want to be a friend? It's strange how he put so much emphasis on the word. He could be pitying me. Or he could be working me to get back into the garden. Or he could actually…mean it.

"Wow," he says with a chuckle. "I didn't think you'd need to think about it so much."

"Sorry, it's…" I struggle to swallow and try to find the words through the nerves. "It's weird to think about. What did you have in mind?"

He shrugs. "Like, normal friend stuff? Talk, joke, hang out, go out?"

"Going out might be a stretch," I say, rubbing the back of my neck. I'm not sure if that's possible.

He narrows his eyes and grins. "When's the last time you went to the movies?"

"Never been." How vague can I be before he catches on?

"What?" he shouts. I recoil, but he keeps going. "How have you never been to a movie?"

"I don't know, I just haven't."

"They're amazing. The popcorn smell, the comfy seats, how you get lost in another world for a couple of hours… They're my favorite thing in the world."

I nod. It's something I've always heard of but never thought too hard about. And the way Liam gets when he talks about it is kind of…cute? "Sounds great. I'll have to try it someday."

"Well, what are you doing tomorrow night?"

I shake my head. "I see where this is going and I don't think that's a very good idea."

"Are you scared?"

"No." I scoff quickly. That's a lie. I kind of am. "I don't

think my mom will let me."

"Then sneak out with me."

I sigh. There's not a chance in the world. "She'll completely melt down."

"Doesn't she sleep like a rock anyway? If that fire escape didn't wake her up, nothing will."

I pause and think about the idea of me going out of my house. For the first time, ever. And with…Liam.

"What have you got to lose?" he asks gently.

It goes against everything I've been told, everything I've agreed to. It's a terrible idea and I'd be ruining every ounce of trust my mom's put in me. Going against how she raised me.

I can only imagine how angry and disappointed she'd be with me if she found out. I've never seen her lose her temper, and I absolutely don't want to. She's told me how dangerous the outside world is since I was little, and I don't exactly have any reason to not believe her.

It's always a question of safety. It may not be the best idea, but I'd be with him. He'd know what to look out for, right? And I mean, the whole reason I'd want to go out is to meet people, make friends… So what if I did it backward? Maybe I've made a friend that'll make going out much easier. I wouldn't be alone.

I want nothing more in this world than to be like a normal human. No plants. No magic. No pressure.

I take a deep breath. "I'm in," I say.

It's time I gamble on something.

Chapter Thirteen

I'm on my hands and knees, tearing out what's left of a field of lilies.

Three giant wagons of blooms already went down to the cooler and it's not even noon. Now, all that's left is ripping out the odds and ends so we can have a clean slate.

My back aches and my muscles burn, skin oily from where my sweat used to be. Going through the motions is a lot harder when I know what's happening tonight. My stomach plummets at the thought of what I agreed to.

Unlike the impression I gave to Liam, I actually have everything to lose.

I could lead humans right to our secret if I act too weird. Do the wrong thing. Say the wrong thing. With the garden thief still at large now that I've ruled out Liam, I can't afford to draw any extra attention to what we were or what we have.

I dig harder and faster, trying to get my mind off it all.

My pocket buzzes twice. I sit up, take a deep breath, and slip my phone out. Probably my mom with another order. *Ugh.* However, my eyes grow wide when it's Liam's name sitting on my screen above TEXT MESSAGE.

I shake my head and stand up, prickles running through my body as my heart picks up speed. My feet lumber over to a rock at the edge of the plot, the granite radiating a coolness through my shorts that calms me down. I tap in my passcode to see what he has to say.

Liam: Morning!

Me: Morning. How'd you sleep?

Liam: Like the dead. Wyd?

Me: Work as always

Liam: Fun. Ready to lose your virginity tonight?

I narrow my eyes at the screen and shake my head. He's almost worse in writing than he is in person.

Me: Wtf?

Liam: Kidding! Sorry. Meant your first movie. Was funnier in my head

Me: And you didn't even need me to tell you that

I shake my head with a smirk. It's kind of fun to poke at him at this point. I don't let him get away with saying weird things in person—I wasn't about to let him text me any differently.

Liam: What do you want to see?

Me: Surprise me

Liam: Perfect. Romance

Me: Or not

Liam: Kidding. Again. Something funny?

Me: Funnier than you?

Liam: Not possible. Action then

How can someone be so ridiculous and attractive at the same time? Normally I'd be frustrated by the back-and-forth, but I can't wait to go out tonight. Is it because I'm finally getting out of here? Or is it because of him?

Me: Sounds good. You're the expert

Liam: Don't worry, I'll go slow

Me: Ugh you're the worst

Liam: Hahaha. You'd better get back to work. Don't want your mom to fire you

I dig through my emojis and find one with a single finger sticking up. He reacts with a heart, starting up the butterflies in my stomach again.

I've mashed them down for days, but I soak them up for a minute and it's kind of…nice? I'd be lying if I said I wasn't hoping he'd write back some more, but I know I'll have all night to hear what he has to say.

I stare at my reflection in the bathroom mirror, willing my hair to go from its forest green to some sort of tame brown. I've been jumpy and distracted all day. But finally, it's somehow been precisely eleven hours, thirty-seven minutes, and forty-two seconds. And at last, my pocket buzzes again.

Liam: Ready when you are

Me: Meet me in the alley?

Liam: Be right out

Deep breath in, deep breath out. A tiny echo of a click bounces off the white bathroom tile as I set my phone on the side of the sink, and the sound makes me jump. For the love of nature, I need to calm down.

It's the night I've been waiting for—I get to escape from this tower. I won't be watched, and I won't be worried over. I get to be…normal. For once in my life.

No matter what, I can't get caught. Because if I get caught… My heart races, and my chest tightens.

My feet move as quietly as possible as I glide through my apartment. The moon cuts through the darkness in the living room, giving me enough light to find the key on the bookshelf right where I left it.

I unlatch the door, lock up behind me, and go down the stairwell at the end of the hallway. I finally arrive at the door at the bottom. The outside world is right on the other side.

My hand trembles and my heart skips as I turn the knob and push it open.

There's nothing to be afraid of. You can do this.

It's now or never.

Chapter Fourteen

Three steps out onto the stoop and the warm night air swirls on my skin.

"About time!"

I jump, completely startled as my senses absorb the outside world, a rush of everything all at once. Sure, I may have been out here plenty of times on the fire escape, but it's different down here, without the smells of flowers and soil flooding out my window behind me, and my limited, top-down point of view.

The outside has a fresh, clean scent I don't think I'll ever get used to. I feel the night air swirling warm on my skin. It's not as humid as the garden, yet it doesn't feel all that different. The sky seems just as tall as it was from the fire escape, but instead of the canopy of trees I'm used to, it's thick brick trunks of buildings and metal branches connecting them.

Concrete in place of soil, trash in place of flowers, chain-link fences instead of walls of leaves. It's another garden, only by a different name.

An urban jungle.

Liam laughs from a parking space thirty feet away, sitting on the hood of a car. I press my hand to my chest to slow my heart and I can't help but smile back.

"Sorry, took me a while to get ready," I say as I walk over to him.

"No worries," he says, standing up and getting around to the driver's side. "We've still got plenty of time."

Somehow he's able to comfort me, the tightness in my chest easing. He doesn't seem worried at all.

"Is this yours?" I ask Liam, going around the black car to the passenger side. I don't know the first thing about automobiles, but it looks too expensive for a high school senior.

"No, it's my dad's. I need to get a job and save up for my own." He opens the door and climbs inside.

Shit. I've never been in one before. Can't be hard to figure out, right? I've seen it on TV. My fingers fit under the handle and pull—way too hard apparently, because the door comes flying open and I hit my leg.

"You okay over there?" he asks with narrowed eyes.

"Yup," I say through gritted teeth as I climb in. I shut the door behind me, again with too much force. This is fucking mortifying.

Liam fights back a laugh as he starts the car, but then pauses and looks at me for a few seconds. "Aren't you gonna buckle up?"

"Oh, uh…yeah." I paw around to my side, grabbing hold of the strap near my arm. I pull from the bottom, but nothing happens. I pull from the top, but it shoots out and goes right back in as soon as I stop pulling.

I yank again and reach around to the other side of the seat, moving as quickly as I can to end this moment as soon as possible. His face catches my eye and I force a small smile, jamming the belt into the buckle without it going inside. I'm burning red.

"Turn it around," he says as he gently reaches out, holding back laughter. His hand brushes mine as he takes it from me, flipping it around in his fingers. He clicks it and leans back, but I sit still—frozen and hoping that's enough embarrassment for the night. He eyes me with a playful smile.

I rub the back of my neck, cringing. "Sorry, it's been a while since I've driven anywhere."

He opens his mouth to say something, but he closes it again and chuckles. "You're so strange. I like it." Somehow the words make my nerves dissolve. He tilts his head down to see where he's putting his hand and I notice he still has the bandage on his face.

"You could probably take that off now," I say, pointing at his forehead.

He looks at me confused and reaches up. "Oh, the cut. You sure? It was pretty bad."

"The stuff I gave you works fast," I say. "I can do it for you, if you want."

Liam smiles and tips his head toward me. Pinching the edge of the tape, I peel it back as gently as possible. The skin is completely healed underneath.

"Worked like a charm," I say, folding the gauze and stuffing it in the cup holder.

Liam still looks confused, but he pulls down a flap from the roof of the car and stares in a mirror attached to it. His eyes grow wide. "Wow, you weren't kidding about that stuff," he says, rubbing his fingers over where the cut used to be. "It looks great."

"It sure does," I say, lost in thought and smiling.

He looks at me with squinted eyes and a smirk.

"Your forehead," I say quickly. "I'm talking about your forehead. Not your face. I mean, your face is fine, too. I guess." My face burns hot, on the other hand, and part of me wishes it would just combust and put me out of my misery right now.

Liam starts laughing and shaking his head. "Let's get out of here."

As Liam drives through the streets, I congratulate myself on thinking to apply extra deodorant before I left, because this whole moving vehicle thing? Terrifying. Sure, I'm not embarrassed anymore, but I'm gripping the edge of my seat with all my strength.

I think he can sense my nerves, because he's being especially slow and careful when it comes to red lights and stop signs. I mean, at least in comparison to the few other cars around us. I'm not quite sure why they aren't doing the same. I remember seeing on TV that both of those mean stop, right? And you get put in jail if you don't?

I calm down after a few minutes, looking all around us. This may be my first and last time going out if my mom catches me, so I want to take in everything about this town. This place I've lived in my whole life yet know nothing about.

I look to my right and see a town square, with benches and fountains and trees that must be at least a hundred years old. I look to my left and I see Liam looking back at me, smiling.

"When's the last time you've been on this side of town?" he asks.

"Never. I stay on the south side." Not necessarily a lie. He doesn't need to know the whole truth.

"Well, by all means," he says, adjusting his body to sit more comfortably and taking one hand off the wheel. "Let me give you the tour." He points at a red brick storefront on a row of shops. "My mom used to take me there for ice cream. Might take you there next time if they have something you can eat." He motions to an Italian restaurant a few blocks down, complete with a comically large sausage on top of the building. "That's where my coach takes us for our end-of-season dinner. They always give us an all-you-can-eat pizza thing if we win State. And there..." he says and pushes his square jaw toward a playground. Entirely made of metal, but embedded in nature—hundred-year-old trees with a riverbank in the background. "Is where I had my first kiss."

I laugh. "On the slide or the teeter-totter?"

He chuckles. "Under the jungle gym, actually. We were six. It was obviously very serious."

Looking around now, it's like I am seeing a whole life I could have been living this entire time. None of it seems nearly as dangerous as my mom always warns me about. No criminals. No doom. It is all actually...quiet and innocent. How different would my life have been if she had let up, just a little?

Maybe I could have been on some kind of team. Maybe I could have had my first kiss at the bottom of a plastic slide. I wish she could have had a Liam to show her the good things—the beauty of people. Why was she always so afraid? Especially of a place like this?

I can't help but feel bitter, but I keep telling myself she must have had a good reason.

"Here we are," he says after a few more minutes, pulling

into an empty parking space next to a cinema.

Movie posters line the outside of the building while the white marquee glows from the level above, surrounded by hundreds of twinkling white lights.

I unbuckle the seat belt, pull the latch to open the door, and push—only much more softly this time. I stand up on the concrete curb and push the door shut behind me. The summer air is warm, and the stars twinkle above behind the soft clouds, exactly like the lights and swirls in the garden—only millions of miles away.

I smile as I close my eyes and take a deep breath. My head falls back, and I try not to make any sudden movements to break the spell. I want to take in every detail and remember it forever. I'm in complete awe. If this is what being normal feels like—being free—right now I'd trade it for anything.

When I open my eyes, Liam is standing in the street and staring at me with a grin. "What?" I ask.

"Just glad you're having a good time. But you know the best part hasn't even started yet, right?"

I chuckle. I'm not sure how much better it can get. "I'll hold you to that."

"Then let's go." He laughs.

Chapter Fifteen

Liam steps up onto the sidewalk and leads the way to the front of the theater.

The streets are empty except for the occasional car passing by. Is this what the world is like at night? *Asleep?* Do people not go see movies on a Tuesday night? Even on summer vacation?

Not that I wish it were different. I kind of like that it's only us.

We get to a glass box in front of the door, an Asian girl sitting inside with bright purple shoulder-length hair. I'm already more at ease by seeing her. I've told my mom for years my hair wouldn't stick out. She looks up from her phone as we approach, a huge smile covering her face as soon as she sees him.

"Liam!" Her eyes cut across to me, grow wide, and snap back to him. "Oh my God, are you on a date?" she asks with a sly tone.

"No," I say from behind him. I'm starting to think that humans assume too much.

Liam chuckles, but his cheeks are redder than they were before. "Hi Max. And no, a friend. This is Quill."

"Hi Quill, nice to meet you," she says. She sighs and looks back at Liam with disappointment. "Man, I thought my night was about to get less boring."

"Sorry," he says with a shrug. "Two for the ten o'clock."

"Sounds good," she says as her black nails tap the computer screen in front of her.

Suddenly what's about to happen next dawns on me. My skin prickles as I lean in to him from behind. "Shit," I whisper in his ear. "I am so sorry. I forgot my wallet." I was so nervous that I completely forgot things cost money. How many more times do I need to be embarrassed around him before things can just go smoothly?

"It's okay," Liam says quietly, gently waving me away with a free hand. "It's handled."

She prints out the tickets and slides them under the glass. "Have fun," she says with a wink.

"Thanks." He hands me my little slip of paper. We walk to the door and he holds it open for me. Cool air rushes along my face and blows my hair around as sweet and salty scents fill my nostrils. My mouth waters a little bit, but I'm more concerned about what went on outside.

"Arc you not gonna pay?" I ask him.

"Friends and family discount," he says with a smile. "Want some popcorn?"

I shake my head. "Vegan, remember?"

"I know," he says and nods. "I called ahead, though. They use coconut oil. You can have it."

"Oh," I say, taken aback. I'm surprised he took the time to check. "Sure." He's turning out to be oddly thoughtful, and I can't help but slip him a small smile.

We walk up to the register, shelves around it full of

brightly colored plastic bags and the counter behind it holding rows and rows of red cups and buckets, glass cases of hot dogs and nachos, and swirling circles of red and blue liquid. It's all so foreign compared to the plants I see every day filling up the walls in my mom's shop.

A Black guy comes out from the back as we walk up, with long braids and as tall as Liam. And, of course, they know each other, too. "How come you always get the cute ones?" the guy asks him and motions to me.

"It's not a date," I say. Ugh. Humans. And what's that supposed to mean, *always*? Liam laughs, but I'm starting to think he may have a reputation. I wouldn't have classified myself as *cute*, either.

"James, this is Quill. Quill, James. He's a friend from school."

"Then if it's not a date, let me know if you want my number," James says to me as he rests his lean arms on the counter. He shoots me a quick wink with a smile.

Liam's jaw tightens in my periphery, but I roll my eyes. "I'll stick to the popcorn, thanks," I deadpan.

James laughs and looks back at Liam. "I like this one."

"He's pretty cool," Liam says with a smile, but a smooth tone to his voice. "Anyway, one large bucket and two large Cokes."

"You got it," James says and goes to grab our food.

Liam's posture is particularly stiff and his cheeks are pinker than normal. Wait, is he embarrassed?

"He reminds me of you a little," I say to Liam. "He smiles at me like you do."

"He does that when he's flirting," Liam says gruffly.

I raise my eyebrows. He's not embarrassed, he's jealous. I'm thoroughly entertained and I can't help but poke at him. "So you've been flirting with me?"

A smile creeps up the side of his mouth and he tips his head to the side. "Why, do you want me to?"

My skin prickles and I instantly regret going down this road. "I—I never said that."

Liam laughs and shrugs. "Besides, I'm cuter," he says with a grin. I'm still flustered, so for once in my life, I don't try to get the last word.

We grab our food—again without paying—and walk down the hallway and into the theater. An army of empty red chairs greets us. Aren't movies supposed to be packed? Because we're the only ones in here.

"Where do you wanna sit?" Liam asks.

"Uh," I pause, overwhelmed by all the decisions. It's better if I leave it to him. "You're the expert."

He nods decisively. "Back middle it is."

I follow him up the stairs all the way to the top, down the row, and grab the seat next to him. He sets down our drinks and popcorn and presses the button on the side of his chair to lie back. I do the same. I think he waited to do that until he knew I was watching.

"Do you like superhero movies?" Liam asks.

"They're okay. Depends on the superhero."

He nods and starts pulling on a light jacket. "Marvel or DC?"

"Marvel," I say. "Big fan of X-Men. I like how they're born that way."

"As opposed to Batman, who's just rich?" Liam asks.

I grin. "You said it, not me." I take a sip of my soda and the bubbles and sugar assault my system. I'm gonna be wired tonight.

"Fair," he says. "So what do you usually like to watch?"

Is this what humans do? Quiz each other on their likes and dislikes? I mean, it's flattering he wants to know, but still weird. "Documentaries. You?"

He laughs and crosses his legs. "Horror. Really? Documentaries?"

"Reality is more than entertaining. But horror? Why do you want to be scared?"

"Who said it's scary? It's all latex and corn syrup."

I shake my head. "That poor corn died for nothing."

"That corn died to make me laugh."

I chuckle and feel my muscles loosen. Maybe I should ask him something back? "Favorite horror movie?"

"That's a good question." He stops, rubs his chin and smiles. *"Cabin in the Woods."*

I tilt my head to the side. "Not *Silence of the Lambs* or *The Exorcist*?"

"Oh no, those are too easy. In *Cabin*, the big bad isn't what you think it is, and it turns out it's been watching them and planning everything the whole time. In every horror movie. Ever. Very meta."

"You've got me there," I say. Maybe it's because we're alone in a simple room—even though the room is huge—but I feel way better now that we're sitting in one place with no one else around. I feel like myself again.

No obsessions about looks or nerves about sneaking out of the house or embarrassment about human customs. I adjust myself in my seat a little deeper and snuggle into the plush red fabric.

"So what about you? Favorite documentary?"

"Oh, that's too hard," I say, shaking my head.

"Okay then," he says. "Favorite subject."

I think for a second. "The royal family."

"Honestly?" he asks. "Like the boring one? From England?"

"Yes, and not boring at all."

He laughs. "I mean come on, it's just a bunch of boring white people in a giant house. What's special about that?"

"I mean, think about it," I answer. "Arguably the most powerful bloodline in the world, all until the day they decided to muzzle that power. How they almost never exert it unless it's necessary."

"But that's the worst part," Liam says. "If you had power like that, wouldn't you try to fix everything?"

"But that's the thing," I say and hold up a finger. "Sometimes the hardest thing in the world is to say nothing and do nothing. Have faith that it'll work out on its own."

He shrugs, chewing on the straw in his drink. I can't help but wonder if it'll even work by the end of the movie. "I mean, if I had that many people listen to me," he says. "I'd be speaking my mind constantly."

"But they're the opposite," I say. "Look at all of the painstaking steps they take to never cause a frenzy and everything they've sacrificed over the years to do what's right. All for a sense of duty."

"And you relate to that?" he asks. "Not doing what you want, only because your family says so?"

I tip my head from side to side. "Well, tonight I'm doing what I want to do. So I'll let you know how that turns out."

Liam grins. "Pretty good so far, if you ask me."

I'm so glad I'm here and that I took the chance to do what I actually want to do, for once in my life. Everything feels so fresh and new, yet relaxing and comfortable at the same time. Like it was meant to be. This whole human world thing? Not so bad, if you ask me. As long as it's always like this.

The lights dim around us as the gigantic screen lights up.

Liam was right—the world falls away.

I've never been so mesmerized by the sights and sounds, and the warmth from his shoulder seeps through his hoodie and into mine. I've also never been this close to a human.

My heart is pounding and I'm sweating, but I still want him to stay where he is and not move away… *What is this feeling? Why is he so close?* And why is his hand palm up on the armrest?

More and more gunfire and explosions rock the seats the further we get into the movie, but I'm having a hard time with how over-the-top everything is.

"I mean, honestly," I lean over to Liam and say. "Why are these cities *always* about to get destroyed? And why is the superhero the only one who can save them?"

He laughs. "Because he's the good guy, duh."

I roll my eyes. "Wouldn't you move away? And what did everyone do before all these superheroes came around? Was it all fine? Because if the danger didn't show up until after the superhero got there, that's a pretty big coincidence."

"Are you saying it's the hero's fault?"

"All I'm saying is maybe the hero is the reason it's in danger in the first place."

Liam props himself up to look at me. "First off, it's only a movie. Second, the universe hates a vacuum. If it weren't that hero or that villain, someone else would have filled the spots eventually."

"If you say so."

I turn back to look at the screen, but something small hits the side of my face from Liam's direction. I look over, but he's staring straight forward. I look forward again, but out of the corner of my eye, I see his hand toss another few pieces of popcorn at me.

"You asshole." I laugh. I reach into the bucket and toss a handful at him.

He laughs and pushes me with the side of his shoulder until I push him back. We slow down, closer than we were, until I look over at him. His eyes are staring right into mine with a smirk, his face less than a foot from mine. Electricity fills the air as he starts to tilt his head to the side and leans forward. Butterflies fill my chest. I think I know what's about to happen. I don't know what I'm doing.

"Bathroom," I say and jump to standing. I march through the aisle, down the flight of stairs, and into the bathroom in the hallway.

My hands grip the cool porcelain of the sink as I look at my own face in the mirror.

I take a deep breath in and exhale, tuning out the bright red and yellow wall in my reflection. It's only me, alone with my thoughts.

What the hell was that? Did he just try to kiss me? Did I…want him to?

This is *not* a date, but…did I kind of want it to be?

Chapter Sixteen

We ride home in silence, and although there's so much of the outside world I want to look at, all I can think of is Liam. And that moment.

That I ruined.

After I'd come back into the theater, Liam's energy was different. He just stared at the screen, more distance between us than before, friendly but closed off.

I rub my palms against the sides of my pants. I desperately want to make this right before we get home and I lose my chance. I want to talk to him, ask something, make conversation about anything but…I can't find the words.

We finally get back to my mom's building. Liam parks the car, opens the alley door for me, and walks me back to my doorstep.

"Sorry about that whole thing in the theater," Liam says, rubbing the back of his head. " I hope I didn't make anything weird."

"Not weird at all," I say, shaking my head. "Don't worry

about it." And that's the truth. If anyone made it weird, it was me.

"Text me later?" Liam asks.

"Definitely."

He moves in toward me again, snaking his arms around my shoulders and waist. I go still at first, stunned he's so close. I'm not exactly used to this whole bodily contact thing. I didn't expect this, but I'm more ready this time.

I mimic him as he squeezes, the scents of his skin and his cologne mixing all around my face. I let myself relax into it, light-headedness settling in. He releases me, waves, and heads back to his apartment.

I'm breathless as heat spreads through my chest.

This was all worth it, right? I went out into the world and nothing happened, and it was worth it. I couldn't be happier right now, so I'd have to say it was…so worth it. And Mom has been wrong all along. And maybe I can actually do this again. I wonder where Liam will want to go next time. It doesn't matter, though—as long as it's with him.

The lock on my door clicks open as soon as I turn the key. The apartment is dark as I walk inside, lock up, and set the key back on the bookshelf.

"What the hell do you think you're doing?" a voice asks from across the room.

My lungs freeze as my eyes zero in on my sister's lithe figure, sitting with her ankles crossed in the chair across the room. *Damn. Shit. Fuck.*

I swear, my spine drops out from inside me. "Uh—" I start, but nothing else will come out.

"Did you leave the house?" she asks with a calm tone. A dangerous tone. "With *him*?"

I walk toward her slowly, hands held up in the air,

trying to defuse her. I'm treating her like a rabid animal because I know when she gets angry, she might as well be. If I can keep her calm, this won't be so bad. "Laurel, it's not what it looks like—"

"It's *exactly* what it looks like!" she says as she shoots up, the blond plait in the middle of her back flying through the air. "Have you lost your fucking mind?"

Okay, we're way beyond calm. "We only went to see a movie. It's really not that big of a deal—"

She rushes toward me, pressing her pointer finger into my chest. "He's enemy number one!"

I roll my eyes. "Laurel, I already told you. It wasn't Liam." My voice stays low, even as I feel myself grow angrier with each word. Why is Laurel trying to ruin this for me? Everything's been quiet for days, and whoever it was must have realized they couldn't get whatever they came for. I have everything under control, *and* I'm finally getting what I always wanted. What I didn't even know I needed—a friend.

Now that I think of it, when was the last time Laurel had a friend? Could it be she's actually jealous of the connection between me and Liam?

"Okay, genius. So if it wasn't your little friend, then who was it?"

"What about the car I told you sped off that night? Did you ever stop to think of that?" I highly doubt it was Max and James, but it's worth it to get her attention away from Liam. "Besides, it couldn't have been him. He's allergic to flowers."

She feigns a laugh. "Oh right, the 'flower allergy.'" She air quotes. "Do you hear yourself? Did you ever stop to consider he could be lying to you? That's what his kind do best."

"His *kind*?" I circle around her, staring her up and down. My temper flares, heat licking at the back of my neck. "What is wrong with you tonight? You're always on my side!"

"And I still am. Someone broke into our house, and your solution for it is to run around with a suspect. Mom will go off the deep end if she finds out." Laurel clenches her jaw and shakes her head. "Do you really want to move again? So you can be stuck even deeper in the middle of nowhere? 'Cause I don't."

I scoff. "Way to make this about yourself, Laurel." I don't know why I'd expect anything else.

"I'm not, I'm trying to help you figure this out. I'm looking out for you. I want only the best for you." She flings her hand in the direction of Liam's apartment. "*That* isn't it."

Who the hell does she think she is, making all of my decisions for me? I'm so sick of her thinking she always knows better than I do. My voice grows cold and my eyes fill with steel. "Says Little Miss Perfect who can't help but manipulate every human she meets."

Her posture becomes rigidly straight and she walks toward me, nose to nose, with her dark green eyes cutting into mine. Her words are barely hiding her rage. "Say that again." The branches and leaves coating the living room rustle, warping around the walls.

I stand straighter as a challenge to her. I'd like to see her fucking try to use her powers on me. "I don't need to," I snap. "Get out of here. I can take care of myself."

She storms to the front door and unlocks it, then turns back to me. "Fuck you. The garden is in jeopardy, but clearly you don't care. I hope Mom locks you up for good." A look of sadness flits across her features before she shakes her head and opens the door. "You're on your own, Quill."

I paw around on my nightstand to grip my phone. My hand holds it above my face, thumbs tapping to pull up his texts.

And next time—because there *will* be a next time—I won't be so nervous. It can only get better from here.

Maybe I'm hyperfocused on proving my sister wrong? Possibly, but my brain is racing from thought to thought. What does she know about liking someone?

For once, I'm happy, and I'm not about to let her take that away. What's she going to do, snitch on me? Highly doubtful. She wouldn't betray me. Or…would she?

What would my mom do if she found out? Evict Liam and his dad? Lock me in the garden? Move the family to the top of some mountain? I wait for guilt and regret to build up in me…but…nothing. I'd do it again.

No. I'm happy, damn it. Tonight was *good.* I got a taste of the outside world—being normal—and I can't stop wanting more. Despite all of my nerves, and even despite my sister, I can't help but smile.

Chapter Seventeen

The frigid air in the cooler is penetrating more than skin deep, no matter how hard my goose bumps try to fight it off.

The longer I'm in here, the more my body fights my brain, starting with my fingers ignoring me. It's a dryad thing—like plants, we don't do well in the cold.

I've been in here for an hour sorting and clipping blooms, but no matter the temperature, my mind has been running rampant with Liam at the forefront. I keep thinking about our text exchange last night, after Laurel finished her little temper tantrum and I got into bed.

Me: My turn to pick next time?

Liam: When's next time?

Me: Same time tomorrow?

Liam: I was hoping you'd say that. Can't wait.

Warmth rushes through me as I remember the feel of his arm next to mine, the smell of his skin, and how soft his eyes were when his face was inches away. I don't need my mom or my sister to tell me what's right. I know I'm not wrong. Last night was one of the best nights of my life. For once, I was free. Free to do and feel whatever I want.

And I'm going to do it again, no matter what.

I put down my shears and take my gloves off, blowing hot air into my palms.

I rub them together for a few seconds, stopping to ball up my fingers and open them again as much as I can. Sure, I may be distracted, but this job would go so much faster if I had a full range of motion.

I've been so conflicted all morning. I don't understand why feelings are so damn complicated. Why can't I just feel one thing at once and then move on to the next? Things would be so much easier to process.

On one hand, I'm on cloud nine from going out with Liam last night. It's like I have this secret that's only mine, making my monotonous daily tasks more bearable. It's this invisible power I'm wearing right beneath my skin.

On the other hand, I'm still so angry at Laurel. She spied on me, judged me, and tried to control me. It's an invasion of everything we've ever shared. She doesn't even know Liam.

Not to mention the fact that the garden is acting weird. I still haven't forgotten about that bush dissolving when I touched it. I haven't seen anything like it since, and I hope I don't again.

The glass door on the other side of the cooler slides open, warm air bursting and brushing over my skin, coaxing my limbs to obey me again. I let out a sigh, soon followed by my mother's voice.

"Has Laurel stopped by today?" she asks as she walks beside me. Her delicate hands pluck individual flowers off the wall in front of me—a little of this and a little of that.

It never ceases to amaze me how she can whip

something up with barely a thought. She always knows exactly what to do.

"Nope," I say, maybe a little too brusquely. "Haven't seen her." And I'm so glad I haven't. She crossed a line last night. I may have said something hurtful back, but honestly, I didn't feel bad about it. If she wants to mouth off about how I live my life, I can do the exact thing. And now I feel like we might have overreacted with the whole break-in thing.

"Strange." Mom agilely waves her thick fingers over the petals, and they all begin to glow. Each different color morphs from yellow and orange and red to become pure white. "She's been dodging my calls today."

"Weird," I say, turning away from her to put my gloves back on.

She pauses behind me, which tells me her eyes are digging into my back. I can feel her doing her X-ray thing again. "Did something happen?" she asks slowly and calmly.

"Not at all." I shake my head and go back to clipping off leaves and thorns. That's a lie, but I can't let her get between us and try to mediate. Then the secret's out and things will get so much worse. It's best if I push my mom past the subject as quickly as I can. "I'll tell her to call you if I see her."

She steps beside me, her palm gently reaching to my cheek. She turns my face toward hers, eyes staring deep into mine as she cocks her head.

"Seriously," I say with the most believable smile. There's this quiet paranoia of my sister ratting me out lingering in my head, but I do everything in my power to squash it down. I put my hand on top of hers. "Brother-sister stuff. It's not a big deal."

She smirks and pulls her hand away. "If you say so." She twirls her finger around the bouquet in her other hand, coaxing the tendrils and stems around the middle to grow into a delicate braid. "Your skin is cold, by the way. Why don't you head back upstairs to warm up? I'll finish down here."

Thank Eden, she bought it. "You sure?"

"Yes," she says with a nod. She walks back to the glass door, stopping and turning her head right before she closes it. "And make up with your sister."

I roll my eyes and sigh. "If I have to." Another lie.

I shiver as I go upstairs, hugging myself and rubbing my arms with my hands. Luckily, I know just where to go to warm up the fastest.

My pocket buzzes just as I'm beginning to doze off amidst the humid air and aroma of the purple blossoms enshrouding the arbor, where I'm sprawled out on a long bench of boughs inside a living gazebo. My heartbeat picks up again as my mouth twists into a smile. It's strange because I'd normally be irritated at the interruption. Except I know exactly who it is.

I dig my phone out and glance at the screen to see his name.

Liam: Wyd?

Me: Taking a break at work. You?

Thirty seconds later, my screen lights up with a picture. My heart skips a beat as his face appears—a selfie with him winking and biting his tongue with a smile. His wavy red hair is somehow sticking up in all the right places, and he's lying in bed with a pillow under his head and a blanket covering his bare chest.

My eyes go wide, and my mouth goes dry. A wave of excitement rushes through my body. I… I… How do I respond?

Downplay?

Downplay.

Me: Looks cozy. Glad one of us gets to relax

Liam: Well there's room for two ;)

Why does he say things like that? Just to see how I'll react? Do all humans do this?

The sides of my face are burning and I'm trying to stop my thoughts, but I can't help wanting to see more. How is he able to make me so flustered? Thankfully my phone buzzes again, because I don't think I would have been able to downplay that one.

Liam: Jk! Where's my picture?

I shake my head and sigh. Something tells me he wasn't totally kidding.

Still, I stand and hold the phone out in front of me. A sheet of lavender petals cascades behind me, shadows from the bright stars above dancing on my skin. I give him a little smirk before snapping the photo and sending it his way. He has no idea where the garden even is, so I think it's safe to give him a sneak peek of one corner.

My body sinks back down to the bench, and he responds in no time.

Liam: Gorgeous…you should post that

Me: Post it?

Liam: Sorry, I forgot you don't have InstaSnap. You should make one. Add me if you do. @liquidliam

Me: I'll think about it

I'm not sure it's the best idea to go public. The internet has a long memory, and it's way too easy for my sister to find something else to be even angrier about. Plus, it's not exactly the same as going into public with Liam and ending up in an empty movie theater. Who knows who's watching?

Then again, isn't this another thing normal people do nowadays? Won't I need to get one to fit in eventually?

Liam: So what did you want to do tonight?

Me: How about this. You took me somewhere you thought I'd like. What's your favorite place in the world?

Liam: Easy. School pool. Might be hard to get into though

The movies are one thing, but breaking and entering? That's a whole new level. However, a little magical intervention would make that easier. It's not like we'd be hurting anyone. Only a quick visit.

Me: I can get around that

Liam: Going from breaking out to breaking in? I like it

Me: Been taking a lot of chances lately. What's a few more?

Liam: Good thinking. Text me after your mom goes to bed?

Me: Will do. And get out of bed. Go be productive

Liam: I'm comfy here. You can be productive enough for both of us ;)

Me: Thanks jerk

Liam sends back a laughing emoji and a heart, and I just roll my eyes.

He obviously likes getting a rise out of me, but there's still so much I don't know—specifically what he's like in public. At school. With his family. I think it's time I found out.

Out of curiosity, I Google his handle.

That chiseled face pops up immediately, and I can't

help but grin. I scroll through post after post, getting a peek into what a normal life would look like. One without gardens and potions and magic day in and day out. One where the biggest worries are friends and homework and social media.

The first photo is of Liam sitting in the same red chairs we were in last night, but next to his two friends I met. Max, was it? She has a mohawk in this photo, but still the same signature purple. James has his hair buzzed short, but still wearing his uniform from the movie theater. I wonder what they were seeing that night.

I wonder what they talked about and laughed about and drank and ate. They're all smiling, and all I can do is imagine what it must have been like to be there with them. Maybe we can invite them next time. If Liam likes them, wouldn't I?

A few scrolls down, and there he is with goggles around his forehead and a gold medal around his neck. A bright cerulean pool sits in the background—a completely unnatural color compared to the ones here in the garden.

His teammates are all gathered around him, cheering. Not a whole lot of clothes on him—and he's in much better shape than I am. It's not a bad sight. I can't help but think back to that selfie he sent me and wonder what it would be like to lie next to someone. Particularly him. Something in my chest craves to find out. Wants it so bad, it clenches. Why am I feeling like this? I barely know this boy.

The last photo I see is of a young boy, maybe six or seven, standing in front of a man and a woman. The bald man is muscular and handsome in a blue suit, and she's tall and statuesque, with long blond hair and an elegant white dress. The boy is clinging to her, almost afraid of the camera, but both of the adults are smiling with a lit-up

Christmas tree in the background.

I snicker, because there are a thousand real trees around me now I could dress up a thousand times better. But then I get to the caption: "Happy birthday, Mom."

I sigh, a slight twinge nicking at my heart. He clearly loved her very much. I can barely remember my dad, but if I lost my mom? I don't know what I would do.

Sure, she's overprotective, but I'd be lost without her. And destroyed. Luckily I have another five hundred years or so before I even need to consider it.

A screen pops up as I go further down, pushing me to sign up to see more. It's not the best idea, I know, but… how much could it actually hurt? I take a deep breath and close my eyes to listen to my intuition.

Fuck it. I'm doing this.

I fill out a few boxes, type in the handle "@quillworks," and hit confirm. I press "follow" on his profile and take another deep breath. If I'm going to do this, I may as well do this right.

With a few more taps, I post the photo he deemed as "gorgeous." I get my first follow back and "like" within seconds.

Chapter Eighteen

It's way easier to get ready tonight.

Most of my closet got to stay on its shelves, thanks to the vision of Liam in the tight-fitting plain white tee and black shorts he wore last time. Nothing too fancy, and nothing to overthink.

This time I even run a handful of water through my hair. Sure, it gets sucked up right away, but at least the patch of grass I call hair looks like there was effort thrown in. My nerves aren't as raw, either—I already know what to expect for the most part. It'll be only Liam and me anyway. No friends, no public, only us and an empty school. I wonder what it'll be like.

I slow my breath and hush my footsteps, rolling heel to toe as I move silently through my house. No Laurel in the living room this time—let's hope she can mind her business so it can stay that way. My fingers swipe the key off the bookshelf, I slip out the front door, and the stairs lead me to the first floor.

A familiar, creeping feeling is starting to return—the

one I do my best to bury and not dread the possible consequences. I stop at the door to the alley and take a deep breath.

One. Two. Three.

I push the door open and see Liam by his dad's car. He turns his head in my direction, and the hugest smile spreads across his face.

"Ready to go?" I ask as I walk to the passenger side.

He beats me to it, opening the door for me. "Been waiting all day."

I get in, and he closes the door before getting in on the driver's side. "Glad to see you got out of bed," I say as I roll down the window.

"Are you giving me shit for my selfie?" He reverses the car, puts it in drive, and takes off out of the alleyway.

I shrug. It's fun to give him a hard time. "So what if I am?"

"Oh please," he says with a mischievous crooked smile. "You saw my InstaSnap. I know you've seen me with fewer clothes than that."

"Just tell me you brought more than your Speedo tonight, and we'll be good."

"Wait," he says, face full of confusion. "I thought we were going skinny dipping?"

My cheeks burn hot, and my eyes widen. "Uh, I mean—I guess—but…"

He breaks out laughing. "You're so easy to work up sometimes." He pushes my shoulder with his palm and turns onto the main street.

The tingling feeling in my chest fades and so does the embarrassment. "I hate you," I say, shaking my head and looking forward, focusing on the black sky. No moon tonight—complete cloud cover, so it's darker than normal.

The wind is twisting and turning the leaves on the trees as we pass. The garden is at perpetual peace, that is, unless my mom or my sister rile it up. I've always wished I could do that. I roll down the window and let my ears soak in the rustling, the smell of a storm filling my nose as it pours in.

"So you got away with it?" he asks, driving through a yellow light. He kisses his fingers and touches the roof of the car.

I pay more attention to the strange gesture than the question. "Hmm?"

"Since you're out again with me, I'm assuming your mom didn't find out?"

"Oh." I adjust myself in the seat, crossing my arms. I'm suddenly reminded that I'm pissed at Laurel. "No, but my sister did."

"Oh shit," he says as a grimace crosses his face. "What did she say?"

I shake my head. "It doesn't matter. Let's just say she wasn't happy about it."

He sighs, leaning back. He pulls one hand off the wheel and sets his arm on the center console. "I don't understand why you can't go out. Be a normal teenage boy."

"They're only protective of me, is all. I get it, but it's too much sometimes." That and my sister kind of hates him.

"Maybe I can meet them someday. Maybe they'll change their minds if they get to know me."

"Maybe," I say. *Doubtful. Besides, I'd rather keep you all to myself for now.* I shock myself as that thought runs through my mind. *Where the hell did that come from?*

We finally pull up to the school after about fifteen minutes. The lights are out in the parking lot, and no cars are left—a good sign that we'll actually get away with this. The car comes to a full stop, and we get out.

"Still not sure how you plan to get in," he says as we walk up to the doors.

Towering oaks darken the front lawn, leaving only a concrete sidewalk lined with large rocks in the shadows. Of course the front doors are the most exposed part of the building. I'm glad there are no houses around, at least.

I smile confidently. "I have my ways. Do you know if there's an alarm?"

"There is, but they never turn it on," he says. "Small town. I don't think anyone's had the balls to do something like this."

"First time for everything, I guess. Keep a lookout in case." I dig into my pocket and pull out an iridescent sprig in the shape of a four-leaf clover. My sister taught me about Rainbow Root a long time ago, but this was my first non-magical reason to use it.

Making sure he's still turned away, I hold it near the lock. It begins to twist between my fingers, snaking into the lock and morphing into the shape of a glass key. It hardens, and I twist until it clicks. "Got it," I say as I pull the door open.

Liam's head swivels around. "How did you do that?"

I roll my eyes. "Magic, duh." He wouldn't believe me, anyway. I havc to admit, this whole mischief thing is actually kind of fun. Mostly because I know we won't get caught, but also because I have someone to do it with.

He scoffs, walking through the doorway after me. "Very funny. Fine, don't tell me."

"I'll teach you one day if you play your cards right," I say proudly.

"I'll hold you to that." I hope he doesn't.

We walk into the main lobby, but I slow my steps to take it all in.

The high ceilings, the pillars, the long hallways—it's incredible. I keep reminding myself to blink every time my eyes start getting too dry.

"What's the matter?" Liam asks.

I shake my head. "Nothing, it's just so…big. I've never been in a building like this before."

Liam chuckles. "You get used to it." He slows his pace to match my stroll. "The library is all the way down to the left…the art classes are all upstairs…but where we're going is all the way to the right. The gyms and the pool."

"I guess we'd better get going if we want to get there by midnight," I say, still marveling. There's so much here I'm curious about. So much I want to see and learn. What's a day here like? Are teachers strict? Are the kids my age nice like Max and James? What else could I learn about if I wanted to?

He laughs again, putting his arm around my shoulder. I tense up at first—this isn't like a hug that I know is ending in a few seconds. It somehow feels like we're closer than that, and I've never had someone touch me like this who wasn't family.

My heart pounds, but his skin is getting damp. Is he… nervous? Am I nervous? But still, it feels…nice. I let his arm stay, even relaxing in to him.

"I didn't think you'd be so impressed," he says. "It's only a school."

"You're just used to it," I say as we walk down the hallway, joined together.

It's a shame the magic of this place is lost on him. However, the same could be said about me and the garden.

The stagnant air hangs around us, clinging to my skin. I wonder when's the last time they turned on the air conditioning, but it would be a massive waste of money.

We're probably the only ones who have been in here for weeks. The magic of summer vacation.

Rows and rows of photos of past students cover the walls near the ceilings. Were they special for some reason? All desks inside each classroom are in exactly measured rows behind glass doors, with each teacher's name on little placards.

Ryan—English. Niccolls—Algebra. Groteluschen—History.

"What's your favorite class?" I ask.

"Eh, I don't actually like most of them."

I look at him, narrowing my eyes. "Why's that?"

"They're hard for me." He sighs. "I fall asleep in class a lot. Insomnia's a bitch."

"Really? I would have never guessed."

"It's weird, actually," he says with a pause. "I've been sleeping like a baby for the last few days. No more sneezing, either. I don't know why."

"That is strange." I can't help but wonder if that had something to do with the potion I gave him. Maybe it wasn't only his face it had an effect on.

"Any class in particular you're excited about?" he asks.

"Oh, that's an easy one," I say. "Science."

"Says the guy who used magic to get in." He laughs. "Besides, don't you kind of use biology every day?"

"It's different when it's the family business," I say. "I'd love to learn about things the legit way."

"Fair enough." His arm is still sitting innocently on top of my shoulders, but his fingers are gently stroking my arm.

My senses are on overload but it's the only thing I'm capable of focusing on. I'm not sure if this is something friends would do, but I don't care. I'm not pulling away this time.

At last, we get to the end of the hallway. He slides his arm down my spine and a shiver runs through me. He smirks as he reaches for the door handles. "Ready for this?"

"As I'll ever be." I laugh. I've seen water before. What's the big deal?

His thumbs press down on the handles, and he pulls, revealing a gigantic body of water. The ponds and streams inside the garden pale in comparison to the size of this. The same bright blue reflects all along the walls as I walk in, but suddenly my sense of smell is assaulted.

I've never smelled anything like this in my life, and it's disgusting. My nose is already getting raw after only a few seconds. I try to breathe out of my mouth, but the same thing is happening to my throat.

"What do you think?" he asks.

"It's beautiful," I say honestly, ignoring the painful aspect of it. "But what's that horrible smell?"

He lets out a goofy laugh. "Have you never smelled chlorine before?"

I shake my head. "I'm used to fresh water." It's awful. Repulsing. Appalling. I'd prefer manure or vomit, but I have a feeling it's best not to say those things out loud when we're at his favorite place in the world.

"You get used to it," he says. I highly doubt that. "Wanna go for a swim?" Liam asks, moving his arms to strip off his shirt.

"I…think I'll pass this time." The last thing I need is to absorb whatever chemicals are in that water.

Liam tosses his top onto the wooden bleachers and kicks off an outer pair of shorts to reveal a pair of swim trunks underneath. "Suit yourself," he says.

The glowing lights from the pool dance on his muscles,

and I'm standing there frozen and staring at him. His pictures don't do him justice. My hands are aching to reach out and bring him close to me again, but… What the hell is wrong with me? Why am I even thinking like this?

He sees me looking, but he chuckles before breaking into a run and diving gracefully into the deep end. He moves with an animal instinct as soon as he falls under the surface—as if he's part fish. He's agile and alive beneath the surface.

I see why he loves swimming so much. He belongs in the water, almost as much as I belong in nature.

I walk up to the edge of the pool and ease myself down, crossing my legs.

Looking around the huge room, the moonlight streams in through the glass ceiling and gives it a soft glow. Murals cover the walls, notably the largest one in the center of two suits of armor jousting. Castleview Knights, it says. Strange how that's the mascot for a swim team. Wouldn't they just sink?

My eyes flit back to Liam, watching him kick and flip about. "You're a natural," I say when he finally comes up for air.

"Thanks," he says, catching his breath and pushing his hair back. He swims to me and crosses his arms on the edge at my feet. "You should come to a swim meet sometime."

It's an interesting thought, but I doubt that'll happen. Still, I'm curious. "What are they like?"

"Loud and exciting," he says. "They're the reason this is my favorite place in the world. Sure, you can swim anywhere, but it's where all my favorite people can be at the same time. My parents always sat in the front row."

"Sat?" I ask. "Does your dad not come anymore?"

"When he can," Liam says quickly, sadly. "Things changed a lot last year." He does that thing again, where he looks off into the distance. His eyes go flat, and he tugs on his bottom lip with his teeth.

My chest tightens and my heart aches to see him like this. "Not sure how much it means, but I'll be happy to come see you swim." Not sure if I'd actually do it yet, though. That sounds like a lot of humans in one place. The two new ones at the movie theater were enough to handle, but hundreds?

He turns back to me with a smile and winks. "Thought I'd give you the private show now."

I roll my eyes and shake my head with a grin, but my heartbeat goes wild.

He swims a foot or two beside me, presses his huge hands into the tile, and uses his thick arms to push himself out of the pool. He turns to sit next to me, but I scoot away to avoid the water trickling off his trunks. The smile fades as soon as I do. He pulls up his knees to his chest and sighs.

"Listen," he says. "About last night…"

He's the one who can't seem to find the words now. I prod him along, trying to help and see where he's going with this. "What about last night?"

"When we almost…" He looks into my eyes and raises his eyebrows.

"When we almost what?" I wish he would spit it out.

He tips his head down and looks at me from beneath his eyebrows. "Are you honestly gonna make me say it?"

"I don't know what you're talking about." I really wish he would just be upfront about whatever it is that he's thinking.

He sighs. "I'm sorry if I've been making you uncomfortable. I wish I knew how to read you better."

I'm taken aback at him saying that. "Not much to read, Liam. I've been totally honest." I may not understand the things I've been feeling, but I'd like to think I've been upfront about whatever's going on between us. Aren't we friends? Isn't that what friends do?

"I know but…" He pauses. "Okay, I'll just ask. Are you gay?"

"I…I don't know. It's something I've never really thought about."

"Well…think about it now," he says, motioning with his hands. "Do you like guys? Girls? Both?"

He's pushing hard with this one, and I'm starting to wonder why. Maybe we started as friends, but maybe that's only what I thought. Is this why he acts so weird and says those strange things sometimes? Does he…like me? Like that? Is he trying to see if we'd be good…together?

On the surface, it seems like the worst idea in the world. But the more I think about it… It's not actually that bad of a thought. I'd be lying if I said I wasn't interested. I don't want to let on too much, so I'll generalize it. "My sister and I were raised to be who we are and feel what we feel, with no judgment and no labels. I know she's been with guys and girls. My mom, too, before she was with my dad. I mean, I've never even had a friend. It's all so new for me."

He nods. "Okay. That makes a lot of sense."

"Why, are you gay?" I ask, knitting my eyebrows.

"Yeah, I am," he says. "And I know it's not something you've thought much about, but…know you can talk to me if you ever need to."

Now he's being careful with his words, but it still makes me smile. "Thank you. I appreciate that."

He smiles back, shaking his head. "No wonder you've been so weird when I flirt with you."

"Flirt with me?" I laugh, my skin flushing. Suddenly my nerve endings light up, but now it all makes way more sense. "Is that what you've been doing?"

Liam shrugs. "All in good fun. Can't blame a guy for trying."

I need time to figure all of this out, so I roll my eyes. "What I can blame you for is if we get caught in here for staying too long. I can get us in, but we're not invisible. You ready to head home?"

"I suppose." He smirks.

Liam pushes his way to standing—the muscles in his arms flexing under his smooth skin. They short-circuit my brain, and it's like I can't see anything in the room except him while he's standing above me.

I manage to shake out of it when he holds his hand out to me and I gently grip it, an electric current running through my arm from the skin contact. I can't help but think of being closer to him, but I'm not paying attention well enough. I pull up on his arm, but my shoe slips on the puddle of water he brought out with him.

And we both go toppling into the water.

Chapter Nineteen

It all happens in slow motion: the smile on Liam's face, then the terror shooting through my chest as my bare skin slaps the surface of the pool, my body traveling down as the waves rise up to wrap me in a cocoon. The water closes in above me, and time restarts.

I flail, struggling to get my head back above water, as the shock of the cold liquid still holds my chest tight. My breath is fighting me, but he's already right side up and laughing, splashing water at me. It's not nearly as enjoyable on my end.

Thankfully I know how to swim, but the chemicals feel like fire. Every inch of my skin, eyes, and nose is engulfed in an inferno. I cough endlessly, scrambling, as spots cloud my vision. I need to leave this place. I don't know what's going to happen if I'm in here too long, and I don't want to find out.

"Quill, are you okay?" Liam calls, all joy wiping from his eyes.

I pull myself out, curling into a ball beside the edge. I

can't think straight. My body is overwhelmed with agony. My breath shudders as my skin soaks up every drop dripping from my shirt.

Liam paddles to me, jumps out of the water, and crouches. "What's wrong?" he asks frantically. He touches my arm, but the pressure makes it worse.

"I think I'm allergic to the chemicals." I clench my eyes tight, focusing on the starbursts behind them.

"Don't move, I'll get you a towel," he says as he runs to the end of the locker area.

I lay there and hold my soaking arms up, watching the droplets disappear into my pores. He's back in twenty seconds. He crouches, moving to cover me. "Here, maybe we can get the rest off you—" He stops. "How are you dry already?"

I clench my teeth, the initial burn already fading. It sounds better, but now the heat's moved inside. "Can we just…get out of here?"

He pauses. "Yeah, let's go." He scoops me up into his arms. Without a word, he carries me out of the pool area and down the hallway of the school.

It's kind of funny. I finally figure out what's going through his head—and maybe mine too—and now here I am in his arms. But still, I feel too awful to pay attention to anything that's happening outside of my skin.

I should be enjoying this, but all I can focus on is how hard I can clench my fists before it distracts me from how awful I feel. Through the front doors, into the pitch-black parking lot, and at last he stands me up next to the car.

The fresh air is already soothing my skin, making the pain inside more manageable. "I think I can get it from here," I struggle to say, but he reaches the handle before I have a chance.

"Nope, I've got you." He opens my door once more and

helps me inside before going around and getting into the driver's side. The car starts, and we're off.

"You feeling okay?" he asks, halfway through town.

My muscles relaxed a few blocks ago, so now I can at least lie there in peace. They feel so heavy and I'm suddenly so tired.

"Yeah, no more burning," I say, breathing through my mouth as I lean against the doorframe. I roll down the window, trying to air out my sinuses with the smell of rain. "Feeling a little queasy, though."

"I am so sorry," he said. "This was a terrible idea."

"Why are you apologizing?" I chuckle, clutching my stomach. He's so worried—even more so than the night we fell off the fire escape. It makes my chest flutter. "It was my idea. And neither of us knew I'd have this reaction."

"Yeah but…still." He's genuine right now. No bravado. No weird flirting. I was kind of doubting it before—like he was trying to put on an act—but maybe he really does have feelings for me.

I shake my head. "It's no big deal. I've just gotta get home and wash off." In the meantime, though, I'm glad he's here with me.

Liam parks the car behind our building and eases me out, putting my arm around his shoulders. He helps me up the stairs to my door, taking extra care and slowing his pace when I need to catch my breath. Once we're at my door, he pulls me into a tight hug. My skin is tender, but the butterflies in my stomach help numb it.

"Text me after you rinse off, okay?" he asks.

I curse this chlorine because I'd be thoroughly enjoying this if it weren't for the extreme nausea. "Will do," I say into his shoulder. I close my eyes and stay still for a moment—maybe longer than I should.

He pulls back and runs his fingers through my hair. “Thanks for a great night.”

“Let’s make the next one better,” I say with a weak grin.

He chuckles. “It’s a date.”

I lock up behind me, bracing myself on every piece of furniture and wall until I get to my bathroom. I’d felt a little better when I was still with Liam, but now that it’s just me I feel like shit. My steps drag, and my mouth is dry, coated in a metallic taste. All I want is fresh water inside and out. My clothes are stiff and reek of a swimming pool. I’d better bring them into the bath with me, so my mom doesn’t catch on to the odor.

Water pours out of the shower head while I wait for it to warm up. I look in the mirror—and it’s ghastly. The golden tan of my skin remains the same, but it’s completely dried out. The whites of my eyes reflect a greenish-yellow.

This is bad. Very bad.

My heart is racing and my nerves are fried. I don’t know if I can hide this from my mom. I don’t know how long this feeling will last, and I don’t know what to do to make it better. I can’t let her see me like this. It’s bad enough that Liam had to.

I strip off my clothes and toss them onto the floor of the tub. With any luck, they’ll wash out quicker than I will. My hands press against the wall as I slowly sit down on the floor, the stream hitting me directly. The clean water runs along my skin, sinking in bit by bit. I open my mouth to rinse out that awful taste of chemicals and spit it down the drain.

Closing my eyes, I try to will the feeling to go away. I hope this passes soon.

Chapter Twenty

"Quill, are you in there?" my mom's voice shouts.

My eyes fly open, and my body jolts on the floor of the bathtub. The icy chill of the water makes me gasp as I flounder to shut it off.

"Y-yeah, M-M-Mom," I manage to say back as quickly as I can through chattering teeth. I can't smell a thing—my nose is raw and stings as I breathe. My muscles are weak, and a heaviness is weighing me down from my chest, but I can't let on that anything is wrong.

"You've been in there since I got up this morning. Is everything okay?"

My hand rips the towel off the wall even though my body is already sapping up all of the moisture. Partly for modesty, but mostly for warmth. I stumble out of the tub and crack the door open wide enough to show my face.

"A-all g-g-good," I say. I hope she believes me.

Her emerald eyes go wide. "Oh my God, Quill, your lips are purple," she says, reaching out to touch my forehead. "How are you burning up at the same time?"

Damn it. There's no way I can fake my way through this. "D-d-dunno," I say. "I'm s-so c-cold, though." I must look way worse than I thought. I did *not* want her to see me like this. I need to keep trying to fight this so she'll back off and let it go.

"Go put some clothes on and climb in bed. I'll be right back." She rushes away from the door and out of my bedroom, the fabric of her dress flying behind her.

My feet shuffle along the hardwood, stopping long enough to reach down and snatch a pair of sweats and a long shirt. My mouth is so dry and I'm so fucking tired.

I plop down on the bed and yank them on, fighting against the shivering. I don't even bother getting under the covers—I curl up on top of them and bury my face in my pillow. The storm must have passed while I was in the shower because the sun is beating down through my window.

My bedding muffles all the sounds in the house, but Mom's panicked footsteps soon hurry back into my room. "Sit up," she says softly. Her weight bounces my mattress as she sits next to me.

"T-t-too b-bright," I say, rolling over and shading my face with my hand. Trying to fight it off is way harder than I thought it would be. My head is pounding, eyelids clenched.

My mom flourishes her hand above her head, and the branches in my room extend toward the glass, crosshatching it with leaves and twigs. "Better?" she asks in the dark.

"Yeah," I say as I push myself up. "T-thanks." Every inch of my body feels like it's put together wrong, but at least everything around me is quiet and dark. It's the exact opposite of what I felt in the pool—going straight from sharp fire to a blunt frost.

Can this get worse? Am I going to die?

"Drink this," she says, holding out a small blue bottle.

I shake my head and whimper. "I'm already f-freezing, Mom." All I want is to lie here and pray this passes soon. If at all.

"That's the fever, sweetie. We've got to get your temperature down." She uncorks it and pushes it toward me once more. "Don't worry, I mixed it with a sleep potion. You'll be out before you know it."

I sigh, wrapping my fingers around the glass and bringing it to my lips. One deep breath and bottoms up.

A sweet minty taste coats my tongue and throat as my stomach and veins fill with ice. I burp, and a white cloud of my breath comes out. My fingers drop the bottle back into her open hand, and I roll back up into my blankets, shivering even harder than before. She smooths my hair, and before I know it, the world is black.

Black.

For who knows how long.

Deep and dark, underground. Little footsteps echo off dank walls, pitter-pattering in the blackness.

"Hello?" I call. A little girl's laughter rings gently from somewhere in the darkness. I spin, small yellow orbs on the ground catching my eye. How curious. I've never seen anything like them before. I bend down to get a better look—mushrooms?

I poke one, and suddenly it explodes into a million sparks, floating through the air like frozen fireworks. It's the hugest cave I could ever imagine. My eyes trace the little balls of light hanging in the air but settle on the little girl in front of me. Six or seven, delicate frame and long hair that's…bright green? It's the color of mine.

This is so strange.

"You'll never catch me!" Bell-like laughter follows her as she sprints into the darkness.

"Laurel?" I yell after her.

I shuffle carefully in her direction, but she's gone. Out of the darkness, two more figures emerge hand in hand. One is clearly my mother—not any different than now—but the second is a man. Tall, thin, and so familiar.

The closer I look, the more I recognize his features. His eyes and hair are as dark as night, but his skin looks like it's never seen the sun. The same straight nose that I have. The same narrow face. He even has my cheekbones. I swear I've seen him somewhere before… And then it hits me.

"Dad?" I ask. Holy shit, it is him. And he doesn't look a day older than Laurel did two days ago.

He reaches out to me with his free hand, but as I step forward to take it, he moves backward. And farther and farther, until he's gone.

Chapter Twenty-One

"Quill. Quill! Wake up." My mom's hand is on my shoulder, shaking me awake.

My eyes crack open, adjusting to the shadows of the room. My hands run over my face and chest, my vision jumping between the walls of my room. *Shit.* Only a dream. I try to take stock of my body, checking whether my mom's potion helped. But the only thing I feel is cold. Icy, mind-numbing, skull-crushing cold.

"W-what is it? W-w-w-what's wrong with m-m-me?"

"You're freezing, sweetheart," she says, trying to pull me off my back. She can barely contain the worry in her voice. "We need to warm you back up."

"C-c-can you just g-give me s-something else?" I ask, refusing to move.

She shakes her head, doing her best to prop me up. "A heating potion will only bring back your fever. We need to do it the hard way. Let's go to the garden."

I take my deepest breath in, and dread pools in my stomach. *Better to get it over with.*

I throw off the rest of the blankets and put my legs over the side. She fits my arm over her shoulders and helps me to stand, guiding me out into the hallway, pulls open the door, and we step inside my family's secret garden. The summer air inside still feels like a winter's night on my skin.

What time is it? What day is it? Doesn't she have places she needs to be? "Who's r-r-running the sh-shop?"

"Laurel," she says, trekking us forward along the path. "Neither of you ever gets sick, so she was happy to step in. She's worried about you."

I keep my mouth shut. I feel awful, but my irritation with my sister is still strong enough to peek through. *Yeah, I bet she is. Only more ammo for her to throw at me later.*

We slowly walk through a stone arch and into a small grove of trees surrounding a steaming hot pool, my mom supporting my weight the entire way.

We come to an abrupt stop as soon as we get to the water's edge. I see the concern on my mom's face and follow her gaze—a thick green film is smothering the spring. Even feeling as bad as I do, worry bolts through me as I take in the murky water. I've never seen it look like this before. My mind flashes back to the dried brown leaves I came across the other day. What the hell is going on?

She looks around, eyebrows knitting together. "When's the last time you were over here?" Her worry seems to have shifted entirely from me to the garden.

"Um…I d-d-don't know," I say. "Y-yesterday. W-why?" Did I fuck something else up?

"It's an algae bloom, but that's impossible. Not at this temperature and not this quickly."

No, this wasn't me. I have a sinking feeling this is the

handiwork of whoever's been sneaking into the garden—it's too much of a coincidence that the garden acting so strangely and the break-in would happen at the same time and not be connected in some way. Was there another attempted break-in while I was out with Liam last night? Maybe Laurel has a point after all—maybe I'm focusing on all the wrong things, like making a new friend instead of trying to figure out what's going on with my family's eternal lifesource.

I wince as another all-consuming shiver racks my body. I need to get better so I can deal with all of this.

"I'm s-sorry," I say, taking the blame. "I'll do b-better—"

She cuts me off. "No, honey, it's not your fault. Hold on."

My mom stands me up in the archway and paces to the spring's edge. She lifts her dress out of the way as she crouches down, sticking a single finger into the water.

The pool quickly fades into the deepest black, all life inside it dissolving away from her touch in under thirty seconds.

Goose bumps run down the back of my neck and arms. It's such a simple use of magic—nothing as flashy as when Laurel planted the Ardor Blossom—but it's exactly as breathtakingly powerful. Once the water is devoid, it turns clear once again with gray stones at the bottom.

It's a rare moment—my mom never uses that side of her powers. She always believes in nature correcting itself. She's such a gentle woman, always focusing on growth and healing, so her even having the ability to wither anything she touches is more than unsettling. Almost like if Santa Claus were a pro at arson. It just doesn't compute.

"C'mon," she says, hurrying back and ushering me to the water. "In you go. Clothes and all."

The water is lukewarm on my skin although I can see the steam wisp around my face. It's nice, though. Definitely warmer than my room.

I tilt my head back, submerging everything except my face. Every inch of my skin relaxes, the pores opening wide to trade toxins for clarity. After a few seconds of light pinpricks and stings from the damaged tissue, I start to feel like myself again. Nature's reset button.

"Better?" she asks, sitting in the grass nearby.

"Yeah," I say with a deep breath as the tension in my muscles eases. It feels like I'm free to breathe again.

She sighs with relief and pulls her fiery hair back into a bun before folding her hands in her lap. "Why were you in the shower so long this morning? Were you trying to warm up?"

I float peacefully, wondering about the best way to cover my tracks. "I must have fallen asleep in there. I wasn't feeling well last night." Not a lie. Except I need to be careful not to tell her more.

"Why didn't you wake me up? I know I sleep deeply, but I could have taken a pep-up. I could have taken care of you." The worry in her voice is unmistakable, and it's becoming a pit of guilt in my gut. I truly scared her.

I lift my head and look her in the cyc, doing my best to ease her concern. "Mom, I'm seventeen. I should be able to take care of myself."

"Normally, sure. But this isn't normal. It's my job to take care of you at times like this."

I smile at her, trying harder to make her feel better. "I know. And you always have. And I love you for it."

Her full lips grin weakly. "I love you, too."

As I study her face, I'm reminded of the face she wore in my dream. "So that sleeping potion you gave me," I say as I look down, dragging my fingers beneath the surface. "I had some pretty weird dreams."

"Like what?" she asks, tipping her head to the side.

I shrug. After all, it was only a strange fever dream. "I was in this giant cave with all these twinkling lights. Laurel was there, but she was very young. She still had green hair like me. And you were there, and…Dad."

She goes silent for a moment and nods. "I'm surprised you remember that. It's a cavern in the mountainside on the outskirts of town. There are these rare mushrooms that grow inside called Light Caps. You crush them, and the spores fly out, except they're little balls of light."

I snap my head to hers. "Wait," I say, swimming up to the bank. "It's real?" I'm shocked that she's telling me this much. Everything pre-apartment has always gone unspoken.

"Oh yeah." She sighs. "I found it back when Laurel was young. It was beautiful. The closest thing to the night sky I'd seen in years without medicinal help. Your father and I took her a couple of times a year to camp as a family. We kept going until you were about two."

I'm wary to dig deeper, but I'm desperate to know. This is the closest we've ever come to discussing how we ended up here. "Is that when…you know…it happened?" I ask carefully, looking down at the water. I don't want to scare her.

She nods again. "Yes. That's when your father and I split up."

He's definitely one subject I don't bring up—I never dared until today. But I can't shake the feeling that now is the time to ask. "Mom…I know this is kind of weird to ask now, but can you tell me about what happened to Dad?"

She clenches her jaw and looks up. Finally, her eyes

meet mine, and she exhales. "I knew this day would come eventually, but I didn't think it would be today."

I feel guilty about dredging any of this up, but I have to know. It's a bad memory for her, but for me, it's now a fresh wound. "I know, it's just… He was there. In my dream. It's the first time I actually remembered him outside of a picture."

She holds up her hand to slow me down. "It's okay, sweetheart. I understand."

I can't believe she actually agrees to it. She's obviously uncomfortable, but she's going through with it anyway. For me. And truth be told, it's a story I've always wanted to know more than anything.

Physically I'm feeling way better, but still, I'd rather not chance it. Staying in the pool for as long as I can, I swim over to her and cross my arms on the bank of the spring. I rest my head, giving her my complete attention.

"When I met your father, I was in a bit of a…rebellious place in my life," she said, staring off into the distance. "Your grandmother had recently passed on, and I hated being alone. I hated this garden for taking her. I avoided coming in here at all costs, actually—I must have let it grow wild for at least a year. I even moved to the desert to be as far away from plants as possible. The place I went, though, was this dingy little biker bar in the center of downtown."

"Wait, was dad a biker?" I ask. Mom dating a bad boy seems so unlike her. I'd have sooner assumed he was an accountant or dentist.

She laughs. "No, but he was the bartender. So kind. So charming. All the regulars there were—very loyal and so welcoming once you got to know them. That was my circle of friends and before I knew it—your father in particular.

My best friend. Things were fine for a long time, until… they weren't."

I knit my eyebrows. "What happened?"

"There was this guy who got a little too attached to me. I tried to turn him down nicely, but he was adamant. One night, after everyone had gone home, it was me and your father and this guy left at last call. Your father had a bad feeling and insisted on driving me home, but I knew I could take care of myself. I left to walk home, but of course, the guy followed soon after. He kept harassing me, wasn't getting anywhere, and then lost his temper. He tried to attack me."

Shock and silence fill me. The idea of my mom anywhere but the flower shop is so foreign, but the idea of a person attacking a being so gentle is beyond my belief. I shake my head quietly, egging her on.

"Your father showed up out of nowhere and tried to protect me—of course getting caught in the crossfire. I used my powers and scooped the other guy up with the branches of a nearby tree. Wrapped him up nice and tight. Your father, on the other hand, wasn't so lucky. He was losing a lot of blood. So I did what I thought was right—I sprinted home and brought back two potions, the strongest ones I knew how to make. One healed your father. The other wiped every memory the other guy had ever had. He stumbled off and was never heard from again. Problem solved, right? Wrong. Your father had seen everything."

I'm so uncomfortable right now. I don't like the thought of my mom in danger, but I *have* to know the rest. "So, what did you tell him?"

"The truth," she says plainly. "What I am. What I could do. I thought he would run and that I would lose my best friend, but no. Nothing changed. If anything, that night was when I realized I loved him. And that he had loved me since the moment he met me. He accepted me for who I am."

It sounds like a happy ending to a fairy tale. How in the world do you go from then to now?

"Fast forward a few years, and your father pushed me to embrace my roots again, for lack of a better term. We opened the first flower shop, and things were great. We even took trips to gather rare specimens—like to the cave in your dream. That changed once we had Laurel, more so once we had you. Suddenly he wasn't so accepting of the garden."

"What do you mean? What about it?" Our garden is amazing.

She sighs. "You know our power is tied to it. So is our lifespan. If it were to get destroyed, we would become human. Suddenly that was the best option in his mind. Now that we had a family, he was terrified of growing old and losing us. He begged me to get rid of it—thousands of years' worth of magic. He wanted us to be a normal family. I refused."

The pieces are starting to come together. "So…you left him instead?"

"Worse. One night I was sleeping, but the strongest dread I've ever felt in my life woke me up in a cold sweat. I turned to your father, but he wasn't next to me. I ran through the house searching for him, praying he wasn't where I thought he was. But of course…I found him. He waited until I was sleeping to burn down the garden, starting with our family trees."

Horror fills my heart. This was worse than anything I could have imagined. I think once again about the break-in, and a shiver runs through me that has nothing to do with being ill. "But you obviously stopped him."

"I did," she says quietly. "It was the ultimate betrayal. He fought, begged, and pleaded, but he couldn't be trusted after that. My children, myself, and my family's legacy were in danger. That night I gave him the same potion I gave to the man who attacked me. I removed all memories he ever had of us, packed up you kids and the garden, and we left. We moved a thousand miles away. I'm not sure why I thought of the cave when we left—maybe it was the last place we were all truly happy—but that's the whole reason I chose this town. And then our life here began."

I'm shocked speechless. The weight of this secret she's kept for all these years hits me full force. My mom didn't leave my dad—she saved us from him.

My heart breaks for her—the love of her life, the father of her children, betrayed her. It's worse than I could have imagined. She did the best she could, but I think of all the damage he did. Doomed Laurel and me to being hidden away. How different our lives could have been if he hadn't been so selfish…

I've always wondered what he was like and what my mom saw in him. I've wondered what it would be like to have a dad. I can't say I missed him, because you can't miss something you've never had, but after hearing this? I'm glad he's not in our lives. I'm glad he doesn't even know who we are. He tried to hurt us—as far as I'm concerned, he's a monster.

My mom has been through so much. A pang of guilt runs through me at letting my obsession with Liam distract me from protecting our garden. I promise myself that I'll find out who was behind the break-in and make sure it never happens again. My mom deserves better.

"Does Laurel know?"

She nods. "I told her when she was your age, and I'll tell you the same thing I told her. It was the hardest, worst thing I've ever done in my very long life. There's not a day that goes by that I wish I had another choice. But everything I learned in those years, everything that happened to me… It's why I don't trust you being out on your own. You can't defend yourself like I could. But to make it worse, sometimes you can't protect yourself from the ones closest to you. Sometimes you don't know what a person is capable of."

I nod. Maybe that's why Laurel runs around the world whenever she gets the chance. Maybe she's scared to form connections with people, because she knows where it can lead. Where it led my mom and our family.

It makes me wonder, can I ever truly trust humans? Can I trust Liam? But not all humans are like my dad… right? Liam's different. I'm sure of it. I do my best to push all the doubt from my mind. "I understand. And I love you. Thank you for telling me."

She reaches out and grabs my hand, giving it a light squeeze. "I love you, too. Always know that." We're quiet, taking in the moment, until she speaks again softly. "How are you feeling?"

I want to know more. I want to ask about so much more, but I see how hard it is for her to talk about any of this. I'm thankful I got this much from her. So I leave it. "Better," I say with a weak smile, and that's the truth.

She smirks back. "This garden's magic never lets me down. But let's get you back to bed just in case."

Chapter Twenty-Two

I roll over in bed, yawning and stretching my arms above my head and feeling about a million times better than the day before.

Note to self: public pools are toxic pits and should be avoided at all costs. At least it was only chemicals. School's out for the summer, so the chance of someone peeing in there is slim. Ugh, Liam had better not have tried to get away with that, either.

Liam. Shit. I never texted him.

My hand swats around at my nightstand, searching for my phone, and I fumble it between my fingers. I tap the screen and expect it to illuminate my face. Nothing. That's what I get for not plugging in my phone.

Liam: Thanks for a great night :)

Liam: I hope you had a good time

Liam: How are you feeling?

Liam: You okay?

Liam: Text me when you wake up

I raise my eyebrows, smiling. It's a pretty wonderful

feeling to know that he cared so much. I'm also shocked by the amount of messages pouring in. But I keep scrolling, and they don't stop coming.

Liam: Still haven't heard from you… You good?

Liam: Helloooo, you there?

Liam: Earth to Quill

Liam: Did I piss you off or something?

Liam: I didn't mean to make things weird last night

Liam: Listen, I'm sorry if I said something to upset you

Liam: Okay Quill, starting to get worried

Shit, I really must have panicked him. A pit of guilt forms in my stomach. I pull up the keyboard and start typing as quickly as I can.

Me: I am so sorry. I got so sick last night, passed out, and my phone died. I've been out of it all day

Me: Everything's fine, I promise. Last night was fantastic

Me: Not upset and nothing's weird. I don't think you could do that if you tried

I sigh, tapping the side of the phone with my index finger. At this point, it could have been *me* who upset *him* with the accidental silent treatment. My phone buzzes.

Liam: Oh God, are you okay? Sorry I was low-key melting down

Me: It's all good, much better now. Slept it off

Liam: I was kind of worried you were just gonna ghost me

I shake my head, smirking. It's reassuring to know that I may not be the only insecure one.

Me: Haha I don't think I could ever do that. Besides, you know where I live

Liam: Haha true. Don't think I didn't consider coming

over there at least a few times today

Me: Probably better that you didn't. Would've been an awkward conversation with my mom

Liam: Good point

I start tapping on the screen with my next message, but the typing bubble pops up on his side. I stop typing and so does he. I start again, he starts, but then we both stop at the same time.

My heart races a little faster at this game we're playing, and I can't help but laugh out loud. Fuck it, I'll just hit send. Both come through at the same time.

Liam: When do you wanna hang out again?

Me: When do you wanna hang out again?

Liam: Haha jinx

I stare at the screen, chuckling, getting nervous at the thought of seeing him again. The butterflies have been getting stronger as the days go on. We keep getting closer—sometimes closer than friends should, I think—but I can't wait for it. Besides, what do I know about friends? Is it normal for friends to constantly want to be around each other?

Me: Haha glad we're on the same page. Tonight?

Liam: You sure you feeling up to it?

Me: Yeah, I'm good

Liam: What did you have in mind?

It isn't hard to decide, because my dream from the day before is still fresh in my mind—a hidden rock room, gigantic and full of sparkling lights. It makes the decision of where to go pretty easy. Why not take a chance? Another field trip wouldn't hurt.

Me: Wanna go on an adventure?

Liam: Hell yeah. See you in ten :)

Deep down, I know I should be focusing on the

garden. I know there are more important things I should be worrying about, bigger things taking over right now. But something about being with him even for one more night and getting my mind off of it all feels so much better than dwelling in this mess my life is right now. I can't pass up the opportunity.

Ten minutes seems like an eternity, and I can't wait that long. I rush around my room, pulling on whatever clothes I can find. I run down the hall to the garden door to give it a tug and make sure it's locked tight before I head out. I feel a flash of guilt: I should probably go find Laurel, apologize, and put our heads together on a plan for the garden. But it's nighttime already, and she might be out. Or asleep. Is there so much harm in waiting until morning?

I'm leaning against Liam's car, pulse quickening to the tapping of my foot, as he walks out of the building. He's looking downward and mumbling to himself, gesturing lightly—playing out some conversation, almost practicing. It's kind of…cute to see how he acts when he thinks he's alone.

His eyes flit up to the car for a split second, then down, and immediately back up. He gasps and the blush is apparent, even in the moonlight.

"Talking to yourself?" I ask with a smirk.

He laughs nervously, scratching the back of his head. "You…weren't supposed to see that," he says. "It's a bad habit. Especially when I'm nervous."

"Oh, so I make you nervous?" Looks like I'm not the only one.

"Maybe," he says with a sheepish grin. "But don't think I haven't noticed that look you get on your face."

"What look?"

"The scared one when I get close to you. Like a mouse about to be eaten by a tiger."

I roll my eyes. "If anyone should be nervous, it should be you."

A warm smile takes over his mouth with a soft shake of his head. "You? Make me nervous in a bad way? I don't see that happening."

Such a simple sentence shouldn't mean much, but it stops me in my tracks. Suddenly I feel so vulnerable as my heart flutters, touching me to my core.

My mom and my sister know how to act in this world, and humans have a natural instinct to stay away from creatures like us. But even if Liam does think I'm strange, it doesn't seem to bother him. He might even like being around me, despite me not being…normal.

"You ready to go?" he asks, walking over and opening my door for me. He waits less than a foot away from me—close enough to smell his addictive cologne. His wide eyes jump down to my lips and back up to my eyes again.

My skin twinges and my heartbeat thunders in my chest, my eyes running back down to his lips as well. I kind of wonder what they would feel like, how they would taste.

"Uh…yeah. Let's go." I break away from whatever moment we're having before it gets too awkward, climbing into the seat. I catch a small sigh escape from his mouth before he gently shuts the door behind me. I can't help but feel so self-conscious right now. *Did I do something wrong?*

Liam walks around, gets in, and turns the key in the ignition. "So where to?" he asks as the engine roars to life.

I take a second to consider my decision one more time before speaking it out loud. I have to see this cave for myself, and Liam being there with me feels right. "Mount

Verdant, right outside of town," I say, trying to act normal.

"Outdoorsy tonight," he says with bravado as he reverses the car. "I like it." The energy in his voice puts me at ease again. Maybe I didn't make anything weird after all.

Right as we're pulling out of the alley, another car turns in. It looks familiar, but from the look on Liam's face, he definitely recognizes it.

"Shit," he says under his breath as it honks twice.

My heart picks up speed. "What?"

"I fucked up," he says. "Hold on." Our car pulls up next to the other, and he rolls down his window. I look through it and see a familiar face staring back at him.

"Going on another date?" a girl shouts.

Wait. I know that voice. It's Liam's friends from the movie theater, I'm sure of it. I roll my eyes. "It's not a date!" I yell back at her.

I hear James howl with laughter on the other side of Max as Liam shakes his head. "Sorry guys," he tells them. "I totally double-booked."

"I guess it's fine," Max says, feigning irritation. "Text us next time!"

Liam cringes. "Sorry, my bad."

James leans over Max, trying to stick his head out the window. "Where are you guys heading at this time of night, anyway?"

"It's apparently a surprise," Liam says, looking back and shooting me a quick wink.

"Just don't do anything I wouldn't do," Max says, putting her car back in gear.

"And do *everything* I'd do!" James says with another boom of laughter as they speed off.

I'm not sure what he means, but Liam goes beet red. "Sorry about that," he says sheepishly.

"All good. Ready?"

"Ready," he says with a nod. Within a few seconds, we're out on the road.

"You sure you know where you're going?" Liam asks, sounding annoyed.

"I could have sworn the turn was near here," I say as I peer through the windshield, inspecting the wall of leaves for a break in the trees. We're on a side road sandwiched between the highway and the forest outside city limits. "It was in my dream."

"Wait," he says. "Dream? Like you don't even know if it exists?"

I shake my head, mashing down my frustration. "I think it's a memory, at least I'm pretty sure it is. My mom told me it's a real place, but it's been a while since I've been there."

He narrows his eyes. "What's a while?"

"Um…fifteen years, give or take," I say with a nervous laugh.

"We're never gonna find it," he says as he shakes his head and starts turning the car around. "I'm sure we can find something to do in town."

"Oh come on, that's part of the adventure!" I say. "I mean, it's fun as long as I'm with you." I take a moment and replay my own words in my head. It's the most honest thing I've said in days.

He slows down again and thinks for a second. "Ten more minutes, but then I'm driving us back. I'm not about to drive around in circles on the highway in the middle of the night, get pulled over by cop, and explain that it's all because of some dream you had."

"Deal," I say with a firm nod.

I start losing hope around the eight-minute mark, but at last, something looks familiar. "Here!" I say with a small jump in my seat. I *knew* it was real.

"Where's here?" he asks, furrowing his thick eyebrows.

I point my finger to a large oak tree at the side of the road. "See those three slices in its trunk? Turn left."

"I'm gonna run straight into a tree!"

"Trust me! Watch." I open the door and he slams on the brakes.

"Where are you going?" he shouts after me.

I walk around the headlights and next to the bushes, pulling the rough branches aside to reveal a dirt path. "Told ya!" I yell back.

Liam shakes his head but turns the wheel to drive through the bush. I jump back into the car and we continue into the forest. I clench my fists to stop my fingers from trembling with excitement.

The path is definitely overgrown—nothing like the garden.

Years of strangling vines adorn the trees, weighing branches down to rot on the ground. Plant carcasses litter the trail, giving us logs and branches to drive over and around. Right about now I'm wishing I had powers to help clear the path.

"My dad is gonna kill me if I fuck up his car," he grumbles.

The incline raises and we drive at the pace of molasses for about twenty more minutes, eyes glued to the faint ghost of a road through the woods.

I feel my breath growing heavier. Eventually the car evens out and after a little longer, we go through a break in the foliage. Liam stops the car in a gravel clearing on the side of the mountain. Straight ahead on the face of the rock sits an opening the size of a door.

A huge smile takes over my face. “There it is,” I say with a booming laugh. I knew I wasn’t making it up. I look over at him, hoping he’s as glad as I am, but his face is blank.

He shakes his head. “Don’t tell me we’re going in there.”

“Of course we’re going in there,” I say, opening the door. “Why wouldn’t we?”

“I’m not into bears, animal or otherwise,” he says. “How were you so nervous at the movies and the school but you’re completely fine in the middle of nowhere?”

I plant my feet in the dust and stand, bending back down to look him in the eye. “It’s nature,” I say with a smile. “And since when did you get so worried? Adventure, remember?”

Liam sighs. “I guess this is how it ends.”

Chapter Twenty-Three

My feet carry me to the mouth of the cave and I freeze. I could be wrong. This could have all been a big mistake.

Liam walks up next to me. “Not so sure anymore?”

“I’m just a little anxious,” I say, a deep breath coming in and out of my lungs. I look up at the night sky, an inky black ocean divided into slices by the treetops. The gentle white light of the moon is the only thing that sets it apart from the garden—that and the fact that the stars and the swirls seem so much farther away.

He reaches down and wraps his hand around mine. My heart jumps, and tingles run up my spine. I can’t believe his hand is so soft, and I do my best to remember the feeling later. It takes everything in me to not inch closer to him.

My insecurity about the cave melts away. I can’t help but grin at him. Thank nature it’s too dark to let him see me blush.

“Let’s go,” he says with a smile, leading the way.

Liam pulls out his phone and turns on his flashlight

with his free hand, guiding me through the rocky tunnel.

Our footsteps shuffle in the dirt and the sound bounces off the walls, but I'm keenly aware of his breath. His soft palm. The heartbeat I feel between his fingers. I keep wanting more from him—more closeness, more heat, more everything—but my nerves are holding me back.

It's almost like the cave reads my mind when the roof and walls begin closing in as we go farther.

Soon we're inches apart, but still, even as he leads me forward without looking back, he doesn't let go for one second. We keep getting closer.

We walk for what feels like an eternity—not that I mind, as long as I can stay close to him. The air in the cave gets cooler and damper, the scent of wet minerals embracing us. The tunnel finally narrows to a small crack in the wall, thin enough for only one of us to fit through sideways. Exactly like in my dream.

"This is it," I say.

"If you say so," he answers.

We slip through the split in the stone, revealing an enormous room the size of the pool house at the school.

Light gray stalagmites and stalactites coat the walls and ceiling, light from his phone reflecting off a large black pool on the other end. Water gently trickles down the wall, singing as it drips and drops delicately below. It's private and infectiously peaceful—my pulse calms as my eyes grow to take it all in.

The thought of staying here for days crosses my mind, soaking in the sounds of the mountain around us. A connection to the earth itself roots deep into my core, and only this moment exists.

It's only us, here, now.

"So we're here," he says. "It's huge and it's hidden, but

I've been in caves before. What's so special about this one?"

"It's a surprise," I say with a wink. "Close your eyes and turn off the flashlight."

He narrows his gaze. "Promise you're not going to club me to death?'

I let out a single laugh. "Oh come on, that was one time. You've gotta let it go."

He snickers. "I trust you."

With a light breath, he lets his eyelids fall shut.

I look at him, wanting to reach out and touch the side of his face, but I resist. His finger taps the screen without looking and the white light suddenly disappears. Without his phone, what were thousands of lumpy mushrooms become golden orbs—lighting up the edges of the cavern along the ground like a marquee on Broadway. The Light Caps.

I crouch down to the nearest bunch and pluck a single mushroom. A steady glow flows from it, illuminating my hands.

I stand up, place it in my palm, and flick it into the air with a finger.

A stream of bright yellow and orange sparks explodes around me. They hang in the air, steadily expanding to the edges of the room. I'm standing in the middle of a galaxy, wishing stars surrounding me. The breath in my chest catches as I marvel at the beauty around us. This is what I remembered.

"Open your eyes," I whisper to Liam. As he does, he gasps.

"Oh my God, Quill." He stumbles around and stares at every ball of light near and far. The stone that was once the color of doves is replaced with that of a sunflower, mellow and inviting. "This is so… I just…" He turns back to me and smiles. "How are you doing this?"

I put my hands in my pockets, rocking back and forth on my heels. "Magic," I say with faux sarcasm. "Duh." I'm so happy I could show him something that reminds me of him. Beautiful.

He twirls in place slowly, eyes trailing from star to star. "This can't be real."

Awe completely clouds his eyes. The look on his face is that of a little kid, living in a world where only joy exists. It's the perfect moment, and it fills my heart with joy to share it with him.

He squeezes my hand and looks at me, and for the smallest second, I feel like he sees me. All of me. And actually likes me for all of it. And I never want to let him go.

A gentle smile on his lips and peace in his eyes, he starts to speak but stops. He tries again, but still doesn't succeed. At last he finds the words he wants to say. "Tell me the truth," he says. "You've been keeping a secret. What is it that you're not saying?"

And the world comes crashing down. "I—" Shit. This was a bad idea. I took it too far and he caught on. My chest tightens and my vision shrinks. Deflect. I need to deflect. "I don't know what you're talking about."

"Quill," he says, taking a few steps toward me. "This is amazing. You're amazing. But this isn't normal. And I think we both know you aren't normal, either."

"So I have a few tricks up my sleeve," I say aggressively—maybe too aggressively. "So what?"

Liam's deep blue eyes soften and he pauses, biting his lip. He shakes his head. "It's not tricks," he says calmly, motioning around us. "Look at this. Look at you. Bright green hair, kept away from everyone. How did you unlock the doors at the school in two seconds flat? How did you heal me, not to mention your messed up leg? And how you soaked up all that water last night?"

"Liam, I—" *Fuck*. He has me. I shake my head slowly, trying to think of a way to get out of this. I'm not sure where this is going, but I don't like it. Last resort: honesty. "Liam," I say with a sigh. "I can't tell you."

"Quill," he says, reaching out and entwining our fingers again. "You can trust me. I'm not going to hurt you. I…I only want to know."

This doesn't feel like my secret to tell. I don't even have powers.

I think of my mom, who was betrayed by the love of her life. Even she got burned by humans. What if Liam lets it slip to someone? Then that person tells someone else? And then none of us are safe.

"Please," he says, giving my hand a squeeze. "I won't tell anyone. It's just me, I promise."

I look into his eyes and my panic fades. Everything inside them is completely honest. Maybe he's right. He's never lied to me before. Liam's my friend, and he seems… different than any other human I've ever seen on TV or heard about. He's special.

"I'm not exactly…" I'm struggling to say it. If I say it, there's no going back. You can't unring a bell, and this is one huge fucking bell. I steel myself and take a deep breath. "I'm not human."

His eyes narrow. "What do you mean?"

I shake my head. I already started, so I may as well finish it. "My dad was human. My mom's a dryad. So is my sister. So am I." I swear, I'm having an out-of-body experience. I hear the words coming out of my mouth, but it's like someone else is saying them.

"What's..." He shakes his head. "What's a dryad?"

I sigh, motioning for him to sit down with me against the wall. My knees are trembling, and this would be an easier conversation if I were on solid ground. I pull my knees to my chest and Liam scoots closer to me, pressing his shoulder against mine.

"You might know them as nymphs," I say.

"Like from mythology?"

I nod nervously. "Yeah. We're tied to nature; in other words, we have a connection to plants."

"So this"—he motions at the swirling lights—"is all from a plant?"

I point at the mushrooms along the wall.

"And the locks? And that stuff you gave me to drink?"

"Yes. Everything came from plants, but those are a little more special than normal ragweed. They're magic. We take care of them in our garden." It's all word vomit at this point—I can't stop talking. But I have to be honest, it feels...good to be real with him.

"The one you work in? For your mom's flower shop?"

I nod. "It's been in our family since the first dryad was born."

"When was that?" he asks.

I shrug. "How old is nature? When was the first tree grown?" I'm starting to actually enjoy telling the complete truth.

He tilts his head and looks at me skeptically. "Are you telling me that your family is older than...everything?"

"I guess so." I laugh. "I mean, my mom is almost five hundred." I'm proud to tell him that bit.

"Shut the fuck up," he says. "No one can live that long."

I laugh. "My grandma was almost twelve hundred

when she passed. Dryads live for a super-long time."

Liam's eyes widen, but all he does is nod in understanding. No panic. No disbelief. Wow, he's actually taking all of this...well. I mean, he's not exactly running and screaming, so that's a good sign.

He looks down at his hands, twisting his fingers. "So you're kinda like royalty?"

I shake my head. "I don't know about that." It's flattering, but no. My sister? Maybe. My mom? Sure. But me? About as far as you can get.

"Sounds like it," he says. "The oldest living bloodline in the world. Are you going to be that old one day?"

"I don't know. That's the weird part. I'm the first male dryad ever born. I'm one big question mark."

"How is that any different?"

"My mom and sister have powers. They can grow things in seconds, shrivel them, make them move, and change how they look. Complete control. I, however, do not. I'm a dud."

"I wouldn't say that," he says, motioning around the room.

I laugh. "You can thank that magical fungus in the corner for the light show, not me. I'm defenseless compared to both of them. I'm more human than I am dryad, probably because I'm a guy. Minus the hair and soaking up water thing."

"So that's why you got sick," he nods. "The chemicals. And that's why they keep you locked up."

"To protect me," I say, resigned. "They think someone might hurt me." This is all so different to say out loud. I accepted it a long time ago, but I understand my mom more now—especially after everything that's happened lately.

Liam takes a deep breath in and puts his arm around me. He pulls me close and squeezes me tight. "I'll protect you," he says.

I want nothing more in the world than to believe him. And cautiously, I let myself. Feeling at ease, I lean in to him. "And I believe you."

He runs his hand through my hair, twirling it around his fingers. "Thank you for telling me."

I close my eyes and lean in to him with a chuckle. "You mean you don't think I'm weird?"

"Not at all. I think you're amazing." He puts his legs out and leans back on the wall, pulling me against his chest. He smells like citrus—only better than anything I can find in the garden. For once in my life, I feel like I'm enough. Like I'm not less than or something that needs to be protected because I'm so weak. With Liam, I feel like I can do anything.

His head falls forward, pressing his face into my hair.

I can feel him breathing while his arms hold me close. I press my ear to his chest, feeling his breathing and hearing his heartbeat. The longer we sit, the more it slows—and mine matches. The light from the room fades from behind my eyelids and I curl in closer to him.

Eventually, I drift off with him by my side.

Images pass through my mind.

I'm standing in the garden on the path in front of my family trees, but another figure is much closer. He seems familiar. He isn't facing me, but I could swear that it's… my dad. How is it possible to miss someone you've never met?

I have so many questions to ask him, so much I want to know. I walk closer, but as I do, he lifts a stick. A bright flame explodes from the end.

His head turns toward me with a somber smile on his face. "I'll protect you," he says.

He throws the torch toward my grandmother's tree, fire engulfing the grove. Hundreds of screams burst out from the canopy above, raining fire down on the garden.

"No!" I scream, terror flooding through my spine. My body flails, kicking the mushrooms at my feet. My eyes shoot open as millions of sparks fly through the cavern.

"Quill!" Liam shouts, startling awake. "What is it?"

I'm breathing deeply, holding my chest as he puts his hands on my shoulders. "Bad dream," I say between gasps. I collect myself for a few seconds, finding that calm place I was in before I fell asleep. I'm here. With Liam. Everything is okay. But quicker than I'd hoped, a new panic sets in. "Shit! What time is it?"

"I don't know." He yawns, rubbing his eyes. "We must've passed out."

I frantically pat myself down in search of my phone. I yank it out and tap the screen. 6:32 a.m. "Fuck!"

"What is it?"

I jump to standing and pull him up with me. "My mom's waking up soon."

Liam's eyes go wide. "We need to go."

As quickly as we can, we maneuver our way out of the cave. The sky is a light purple, the sun threatening to break the horizon on the other side of the trees. I'm so angry at myself, but I'm more worried about what'll happen if we don't get back quickly enough. The worst will be yet to come. We sprint to the car and speed back down the mountain and to the highway.

We're silent on the whole drive, both of us understanding what will happen if my mom catches me out. Somehow a trip that took us thirty minutes took us ten to return, and thank everything in nature there was no cop along the way. Liam swings the car back into its spot and shifts it into park.

"I've gotta go," I say, throwing my arms around him while he's still in his seat. I squeeze him as tight as I can. "Thank you."

"You're welcome," he says as he presses me close. "Now go, before she wakes up."

I jump out of the car and run through the alleyway, wishing the sky would stop lightening until I'm back in bed. Will my mom catch me? Will she catch Liam? What if she does? When will I see him again? I'm already aching at the thought of him going away.

Up the stairs, down the hallway, and a little turn of a small silver key.

I crack the door open, and thankfully there's no noise from inside. *Holy shit. I made it.*

One deep breath to quell my nerves before I put the key back. It was the best night of my life, and everything is okay. I pop off my shoes and tiptoe back to my room, pushing the door closed as slowly as I can.

"I wouldn't bother trying to sneak back in," my mom says from her bedroom. My stomach twists as ice floods my veins. Her figure appears in the doorway, eyes steely and voice sharp. "I'm not as dull as you think, and you're not nearly as slick."

Chapter Twenty-Four

"I'm giving you one chance," she says, holding up a single finger. "Who were you with?"

"No one," I say quickly. Probably too quickly. *Damn it, Quill, great start.*

She shakes her head, pursing her lips. "Then where were you?"

It's taking everything in me to act casual and not let on that I'm a raw pile of nerves. I do my best to wipe it all away and seem as honest as possible. Actually, honesty may be the one thing that saves me. "The cave. The one from my dream."

She narrows her eyes, shaking her head. "How did you find it?"

It looks like she's buying it. I shrug. "Looks like I remembered the way."

"The opening by the gravel?" she asks.

"Yes."

She purses her lips. "Through the forest?"

"Yup." My confidence is growing. I may actually get out

of this unscathed. Mostly.

She narrows her eyes. "Where did you turn?"

"The oak tree with the slits in the trunk." So far so good. Facts. I need to stick to the facts.

She nods her head, crossing her arms and leaning against the wall. "Okay then. So tell me, how did you manage to get down the highway with no car?"

Fuck. My brain stalls on the answer and my mouth opens, words run dry. I close it and stare at her, clenching my jaw. Here it comes.

The leaves around the room give away her fury as they twist and rustle. It's like I'm in a room full of rattlesnakes, nowhere to escape. "That's what I thought. It's the neighbor boy, isn't it? Liam is his name, right?"

Her saying his name makes my heart stop. I jump into protection mode. "He has nothing to do with this," I say, stomach dropping.

She rolls her eyes. "For Eden's sake, Quill, it's not even the first time this week. Laurel already told me all about it when your bed was empty and I went looking for you this morning."

My stone-cold exterior shatters as heat rushes over my skin. "Ugh, fucking Laurel!" I say, kicking my door.

Her nostrils flare and her eyes go wide. "Language! And don't you dare blame your sister for this! One rule, Quill—one rule! Stay. In. The. House. How hard is that?" Her words are sharp, yet she doesn't raise her voice. She doesn't need to. It's like I can feel everything she's feeling, pulsing off of her.

"I've been in this house for my whole life, Mom!" I say, motioning all around me. "I'm not as helpless as you think!" I think of all the things I could have had, all the things she robbed me of, and the resentment constricts my throat.

"Oh yeah? Is that why you were so sick yesterday?" she asks, her youthful face full of anger. "Practically on your deathbed while I tear my hair out at the thought of losing you! Blaming myself, wondering what I could have possibly done to cause it! Let me guess, you went in a swimming pool?"

That's one thing I didn't expect her to say. I bite my tongue, forcing myself back into my normal stoic shell.

"How did you know?" I ask quietly. I'm still angry, but I'm doing my best to proceed with caution.

"Because the same thing happened to me once," she says, pressing her hand to her chest. "I'm five hundred years old, Quill! I've seen it all! The only problem was that I was too worried to put it all together!"

I stare at the ground, doing my best to keep my feelings under control, but it's getting harder the longer this goes on. "I just wanted to see what the world was like." Fine, she thinks she knows everything there is to know. But why does she get to find out and I don't?

"I'm aware, Quill. We're all aware you want out. You never let us forget it. But when did you become so selfish? So impulsive? I didn't raise you to be like this."

I stay quiet. I've never fought with my mom before. I know I can't hold my ground against her, so all I can do is wait for it to pass. The helplessness feeds my rage.

She shakes her head, motioning for me to follow her to the kitchen. A gorgeous sunrise bleeds through the windows, cheering up the whole room. It's kind of ironic it's such a beautiful morning in the middle of our war.

We sit across from each other at the table, letting silence take over. This is different than every meal we've shared here. Brutal. Hostile. After a while she sighs, closing her eyes and pinching the bridge of her nose. "So when did you meet him?"

I cross my arms. I may as well tell her some of the true story. "Last week," I say with a clipped tone. "He was on the fire escape outside my window."

"And then what?"

My fingernails absentmindedly scratch the wood grains on the surface as I refuse to look at her. This is so uncomfortable. "I don't know, he kept talking to me after that. We hung out, he took me to a movie, and then the pool thing happened. You saw how well that went."

She nods, obviously mincing her words. The constant looking up at the ceiling is giving away how much she's struggling to stay calm. "And then you went to the cave with him. What next?"

"We went inside and fell asleep," I say.

"Did you show him the Light Caps?"

Again, Liam is my first priority here. And the truth didn't get me very far, so I'll try another approach. "No."

She stares me down, tilting her head to the side. "More lies? Really? The Light Caps are the whole reason to go there."

I sigh. Goddamn it. I sit up tall as my ribs tighten. "Fine," I say defiantly. "Yes, I showed him the mushrooms."

She nods, clenching her jaw, but keeping her words deliberate and sanitized. "And how did you explain it?"

Think fast, Quill. A documentary I watched a year or so ago pops in my head. "Bioluminescence. Completely natural."

She burrows her green eyes into mine, never looking more serious. "So you didn't tell him about what you are? What we are?"

Shit. Deflect. I scoff and venom coats my words. "Why

would I do that? So you could brainwash him like you did Dad?" The words are out of my mouth before I can stop them. Even as I hear myself, I cringe inwardly.

Her eyes widen with pain and surprise, then narrow. "Wow. I had no idea I could have a child who could be so hurtful." She stands up from the table, her chair screeching, and she walks away. "Telling you was a complete mistake. I was worried you weren't old enough. I was right."

A pit twists in my stomach. I didn't mean to hurt her like that. Damn it, I'm making this so much worse than it ever should have been. "Mom, that's not what I meant— "

She turns around and holds her hand out to cut me off. "You know what, maybe I was wrong to let them move in. Maybe I need to ask them to go."

My eyes go wide and panic wells in my chest. "No! Please don't!"

"I don't know what else to do," she says, throwing her hands up as she starts to pace. "I'm sure you know they're in hard times right now, but I'm not about to sacrifice my own family for theirs. He's obviously a bad influence on you, and you're too young to be playing these games."

I ignore the comment about hard times and focus on the immediate problem. I'll make sure to ask Liam about it later. I'm too concerned with how my skin is prickling and how my pulse picks up speed at the thought of losing him. "Mom, you're being ridiculous. He's a good guy and we're friends."

"Don't be naive, Quill," she snaps. "Friendship is one thing, but this is something else entirely. I haven't even met him and I already know that."

"Oh and you know this from all your years in a biker bar?" I say sarcastically through gritted teeth. "I'm honored to be the son of such a mind reader."

"Why are you being so difficult?" she shouts, flinging her hands in the air. She's losing control—the louder she gets, the more the vines around the kitchen writhe and rustle on the walls.

"Because, Mom, he's nice. And he's funny. And he likes me for who I am. What's wrong with that?" I'm speaking earnestly now, praying that some of it gets through to her.

She shakes her head stubbornly. "You don't know people like I do, and I don't like it," she says. "I know I say humans are inherently good, but they don't mix well with our kind. I'm old enough to know what that boy is thinking, and trust me when I say that he's no good for you."

That's it. She's kept me trapped for my whole fucking life, feeding me one lie after the next. The world isn't nearly as dangerous as she'd led me to believe, and here she is doing the same thing to Liam. She thinks she can make all my decisions for me? Tell me what to think and what to feel? I've fucking had enough of this.

I stand up and stomp past her to my room. "Oh, okay," I shout on my way. "So, since you're alone, the rest of us need to be, too. Gotcha."

She spirals around and stalks me down the hallway. "You think I don't ever get lonely? That I've never wanted someone so badly that it killed me to let them go? Don't think you're the only person in the world with feelings, Quill!"

I'm not giving her anything else. I turn around as soon as I get through the door, about to close it behind me. "Are we done?" I ask with a flat tone. "Because I'd like to go to bed now."

She stops in her tracks and puts her hands on her hips, an indignant smile growing. "You know what? Go ahead.

And you can stay in there until I'm ready to look at you again."

I narrow my eyes. "Oh, so I'm a prisoner now?"

"Apparently you've thought you were a prisoner this entire time. But trust me, son, you haven't seen anything yet."

Anger swells again as I scoff and slam the door, stomping over to my bed and throwing myself on it. But as soon as I do, the branches on my ceiling and walls warp and snake to barricade my room shut behind me. An errant vine even scoops up my phone from my nightstand when I'm not looking—I notice right as it gets sucked underneath my door.

"You can't keep me in here forever!" I shout through the wall of leaves, but my mom doesn't respond.

I'm fucking *livid*. I can't believe she'd ever treat me like this. I wasn't hurt and I didn't cause any trouble. What's the big fucking deal?

There are other kids out there doing *so* much worse. And who is she to be the judge of that? Didn't she used to hang out with gangs in a bar?

I pace back and forth for hours, raging. I'm thinking of all of the things—both helpful and hurtful—that I wish I'd said but was too slow to think of at the time. Maybe I could have calmed her down. Maybe I could have gotten my point across with brutal honesty. I guess I'll never know.

But sooner or later, as I calm down, the more I think about it, the more I'm angry at myself for how I behaved with her. The low blows I took. *Do I think she's being unfair?* Yes, but that isn't new.

What I didn't realize was that any of this would hurt her so badly. I didn't know guilt could run this deep. Ugh, I'm the *worst*.

There was one thing I wasn't budging on, though. Liam. As far as Liam goes? I know she's got it all wrong. She doesn't know him at all.

I don't want to hurt her, but I won't stop seeing him. She can't make me. We have this connection I can't explain, and the thought of losing him literally hurts my chest. It's an ache that seeps down to the bone.

She doesn't even know him. Just because my dad betrayed her doesn't mean Liam would do the same. Whatever she may think, she'd better realize that she can't keep us separated forever.

Chapter Twenty-Five

The sound of scratching fills my room as the doorknob turns and the door cracks open.

"Can I come in?" Laurel appears, looking soft and hopeful. It's annoying.

"Oh look, it's my traitor of a sister." I cross my legs and link my fingers on my stomach, head resting on my pillow. It's the first time we've spoken since our fight the other evening. My face may be calm, but if she can't feel the bitterness coming off me, then we truly have grown apart. "What do you want?"

She cringes and steps inside, a flowing sapphire gown hung on her thin frame. "I guess I kind of deserved that one."

My eyebrows raise as I tip my head to the side. "Ya think?"

She sighs, walking over to my bed and sitting next to me. "I know we fought, but I didn't want to sell you out. Seriously, I didn't. But there was no way I could cover for you after last night."

"Seriously?" I say, keeping my voice as calm and reasonable as possible. It's harder than I expected. "You pretty much told Mom everything."

"I mean, can you really blame me?" she says. "You disappeared. And then look at what happened when you went out with him the night before. Mom told me how sick you got. I could basically hear your teeth chattering from downstairs in the shop. She was incredibly close to brewing another cure-all as a last resort." She lowers her voice. "Not to mention I still don't agree with you about the break-in—we don't know for sure that it wasn't Liam, and we don't have any new leads. We're stuck, Quill, and we're in danger. And you're too distracted with Liam to care."

A pang of guilt hits me again at how I've prioritized Liam over the garden, but I'm not about to let it show. I've beat myself up enough for the last few hours, and I don't need her two cents. It's not like I totally disagree with her, but I still answer her with silence.

"But I was pretty nasty the other night, and that was wrong, too," Laurel continues. "So let me make it up to you."

I try to look like I don't care, but she's piqued my interest. "How?"

"Well, seeing as how I'm your new babysitter for the foreseeable future—"

"Wait." I cut her off. "*You're* guarding my jail cell?"

She shrugs. "I'm staying here to make sure you don't go sneaking out with your boyfriend again."

I scoff. "He's *not* my boyfriend." Damn it, I wish everyone would cut that shit out.

She closes her eyes. "Shit. Sorry. Again. That came out way snarkier than I meant it to."

"Whatever," I say, rolling away from her. I hope she'll take that as her cue to get out, but unfortunately, she doesn't.

"Listen. I know friendships and I know hookups, but I don't think he's either one of those. He means something to you, doesn't he?"

"Why do you care?"

"Because you're my brother and I don't want you to be unhappy," she says. I roll back around to face her and she sighs. "I have an idea if you'll hear me out."

I don't trust her, but I can't help but be curious. "And what might that be?"

"Ever heard of the Reverie Tree?"

I nod. "The one with the giant blue flowers. What about it?"

"It's used to control dreams," she says, wringing her hands. "But if two people split the same flower, they share the same dream."

I stare at her, and I can't believe what I'm hearing. "Are you trying to help me see him?"

She looks down at the ground. "It's not like you're leaving the house. I'm still doing my job."

Is this some sort of test? Another thing she'll snitch on me about? But the look on her face and her tone seem genuine. Recent events aside, she's still my sister and she's always been there for me. Plus I'd do anything to see him right about now. Even one wall apart feels too far. Our eyes meet and I give her a small nod. "That would be great. Thank you."

"I'll leave it on his doorstep," she says, standing up. She pulls my phone from her pocket and holds it toward me, other hand on her hip and head cocked. "Text him and tell him to eat it tonight and go to bed. You do the same."

"Why are you being so nice all of a sudden? I thought you hated him."

She presses her lips together, looking at me with soft eyes before she answers. "I don't like seeing you miserable, Quill. And obviously, you actually care about him. Trust me…I know that look on your face."

"So…you don't think he's the one who broke in?"

She shakes her head. "He's a little too preoccupied with whisking you all around town on dates. Can't exactly break into the garden if he's with you."

"So if it wasn't him, who do you think it was?"

She sighs. "I don't know. But I think someone tried to break in again last night when you were gone. I kept seeing this car circling the building from my apartment in the middle of the night. They sped off as soon as I came down."

A cold chill runs through my spine. So this isn't over.

"I'm working on a theory about who it was, but don't worry about it right now," she says. "I just can't figure out how they're getting into the apartment or what they're doing when they get there. The plants are acting stranger and stranger each day."

"Did something else happen?"

"Not as long as you don't count things growing in places they shouldn't be. Mom told me about how the spring was full of algae. Not normal. So I'm keeping a closer eye on things. You don't need to worry about it tonight, though. Let me go grab the flower so you can see Liam, and I'll drop one outside his door, too. Don't forget to text him."

"I won't," I say.

Laurel walks out of my room, heels clicking down the hallway before the garden door creaks open. I turn on my phone and already have a message waiting from Liam.

Liam: You okay? I'm assuming you got caught

Me: How did you guess?

Liam: Your mom called my dad

Me: Shit. What did she say?

Liam: Not sure. Something about me running around town in the middle of the night with her son

Ugh. My mom is already meddling and making things worse. I'm still guilty for going off the way I did, but it doesn't make me any less pissed.

Me: What did he say?

Liam: Again, not sure. But he's pretty upset with me right now. I'm on house arrest

I look around my room, both window and door encased in thick trees. Something tells me his prison has a little less security than mine does.

Me: I know the feeling

Liam: Well I don't know about you, but I think it was worth it

I smile at the screen, butterflies coating my stomach again. It's amazing how he does that without even trying.

Me: Definitely. I wanna see you again

Liam: Something tells me that won't happen for a while

Me: Sooner than you think. I'm leaving something on your doorstep. Eat it before you go to bed tonight

Liam: Are you drugging me?

Me: Yeah, but I ran out of horse tranquilizers. I had to improvise

Liam: Damn, those are my favorites

I chuckle, shaking my head. It's like I can hear the exact tone of his voice, and see that same sparkle in his eye whenever he gives me a hard time. It feels like he's the only person who actually gets me.

Liam: What does it do?

Me: It's a surprise. Don't you trust me?

Liam: Always

My face grows hot, and my heart beats a little harder.

Me: See you tonight

Liam: Can't wait

Laurel comes back right then, walking in and standing above me. "All good with lover boy?" I give her a flat stare and hand the phone to her. "Geez, tough crowd. You're welcome."

I sigh. "Thank you. It means a lot." I really do appreciate her, and I'm so tired from being negative all day. I try to focus on this one positive.

"So does this mean you forgive me?"

I smirk. "I'm beginning to." She flashes a bright white smile and sets the vibrant blue flower on my comforter. "It's a start." She walks out of my room, closes the door, and the branches seal up the room once again.

Chapter Twenty-Six

A soft click resounds in the hallway as my mom's bedroom door closes across from mine. She'll be fast asleep in the next ten minutes, but I know I'm not alone—Laurel's camped out in the living room.

I'm way more calm than I was when my mom and I waged war this morning, but the wound is still raw. The guilt's been growing as the clock ticked on, and it's one of my least favorite feelings in the world. I know the fight isn't over, either. I swear they were talking about me only a few minutes ago.

Either I pissed my mom off worse than I thought or she thinks I'm a better escape artist than I am because she didn't bother relaxing the plants strangling my room shut. A few apples grew from one of the branches earlier, so I can't say this is *completely* inhumane. It's still awful, though.

I rub the delicate blue petals between my fingers, soft and smooth as silk.

Laurel didn't exactly give me the full rundown of

what it's going to be like. My mouth is dry and I can't stop fidgeting, distracted by the worry sitting squarely in my chest.

Can we get hurt wherever I'm going? Will we be trapped, like some kind of sleep paralysis? What if something goes wrong? What if we need to get out?

I guess I'll find out soon enough.

Deep breath in, deep breath out. I fire off a text to Liam.

Me: Ready?

My phone pings a moment later.

Liam: You bet

I send Liam a flower emoji, and then my mouth envelops the blossom, which dissolves the second it hits my tongue and coats my throat in something that tastes like honey. Sleep begins to overtake me—a haze spreading from behind my eyes through each of my limbs. All strength disappears from my muscles as I lie back and curl up, clutching a pillow to my chest.

The white noise from my fan gets farther and farther away as I drift into darkness, letting go of everything that happened earlier today.

"Quill!" Liam's voice calls from the distance in the back of my mind. I swear he's close by. Is it working already? He shouts again, louder. "Quill!"

My eyes fly open, but I'm not in my room anymore.

No trees, no bed, nothing—I'm not even lying down. I'm standing in a scentless white fog, rolling and floating and blotting everything out farther than ten feet from me.

Where could he be? How far is he? I can't wait to see him.

"Hello?" I say, walking forward. "Liam?" The mist swirls around my hand as I try to push it out of the way, but it does no good.

"There you are," he says right behind me.

I jump and press my hand to my chest, steadying my heart and lungs. "Don't do that!"

"Don't do what?" he asks innocently. "You're the one who popped up out of nowhere!"

"I did not!" I say, pushing his shoulder.

He pushes me back lightly, a crooked smile growing on his face. "So you did drug me. I mean, not that I mind."

I shake my head, amused that he's taking this so lightly. "No, it's a plant from the garden. It lets you lucid dream with another person."

"It's pretty cool," he says, nodding and spinning around. "Where do you suppose we are?"

It's a good question. I twist my head in all directions, trying to figure out the most logical answer. "Our brains, I guess."

"Think we're stuck in all this cloudy stuff until we wake up?"

"It should work exactly like a dream. We should be able to go anywhere. Do anything."

"Anything?" he says with a devilish smirk and the raise of an eyebrow.

A rush runs through my spine, thinking of the pic he sent me the other day, and my blush immediately gives me away.

He bursts out laughing, and I'm so thankful he doesn't know what's going on in my head. "You're too easy to mess with sometimes."

I roll my eyes. I swear, I'll be immune to him saying things like that sooner or later. "Since you're too busy thinking about things you shouldn't, I guess I'll try." Closing my eyes, I try to decide where to start.

Liam. Pool. Door. Garden.

"Whoa! What the hell is that?"

My eyes fly open and look between us—a mound of shimmering four-leaf clovers, refracting every color the eye can see. I bend down and run my fingers along the patch, watching them sway back and forth. They seem so *real*.

"It's the plant I used to get us into the school. I was trying to think of the pool, but then I got stuck thinking of us being locked out, and then thinking about how I fixed it… It barely crossed my mind." My fingers pluck one and twist its shimmering leaves, as bright and iridescent as if it were actually there, but it's only a mirage.

"I guess I'd better be careful what I think of," he says with a grimace.

I laugh, carefree for the first time in days. Problems don't exist here—only the things we create. "You'd better keep it clean. Or at least give me some warning in case I need to look away."

"Oh please, you'd love it." He closes his eyes, holds out his hand, and a can of Coke appears. He opens his eyes again with a smile. "Awesome," he says, pulling the tab with a little hiss and pop. He brings it to his lips to drink but pulls it right back down, dissatisfied. "It doesn't taste like anything. I can't even feel it in my mouth."

"It's a dream," I say, laughing. "What did you expect?"

"Then how come I can feel you?" he asks, eyeing the can and swirling it around.

I shrug. "Maybe because I'm real? And so are you. Everything else is an illusion."

"Try something else," he says. "Go big this time."

"Challenge accepted." I concentrate as hard as I can on photos and videos I've seen of a place I'd kill to see in real life.

Thick, rough, red trunks surrounding us and reaching up to the sky. Sunbeams cutting through a canopy of needles, birds calling from the treetops, and lush ferns covering the ground by our feet. I open my eyes to find us in the middle of a gargantuan forest.

Liam is spinning around, mouth gaping. "Holy shit, you did it."

"I've seen pictures of this place and seen it on TV," I say with a high chin and full chest, exceptionally pleased with my own memory. "It's not completely accurate, but I know enough about the woods to fill in the gaps."

"I honestly wouldn't know the difference," he says, looking back at me and smiling. "Where are we?"

"The Redwoods in California." I close my eyes, soaking up the rays breaking through the canopy. When I open them again, he's just staring at me with a grin on his face.

"Wanna go for a walk and see how far this place goes?"

"Why not," I say, moving shoulder to shoulder with him.

We're back in the same limbo we were in at the movie theater—a magnetic attraction, but not quite touching despite the pull. It's making me itch to touch him already.

"So I'm assuming your mom is completely pissed," he says, hands in his pockets.

I nod. "You could say that. I broke her one rule. And then I said some pretty awful things when she called me out."

His brow furrows. "Like what?"

"Like what happened between her and my dad," I say. "How she left him. I just found out so I haven't had time to process it, but I threw it in her face." The words echo in my head. *So, since you're alone, the rest of us need to be, too.* The guilt I thought I left behind in the waking world claws its way out. Ugh, I'm such an asshole.

He nods. "Wanna talk about it?"

I shake my head, staring at the footprints we're leaving in the soft earth below us. Rehashing it out loud would only make it worse. "Let's just say she'll do anything to protect my family."

"You know she can't keep you locked up forever, right?"

I laugh bitterly. "Tell her that." She's already had fifteen years of practice.

We walk in silence for a few moments, dangerously close to touching, but still managing to keep our distance. I do my best to focus only on him and not any of my other problems. Life seems so much easier when he's around.

"I have a question," he says suddenly. "I'm curious. If she changed her mind and let you out, what would you do?"

The possibilities tie my tongue for a second, but I manage to find the words. "If I were totally free?" I ask. "Anything. Everything. I want to get out and explore. Find out what else I'm good at. There's so much I want to learn and so much of the world I want to see."

"Like where? It's not like we aren't in the best place to make that happen."

I sigh with a toothy smile. "A city. A big one." I've seen pictures and videos my whole life, but nature is all I've known. That's the polar opposite.

"You're in luck. Because I have the exact memories to make that happen."

He links our arms to stop me from walking, and I swear a current runs straight from my elbow into my heart. He faces me, shutting his eyes. I've never realized how smooth his skin is, especially in this golden light. How his thick eyelashes are the perfect detail to his face, offsetting his full lips.

While I'm busy studying him, the trees melt where they stand—some morphing into metal and glass while others sink into the ground.

Figures of dark mist swirl around us, becoming a giant crowd. We're surrounded by skyscrapers, all with giant screens blaring above us—and it thrills me. I can't believe I'm actually getting a chance to see what I've always dreamed of. The air fills with voices and horns, cars driving out of the ground onto the pavement that was once loamy soil.

"Welcome to Times Square," Liam shouts above the noise, proud as can be. "Looks like I'm getting the hang of this."

I may have always wanted to go here, but I'm instantly regretting it. I didn't realize what I signed up for. I cling to his arm, chest tightening. "There are so many people."

"Biggest city in the world, what did you expect?"

I shake my head, desperate for him to understand what I'm feeling. "Liam, there are too many people." I'm getting dizzy and all I want is for it to stop. I reach down to the ground to sit. I'm losing my balance.

"Oh shit, hold on." He scrunches his eyes shut, all the people around us fading into wisps of fog.

The sounds disappear, leaving us alone in an empty canyon of buildings.

"Better?" he asks, sitting down next to me.

The air clears once again after a couple of seconds.

I nod, feeling the burning blood rush into my ears. I wish he hadn't seen me like that. "Sorry. I know it's not real, but…it's one thing to see pictures, it's another to be in the middle of it."

"It's okay." He laughs while rubbing my shoulder. "It's

nothing to be embarrassed about. I remember my first time here, and I probably would have felt the same way if my dad weren't carrying me."

Hearing him say that helps me calm down, letting me relax into the memory around us. My eyes move around the mirage, amazed at the details in every corner. Every bright lightbulb. Every word on every sign. Every minute detail—he's thought of it.

"Are you telling me you remember this all from when you were a little kid?"

"Oh no," he says modestly. "We used to come here all the time when my mom was still alive. He does a lot of business in New York, so she and I would spend a lot of time together."

"What exactly does he do? He must be pretty important to go on so many business trips."

"Stock market," he says nonchalantly. "I've never actually understood it."

I pause, noticing a slight change in his voice. He's lying. I distinctly remember committing it to memory the first night I came to his house. "I thought you told me that he does medical stuff last week." I was desperate for him to trip on his words, to change his story. Why is he doing it now?

"Uh…yeah," he stumbles. "He does a little of this and a little of that. It's complicated."

I stare at him, but he avoids eye contact. "What aren't you telling me?"

He shakes his head, closing his eyes. "I really don't want to talk about it," he says, but the dream betrays him. The city dissolves and the space between us grows.

In place of skyscrapers, white walls build up and close in to become a small room. A chair forms beneath each of us, end tables against the wall, and the skeletal frame of a bed in the middle. Metallic poles shoot up near the edge of it, fog becoming monitors and IV bags.

At last, the details of blankets and sheets create themselves, ballooning up to fit the thin and weak figure of a man beneath them.

Eyes sunken into the skull, skin as thin as paper—he barely looks like a real person.

"Liam..." I say slowly, not understanding any of this. "Where are we?" I can tell this is a hospital, even though I've never been in one. But I've watched enough TV to know. What I don't understand is why Liam's mind brought us here.

His eyes fly open, he gasps, and he rushes to shut them once more and changes the scene.

"No, stop." I lock my concentration onto the room and mentally fight his efforts to make it disappear. "Answer me."

His eyelids flutter open again, jaw clenching as he stares at me. He isn't saying a word, but I don't think he needs to. I'm starting to put the pieces together on my own.

"Is...is that your dad?" I ask, tipping my head to the shell of a human being between us. Liam hesitates but nods once and looks down. I shake my head. "I don't understand... Why didn't you tell me?"

"Because"—his voice grows hard with emotion—"I didn't want you to feel bad for me. I know the look people at school give me—my teammates, my teachers. I didn't want to see that same look on your face when you talk to me. It's awful."

I don't know what to say. He's humiliated by this, but I don't understand why. "How long has he been like this?" I ask quietly.

"Since before we moved into your building," Liam says.

"I lied to you. He hasn't been away on business. He's pretty sick."

Shit. If the memory is accurate, he must be in horrible shape. I've never seen someone as sick as this. "What's wrong with him?" I ask, my eyes prickling.

Liam sighs. "After my mom died, he threw himself into his work. He said he wanted to provide for us, but I think it was a little because he wasn't taking her loss so well. Back then he did go out on business all the time. Being at home by myself was normal.

"Then he came home from one of his trips, way more tired than usual. He didn't think much of it. Then came the dizziness and getting winded from a flight of stairs, but he kept working as hard as he could. He started losing a ton of weight, but then he got a bad rash and a fever. Finally, he went to the doctor. Leukemia."

"But he's getting better…right?" I'm hoping he says yes. He has to say yes. He's already lost so much.

Liam shakes his head. "Chemo. Blood transfusions. Radiation. It's been going on for some time now. He's not working, so we had to sell our house. That's why we moved into your building. He met your mom when he decided to try some natural remedies. They got to talking after a couple of months and she offered us a free place to stay."

Suddenly it all made sense. Why my mom made an exception for them. Why Liam was always alone. I have no idea what the medical terms he's saying mean, but judging from his face as he watches his dad, I can tell things are really bad.

While my heart breaks for him, my mind drifts to my mom.

I've made her out to be this awful person all day, but she's actually the opposite. She knew this whole time and put our secrecy at risk to help them. If she was able to do something, maybe I can, too.

"How can I help?"

This time he looks at me, but the tiniest smile accompanies it. "You already are."

"What do you mean?" I ask, shaking my head.

He sighs. "You make me feel like I'm not the most selfish person in the world. He's alone in this room," Liam says, motioning at the medical equipment. "Hooked up to tubes and wires day in and day out. But I…I can't bring myself to see him like this. It hurts too much. It wrecks me. Fifteen, twenty minutes tops before I need to leave to avoid breaking down."

I couldn't imagine what he was going through. Although we were fighting, I know if the roles were reversed and it were my mom in that hospital bed, I'd never leave her side. But I wasn't going to tell him that. Who was I to judge how he copes?

But there has to be something I could do. I go through each section of the garden in my mind, trying to figure out something that my mom might not have thought of.

Mint for nausea, valerian root for sleep, white willow bark for pain…

Liam's voice pulls me out of my mental gymnastics. "What's that on the nightstand beside you?"

My eyes flit to my left, widening on a handful of crimson berries. "Shit," I say, closing my eyes, disappearing them as fast as I can. Those berries aren't an option to help him. "Sorry. Nothing. Just another plant from the garden." I try to answer as quickly and confidently as possible, but he doesn't buy it.

He narrows his eyes. "What do they do that made you think of them?"

"It doesn't matter," I say, shaking my head.

His eyes stare firmly at mine but cut back over to the table. A single glowing pink vial stands where the berries were. I close my eyes again, wiping them from sight.

"Wait. Was…was that the stuff you gave me when I got hurt?"

I clench my jaw. I can't lie to him, but I know where this is going and I don't like it. "Yeah, but…"

"Would it work on my dad?" he asks, cutting me off.

I shake my head. "I—I don't know." And I honestly don't. But it's already too late—I think I gave him false hope.

"Do you think we could try it?" A hopeful smile crosses his face.

I grimace, taking a deep breath. "I learned about it only last week." *Shit.* I need to quit while I'm behind.

He keeps pushing. "Maybe you could ask your mom?"

"I broke, like, a million rules giving it to you," I say, shaking my head. "I'm not even supposed to know about it. That plant's locked up tight anyway, plus I don't know for sure if it would work." I feel like the worst person in the world for telling him no.

"Oh," he says, looking down. "Okay. Never mind."

I sigh. "I'm so sorry Liam, it's not that I don't want to—"

"It's all right," he says, looking back up with a smile that doesn't quite reach his eyes. "I don't want to get you in trouble more than I already have. We haven't run out of options yet."

It hurts so much to see him like this, it's easy to change my mind. Maybe I can convince my mom to do something. It's worth trying. "I'll bring it up to her," I tell him. "I promise."

He nods. "Thanks, Quill. It means a lot."

"I know you didn't mean to, but thank you for sharing. I'm here if you ever want to talk about it." I'm not the most sensitive person in the world, but I do have feelings. Especially feelings for him. If he needs me, I'll be there. I can at least do that much.

He returns a small smile and looks away, and I swear for a second that his eyes look glassier than they should be.

I hate seeing him like this, and I'm desperate to make him feel better. Give him something that may help. "I can show you something in return," I say carefully. "How would you like to see the garden?"

He laughs and nods, wiping his face. "I'd actually like that a lot."

I smile weakly and close my eyes, focusing on every inch of the garden. Every vine, branch, leaf, blossom that I know like the back of my hand. But when I open my eyes… only white fog remains.

A quizzical look covers his face. "What's going on?"

"I don't know." I close my eyes once more, picturing the ponds and waterfalls and swirling sky. But again, nothing changes once I open my eyes.

"Why isn't it working?" he asks. The fog grows darker and thicker all around us.

"I think the flower is wearing off." I walk up to him and lace my fingers with his. "What if… What if I brought you there sometime? To the garden?"

"You'd actually do that?" he says, an excited smile spreading over his mouth. The light quickly begins to disappear from the clouds around us.

I nod. I regret saying it, knowing that I may have made a promise I can't keep, but I try to play it off. "The real thing is better, anyway."

“I can believe it.” He reaches his free arm around me and pulls me into his chest, squeezing hard. “You’re amazing. I want you to know that.”

I rest my head on his shoulder, and everything fades to black.

Chapter Twenty-Seven

Gentle creaking rings around my walls, pulling me out of the best dream I've ever had.

One of my eyes cracks open, watching as the trees coating my walls like veins begin to tremble and twist. The thousands of leaves above me whisper as they rustle, moving like fluid.

They zigzag and curl and coil back to their original homes, peeling away from my window and door and letting the light beam in. They freeze again once they're back where they belong, and the faint hiss of a frying pan reaches my room from the kitchen.

I don't completely trust this. There's the gentle aroma of vanilla luring me out, but this could be a trap. Mom could be lulling me into a false sense of security before tearing into me again. But that doesn't seem like her… This could be a genuine peace offering.

I swipe up some clothes from the floor, throw them on, and carefully crack the door open so I can tiptoe out without being noticed. I round the corner and see my mom's curly red hair swaying gently while she faces the stove—so far, so good.

"Good morning," she says in a calm voice without turning around.

I sigh. I'm not nearly as good at sneaking around as I think I am. "Good morning," I say hesitantly, crossing the room into the morning light.

Another beautiful day like the last time we were in here, but there's a little more hope in the house today. I pull up a chair and sit down as calmly as I can.

With a flick of her index finger, the long vines from the houseplants come alive and gently dance around the room.

Each has its own job—grabbing a plate from the cupboard, lifting a glass from the dishwasher, opening the fridge, pouring me a glass of orange juice, and setting a napkin on my lap. My eyes can't move that freely to watch them all.

Within five seconds, she sets the table for me before turning around and sliding fresh pancakes onto my plate. With one more flick, the tiniest pair of leaves helicopters out of its pot to the syrup, wraps its roots around the bottle, and drops it off on the table before flying through the air and repotting itself.

"So...does this mean we're okay?" I ask her warily. It can't be that easy.

She sighs and pulls my phone out of her apron, holding it out to me. "I overreacted. If you're old enough to be sneaking out, then you're old enough to have friends."

"Really?" *Wow*. I guess it is that easy.

"I mean, I'm not thrilled with you lying to me about it," she says. "But I have a feeling I'm not going to be able to stop you. And with his dad as sick as he is, I'm not going to evict them."

I pause. "So you know about his dad?"

She squints and shakes her head. "Did you not?"

"I'm just surprised you didn't mention it earlier," I say, lifting my fork and knife.

"It wasn't my news to share," she says. "But I'm glad Liam has someone to talk to about it. His dad's been worried about how much Liam's struggling with it."

I remember the image I saw in the dream—the frail skeleton of a man, attached to so many machines. The look on Liam's face when he was trying not to cry. Struggling was an understatement. It was shredding him apart.

I can't help but let my mind wander, replacing his dad with my mom. Alone in that bed, kept alive with cold, hard machines… It only magnifies my guilt for all the horrible things I said to her.

"Mom," I start, but as soon as I look at her, I don't know what to say.

Why is it so hard to figure out what to say? My mouth's always had a mind of its own. Maybe I can let it do the work for me. "I'm sorry," I tell her, word vomit pouring out. "For everything. For lying. For sneaking out. But mostly I'm sorry for saying any of that stuff. It was cruel and awful and I wish I could take it back."

When my eyes come to meet hers, she's nodding gently. "You said some pretty brutal things," she says, taking a cleansing breath. "Even if there was some truth in there."

I wince, shaking my head. Though she means it, it doesn't make it right. "I won't do it again. I promise."

She lets out a small laugh. "Yes, you will." She looks me right in the eye and smiles. "You're young, and I'm not faulting you for that. Your emotions are bound to get the best of you from time to time, whether you like it or not, and you're going to say things you regret. It's something you'll need to learn to control."

She cups the side of my face and I put my hand on hers. I always forget how reasonable she is—probably because we never fight. Doesn't change that this all could have been avoided if I'd been honest with her. Well…honest to a point.

I still can't tell her Liam knows what we are. I'll save that for another day.

We stay there for a second until she ruffles my hair and pulls up a chair next to me.

"Okay, so." She laces her fingers on the table while I turn my attention to my breakfast and fill my fork. "We need to set ground rules. Boundaries. Understood?"

I take a deep breath from my nose and swallow, doing my best to focus on the syrup and salt. I should have expected this. I'm not thrilled, but I nod. I guess it'll be nice to not have to sneak around anymore.

"First of all, no more going out whenever you feel like it," she says. "If you want to go somewhere, you need permission from me. Otherwise, you stay in this building. You can come and hang out down in the flower shop, and you can even go up to the roof if you want privacy."

I'm thrilled that she's giving me more freedom. Finally! It's what I've always wanted, but maybe I could push a little more and go one step further. After going around town with complete freedom—even if it was sneaking around—I'd like to keep that going.

"What about me going over to his house?" I ask, cautiously hopeful. "Or…him coming over here?" My heart flutters at the idea of him coming to visit, but I do my best to ignore it.

She purses her lips. "You can go over to his house if his dad is there, and the same goes for over here if I'm home.

But doors stay open. Understood?"

I roll my eyes and take another bite. "Mom, it's not like…"

She holds up her finger. "You're a teenage boy, and so is he. Expect an incredibly thorough sex talk in the near future."

I choke on my pancakes and cough them up on the plate. I chug down a gulp of juice, my face growing hot. This is so embarrassing.

I haven't even thought about that. If there were any time for a natural disaster, I could desperately use one as a distraction right about now.

"Anyway, any other demands?" I have never wanted to get away from a subject so fast in my life.

I think she sees the blush taking over my face because she's stifling her laughter. "Only one more," she says, composing herself with a kind smile. "Most of all, I want to meet him first."

That one's almost worse. It scares the shit out of me, but she's calm about it. I have a feeling I'm not getting around it, so I give up the struggle before it starts. "Deal." I'm already thinking of all the things that could possibly go wrong in one conversation.

"You know I'm going to tell him the same exact rules, right? Especially the one about the doors—"

"Ugh, MOM!" I yell, shuddering and throwing my napkin at her.

She howls with laughter, pushes away from the table and comes over behind me. "I love you, sweetheart," she says, linking her arms around my chest and kissing my forehead. "Even if you are terrible at sneaking around."

"I love you, too," I say, holding her hands.

She rests her chin on my hair and we remain like that

for a moment. "Now then. I need to go open the shop. I'll see you later." She takes a few steps, but I stop her.

"What changed your mind?" I ask hesitantly. I truly am curious how we got here from the war we had yesterday.

She doesn't seem cross when she turns around—she seems amused. "Laurel talked to me," she says with a small smile. "She…reminded me of some things."

I tilt my head to the side. "Like what?"

"Like what it's like to be young and take chances. And make mistakes." It's vague, but for now, I'll buy it. She turns once more, but I stop her again.

"One more question." The hospital's been sitting at the back of my mind. My mom and I make eye contact, and I say the next part as carefully as I can. "About Liam's dad… Do you think…there's anything you could do to help him?"

She sighs, a somber look taking over her graceful features, shaking her head. "No, sweetheart. Nothing that I haven't already tried. Nothing safe." There's a finality in her voice that tells me not to push it.

I nod my head. "Okay." My gut twists at the thought of how the man's story is going to end, and there's nothing I can do to stop it. I'm crushed, and it's not even my dad. Liam's going to be devastated.

She sighs. "Quill, there are…things about the garden that you don't understand yet. Chances we can't take. You'll understand one day." She gives me one last sympathetic smile before heading downstairs to the shop.

I get up to rinse off my plate. Nothing *safe*? What did she mean by that? And what don't I know about the garden?

I know she was about to brew another cure-all the other day when I was sick—Laurel told me—so why can't she do it for Liam's dad? She knows how bad off he is.

Does it do something different to humans? How bad did I fuck up when I gave it to Liam?

I'm worried it already could have changed him, and I may have not even seen it. It's not like I knew him very long before I gave it to him.

My pocket buzzes before I can spiral out of control. I smile, shut off the water, and shut out the thoughts.

Liam: Morning :)

Me: Morning :)

Me: How did you sleep?

Liam: Haha you should know, you were there

He's right, I was. And I wish I could be there every night, but it's too early to say something that heavy.

Me: Fair enough haha. What are you doing up so early?

Liam: Just started thinking of you and couldn't get back to sleep. You still in prison?

Me: Released for good behavior, actually. With more privileges

Liam: Oh? Like what?

Me: Like no more sneaking around. My mom wants to meet you first. You free now?

Liam: When?

My heart jumps—it's an answer I didn't expect to get out of him easily.

Me: How about now?

Ten minutes later, I rush through the house and out the back door, down the stairs and into the cooler of the flower shop. I hurry and glance around the shop through the glass, and it's easy to see that my mom and Laurel are the only ones there. I slide the door open and poke my head out.

They're both bathed in a peaceful sunlight, the kind that comes only the morning after a brutal storm. An earthy scent weighs down the room while bright blossoms coat the shelves.

Laurel's delicate fingers are in a flowerpot on the counter, covered in soil, her eyes closed in concentration. My mom is right next to her, watching her intently.

"Embody the decay," she tells Laurel. "Imagine the power of the sun pulling away. You're winter incarnate, calling the summer home. The magic of life, traveling back to you as its source."

Laurel sighs and shakes her head. "This is impossible. You know I can only grow things. I've never been able to do this."

"Sorry to interrupt," I say impatiently.

Laurel's eyes fly open and both of their heads snap to me, Laurel yanking her hands out of the soil.

"Not at all, love," my mom says, smiling and patting Laurel on the arm. "Your sister's learning some new tricks."

"Poorly," Laurel says under her breath, walking to the sink and washing her hands.

"Not poorly, just new," my mom says before looking back at me. "I thought you were taking the day off?"

"Yes," I say, careful of how to say the next words. I know my mother is full of grace. I know she sees the good in people. I know she technically gave me her blessing already. But I'm so nervous that my foot is tapping incessantly. I lock my knee, bring it to a stop, and focus on what to say to her. "But do you remember your rules for me seeing Liam?"

She nods. "I'm the one who made them, so I'd hope so."

"When do you think you could possibly meet him?" I ask, hopefully.

She chuckles, crossing her arms as she sits behind the register. "When did you have in mind?"

I force a smile as best as I can, hoping she'll take it well. "Sometime in the next sixty seconds."

Her eyebrows raise as Laurel laughs behind her. My sister shuts the water off and faces me, straightening the straps of her bright yellow sundress. "This oughta be good."

A figure appears in front of the shop, mostly hidden by the broad leaves inside it, but I'd recognize the letterman jacket anywhere. Oh fuck, it's about to happen.

What if it doesn't go well? What if she doesn't like him? What if she changes her mind?

Ten more steps, and it's clearly him reaching for the door handle outside.

"Thatshimpleasebenice," I blurt out as he pushes the door open and the bell above it rings.

My sister and mom laugh. I honestly don't see what's so funny.

Liam walks into the shop and his eyes zero in on mine. "Hi," he says with a sweet smile.

"Hi," I say back, nervous as hell.

It's quiet for a second, my mom and sister watching us closely before my mom finally decides to speak up. "You must be Liam," she says, standing up behind the counter.

Liam breaks eye contact with me, looking straight at her and extending his hand as he walks up. "I am. And you must be Ms…" Liam stops, the words caught in his throat. His eyes grow wide, moving between me and her. "I'm sorry, I just now realized I don't know your last name."

She lets out a kind laugh. "It's Layton," she says, taking his hand in both of hers. "But you can call me Ceres. Have you met my daughter, Laurel?" She motions to my sister, who, by the look on her face, is eating all of this up.

Liam shakes his head and waves to her with his free hand. "Hi."

Laurel giggles and waves back. "Hi there." I know her. She's already picking apart every inch of him in her mind. She could at least *try* to not be so judgmental.

I start going through all the things she's going to tell me later—about his messy hair, his goofy laugh, his ridiculous jacket. I get so angry at her and protective of him, but then stop myself and realize that none of it's even happened yet and I need to get a grip.

"Come and grab a chair," my mom says, waving Liam around the counter. "Quill and Laurel can work while we talk."

Laurel takes the hint. She grabs a pair of shears and a watering can, walking up to me and pulling me by the arm.

Sorry, I mouth to Liam's panicked face as she pulls me away to the other side of the shop.

"You sure didn't waste any time," she says softly in my ear.

"You're not helping," I say with a forced smile as I look back at him over my shoulder.

She shakes her head and pushes me along. Once we're out of earshot, she hands me the shears and nods to a shelf full of flowerpots. "I water, you cut."

"These all look fine." This is so frustrating. I should be over there with Liam. He doesn't know how she thinks, so he doesn't know what to say. I should've prepared him.

Laurel rolls her eyes and flourishes her hand, causing all of them to burst with errant stems and leaves. "How about now?"

I gasp, my eyes growing wide. I can't believe she'd use her magic so close to a human. "He's sitting right there," I hiss.

“Oh please, he’s so nervous, an airplane could crash out front and he wouldn’t notice.”

I grunt in protest but reluctantly start clipping them back anyway. My nerves twinge each time I feel the shears snap shut in my palm. “Can’t I just pretend to be doing work?”

She laughs. “No, you need something to keep yourself busy while she interrogates him.”

I stop and look at her, not amused in the slightest. “Interrogates? Seriously, Laurel?”

She keeps watering the pots around her, chuckling. “Relax, it’s a joke.”

“Not a very funny one,” I say, plucking off errant leaves. “What were you and Mom doing when I came down?”

“Ugh,” she says, shaking her head fervently. “She was trying to teach me how to suck the life out of the poor plant. Barbaric.” I’m kind of taken aback to hear her talk about our family magic like that. It doesn’t seem like her.

I knit my eyebrows and shake my head. “What’s so wrong with that?”

She pauses and looks at me like I have three heads. “It’s a dark art, Quill. It’s unnatural. It goes against everything we stand for.”

“But Mom can do it,” I say defensively. “I don’t know what the big deal is. That’s literally how she cleared the hot spring when I was sick.”

“Yeah, but that was an emergency,” she says, refilling the watering can from a nearby hose. “I can count on one hand the number of times I’ve seen her do it. It corrupts whatever it touches. I’d rather be as powerless as you than be able to do that.” I clench my jaw as it freezes with a grimace. “Sorry, that was rude. Not what I meant. I’m only frustrated. I wish she would come to terms with the fact that I can't do that."

"It's fine." But it's honestly not fine—that was pretty offensive. It leaves me wishing she would drop it entirely. Being the family dud is always gonna be a sore spot for me, and she shouldn't have brought it up.

"He's cute, by the way," she says, moving from plant to plant. "Not what I expected, though. I didn't think you'd have a thing for gingers."

"I don't have a thing for him," I lie, almost clipping my entire damn finger off. For now, as far as my family goes, they need to think we're friends. I haven't even figured out what we are yet.

Laurel laughs. "He sure has a thing for you. He's looked over his shoulder four times since we've been over here."

I pause and look back at Liam and my mom and catch him staring before he snaps his attention forward again. "I don't think it's what you think it is," I say, although she's right. I won't give her that satisfaction, though. I'm still irritated at her running her mouth a minute ago.

Laurel shrugs. "Whatever it is, you've got that boy wrapped around your finger. I've gotta say, you're better at this than I thought you would be."

I shake my head. "I honestly have no idea what 'this' is."

She stops and puts her hands on her hips, smirking. "Oh, you know. Romance. Attraction. Most people never completely figure it out, but you seem to be a natural. Whatever you've said or done worked beautifully. Now just enjoy it."

It's so strange to hear my sister talk about this kind of stuff. To me it's sweet and exciting and new. Her? She seems jaded, like it's a game she's played and won a thousand times. And maybe that's true for her.

I've never seen this side of her, and I kind of wish she wouldn't push any of that on me. It makes her seem cold and calculating in a way I've never caught on to, and that's not how I want to be with Liam. At all. This actually means something to me.

We work in silence, but I'm obsessed with what's happening on the other side of the shop. I'm hyper focused, doing everything I can to eavesdrop, but all I can hear is a gentle rustling of leaves all around us.

I swear my mom is doing that on purpose—muffling her and Liam so she can get some privacy with him. She's always one step ahead. It's smart. Frustrating as hell, but smart.

"What do you think they're talking about?" I ask Laurel.

"Boundaries. Rules. She might even be having the 'no sex' talk with him. Who knows?"

I stop and look her dead in the eye. "I hate you so much right now."

"Oh, calm down." She laughs. "I'm sure it's nothing bad. I doubt she'll scare him away, so don't worry about that."

The thought of last night crosses my mind again and I clench my jaw. This probably isn't the best timing, but I don't know when I'll get another chance to talk to my sister with my mom distracted. "I need to tell you something," I say quietly. "Whoever's been breaking in came back last night."

Laurel freezes and stares at me with wide eyes. "Did you see who it was?"

I shake my head.

She bites her lip, pulling her long blond hair to one side. "I have a theory, but I'm not so sure anymore," she says, twisting the strands in her hand.

"Why didn't you tell me?" I ask, surprised.

"What do you know about those friends of his?" she asks quietly. "They seem to be around pretty often."

I completely disagree with where she's going with this. "They seem nice. They also seem normal. Why?"

She raises her eyebrows and puts her hand on her hip. "Can you confidently say you know what *normal* looks like?" she asks knowingly. "You literally met your first human this month."

She has a point, but I won't let her pin this on them. "No, I can't. But it can't be them. They seem too… I don't know, but it doesn't fit." I know in my heart Max and James wouldn't do this.

Laurel sighs and shakes her head. "Whoever's doing it obviously knows a lot about rare plants," she says. "Keep an eye out. In the meantime, let me work on my hunch. I'll do my best to handle it so Mom doesn't ever need to know."

Just as I'm about to ask how I can help, the rustling fades and my mom's voice carries across the room. "Quill, can you come here for a second?"

She waves me off. "Don't worry about it. Here comes the verdict." Laurel smiles and lets out a tiny giggle, not looking up or pausing her work.

I set down the shears. If she says she's got it handled, I trust her. I walk over to the counter and focus on Liam.

He looks at ease as I approach, even happy. I guess my mom has that effect on people. I perk up, seeing that the conversation went as well as I had hoped.

"Liam tells me that he's really been enjoying spending time with you," she says. "And I can't tell you how happy I am that you have a friend."

I feel my ears heat up like they're sunburned. "Mom, this is so embarrassing."

She chuckles. "Oh, calm down." She turns her head back to Liam and smiles. "Thank you for coming by today to meet me. It means a lot. I'm sure I'll be seeing more of you soon."

"Looking forward to it," he tells her with a sheepish grin. He turns to me and starts to move in for a hug, but stops himself and blushes. "I'll text you later."

"Sounds good." I watch him turn away and walk out of the shop, the bell jingling after the door closes. I look at my mom, wondering what she has to say.

She nods. "Ah. Text. Technology. I was wondering how you two were keeping in contact. I should have figured that one out a while ago."

I cringe, a pang of guilt running through me. "Sorry. I should have told you."

She shakes her head and smiles. "It's fine. Too late now."

"He was incredibly nervous to meet you," I say. "He said he's not good with parents."

She laughs and puts her hands on her hips. "He should give himself more credit. The anxiety was cute. He was trying so hard not to say too much, but he likes you a lot. He's charming."

"So…you approve?" I ask, eyebrows rising in hope. *Please say yes. Please say yes. Please say yes.*

"Yes, I approve." She laughs, causing my heart to leap. "Now go upstairs and enjoy your day off."

My heart is light the rest of the day as I think about the smiles on my mom's and Liam's faces when I'd walked over, how at ease they already seemed with each other.

And the best part is, now that Mom has met and liked

him, I feel way less guilty about where I'm planning to take Liam tonight.

I wait for my mom to fall asleep, and as soon as I'm sure, I invite him over. I greet him with a huge hug at my doorway and lead him inside to the garden door.

I smile. "Ready?"

He takes a deep breath in and grins. "Ready."

I open the door, and the sweet summer air swirls around us. Liam's jaw drops as he looks inside, slowly walking through the doorway. "Quill… This is incredible."

We've been in the garden for under a minute, and Liam's entire vibe has already changed. His joy is infectious, washing over me. I stand next to him relaxed and relieved, staring deep into the woods and laughing.

"You get used to it," I say, doing my best to be modest when I know it's unlike anything his human eyes have ever seen. So far, I think I made the right decision bringing him in here. I shut the door behind us and walk past him, but he stays in place. "You coming?" I ask.

He nods and eventually follows me down the cobblestone path. "So…where are we?" he asks. "Like, I know we're in the garden, but there's no way this is all still in your house."

It's one of those human questions I never think about anymore. This is just my way of life. "It's kind of like a pocket world," I say, looking up at the swirling cosmos above us—the mother of Mother Nature herself. "It's outside of time and space. Everywhere and nowhere, where days and months and years don't exist. Eternal summer with the best growing conditions."

"Wow. And I knew this place would be big, but…this

is unreal. How far does it go?"

I laugh. "About a mile deep and a mile across. But my mom tells me it used to be a lot smaller when it was first created. Only a few trees and a few patches of soil. It grows to fit what we need."

"Hold on," he says, coming to a stop. He digs in his pocket and pulls out his phone, holding it up to the ceiling. "Wow, it even has great reception. Full bars."

My jaw clenches. "Please don't tell me you're taking pictures of this place."

His eyes find mine. "Don't need them. I already have the most gorgeous thing in here with me." He winks.

I roll my eyes and groan, but my heart skips a beat. "Do you want a tour or not?"

"Yes! Yes. Sorry," he says, catching up to me.

"So this is the orchard," I say, motioning around us. "Every fruit you could want and then some."

"I'm guessing this is where you get all of your food?"

I nod. "Better than any farm in the world. Here, let me show you something." I walk over to a tree on the right and reach up, pulling down an orange bulb, except I gasp. It falls to mush in my fingers. I freeze, shock gripping my heart. That's never happened before.

Laurel wasn't kidding when she said it's getting weirder in here by the day. I clench my jaw, worrying about how much worse this is going to get before we figure out who's been doing this and how to stop them. I had better tell her about this tomorrow.

"Everything okay?" he asks behind me.

"Uh, yeah," I say, throwing it on the ground and doing my best to hide my discontent. I don't want to poison this moment for him—I'll deal with it later. I reach back up, gently squeezing another, and it's firm. I pop it off the branch and hand it to him. "Try it."

He takes it in his hand with a skeptical look. "I'm sure it's great, but I've had a peach before."

I shake my head. "It's not a peach. Seriously, try it."

He looks down at it, smells it, and takes a small bite. He chews for a second, and his face lights up. "Holy shit, this is delicious. I've never tasted anything like this."

I laugh, chest out, smiling proudly. "My mom made it for me. Mango and pineapple and guava in the body of a peach. And no pit."

"I'll take one anytime," he says with his mouth full, chomping down with huge bites.

I laugh. "Let's keep going." We walk farther down the path out of the orchard and hang a right. "I'm surprised you haven't sneezed once since you got in here. This place should be driving your allergies wild."

His eyes jump from tree to tree, answering without looking at me. "I would have thought so, too, but they haven't bothered me since you gave me that potion."

Interesting. Looks like it healed more than just the cut on his face.

"So, how come your mom sleeps at night, but you don't?" Liam asks.

"My sister and I are also human because of my dad. We aren't as powerful as her, but some of the rules don't apply to us."

He furrows his brow and tilts his head. "What about your mom? Didn't she have a dad?"

More human questions that don't cross my mind anymore. "Dryads don't necessarily need someone else to have kids. There's a potion for that."

"And what would happen if you took that potion?" he jokes.

"Let's not test that theory." I laugh.

We keep walking farther into the garden, but Liam pauses. "Are you not burning up in here?"

I shrug. "I guess not. I must be used to it."

"Ugh," he scoffs. "Hold on." His hands cross in front of his waist, grip the bottom of his shirt, and he pulls it off in one smooth motion.

I gulp at the sight of his naked chest. I know I've seen it before, but for some reason it stuns me today. I'm at a loss for words as I try to swallow with a dry throat.

"Much better," he says, tucking it into the waistband of his shorts. He looks up, stops, and grins. "Like what you see?"

Truthfully? Yeah, I really do. Something in the back of my mind is begging me to reach out and touch him, but I shake myself back into reality. "I, uh… Wow. Sorry," I say, turning back down the path. "Here, there's something up ahead that might help."

I walk forward, and he catches up right next to me. I see his perfectly sculpted chest out of the corner of my eye, but I keep walking. His sweat starts invading my senses—sweet and woodsy—and it's driving me wild. What is happening to me? *Keep it together, Quill.*

"What's that sound?" he asks as we get closer to the corner.

"You'll see."

We finally turn the corner and arrive at our waterfall.

Liam's eyebrows rise, and he starts laughing. "This place keeps getting better and better."

I'm actually having a blast with Liam here. I'm so happy I can show him all of this, partly out of pride, but he's making me appreciate the magic that work's made me take for granted over the years. "Wanna get in?" I ask him.

He nods, completely excited, and starts stripping off his shorts. He runs forward in his underwear and cannonballs into the pool under the falls. He floats under the surface for a few seconds before coming back up and smoothing his hair back.

"You gonna join me?" he yells after me.

I shrug with a smile and peel off my shirt, walking to meet him. I can feel his eyes dragging across my chest and down my stomach, but as long as I don't make eye contact with him, I won't lose my nerve. I drop my shorts at the water's edge and smoothly slide under the cool surface. I finally look him in the eye again, but he's biting his lip with one eyebrow up.

"Like what you see?" I say in a mocking voice. He's able to make me so flustered and embarrassed whenever he says stuff like that, now I want to return the favor.

Liam tips his head. "Now that you mention it..."

Not the answer I expected.

I playfully scoff and splash him, but he sends back a wave of water the second after he flinches. We go back and forth until he finally lunges at me, wrapping his arms around my bare waist, and pulls me under.

We come back up laughing, our chests pressed together.

We're both in the middle of a beam from the starlight above, and I can't help but notice the freckles on his skin and how they make constellations of their own. I want to trace my finger along each one, drawing lines to connect them. But the moment I realize how close we actually are, I push backward in the water to put space between us.

The last thing I need is for my body to embarrass me while he's pressing up against me.

He opens his mouth to say something, but I cut him off. "Try the water," I tell him in an effort to distract him.

Maybe to distract myself, too.

Liam pauses but ends up shrugging. He cups his hands, brings a few gulps to his lips, and throws his head back with a sigh. "You could bottle this. I didn't know water could taste so clean."

"Better than the school pool?"

"No comparison," he says. "I can't wrap my head around all of this. Does this mean other things exist, too? Vampires? Werewolves?"

I laugh. "Not exactly, but yeah, my mom's told me stories of stuff my family's seen over the years."

"Like what?" he asks, eyes brightening.

"So you've heard stories of gods and goddesses, right?" I drag my hand along the water. "Immortals who were worshipped and ruled entire civilizations. But they were only humans who could do magic."

"Really? Magic like yours?"

I shrug. "More or less. Sometimes they got it from rare creatures like us. We were all actually here first, followed by people much later. But there are way fewer of us nowadays, and we all stay away from humans. Either that or we hide in plain sight like my family does."

He nods. "And no one ever discovers you?"

"I mean, you'll see sightings of things like 'Bigfoot' or 'The Loch Ness Monster' every now and again, but that's about it," I say, lying down to float on my back. "Technology made secrecy super hard—my mom tells me all the time how much she hates it. 'The internet's the worst thing to ever happen to this planet since that rock that killed the dinosaurs.'"

Liam laughs, looking around at the forest. "It's all so amazing. It's hard to believe."

"I haven't even shown you the coolest part yet. Ready

to move on?" His excitement is intoxicating, and I can't get enough of it now.

"Can't wait," he says, swimming to the edge.

I can't help but watch as he gets out, wet fabric clinging to every inch of his legs. I look away once I realize what I'm doing—the least I can do is give him some privacy.

I follow him out with my head down, skin and hair dry by the time I reach down and pull on my clothes. I look back at him, fully clothed again, but the water's soaked through his shirt and shorts. He doesn't seem bothered, though—I mean, he is a swimmer.

We walk in silence for a few more minutes. I watch him examine all the plants around him in awe, but he catches me staring at him. I look away as fast as I can, a sheepish grin taking over my mouth.

I can't help but wonder, was what happened in the pond like what almost happened in the theater? Did I miss a moment? Fuck it up again? I guess I'll never know, so I do my best to push it out of my mind and keep walking. At last, we turn the final corner at the farthest reaches of the garden.

"Here we are," I say, walking into the center of a cozy courtyard. It's all circular—trellises creating a tiny maze in the center encircled with stone benches. Various pots of strange leaves decorate the edges, carefully crafted plots rooted between each one. Flowers of every color and shape populate the canopies and ground around us, like a botanical rainbow.

"Whoa," he says, spinning. "I've never seen plants like this before."

I laugh and shake my head, doing my best to be modest. "I doubt you would. These are the rarest ones in our collection. Magical, extinct, or impossible to find without powers. That's my sister's job nowadays. It's why she's always off traveling the world."

"I recognize that one," he says, pointing to a giant tree with sharp leaves and bright blue flowers. "We ate that last night. And that one." He points to a large circular pot full of clovers of every color. "What about the rest?"

"This one's called a Midas Vine," I said, walking him over to a small trellis. Metallic tendrils and leaves coat the rods, dripping in crystalline berries. "It's real gold and real diamonds. My mom used clippings of this thing to pay for the building."

His face goes flat. "You can literally grow money?"

I laugh. "I'll give you a bracelet for your birthday." I walk farther to a bush of broad, red leaves. "This one's called Dragon's Hide. It grows in the arctic. Just don't touch it—third-degree burns."

He crouches down next to the patch next to it. "What about this ugly one?" He points to a lime-green, matte, sickly looking fern.

"That's my sister's latest find, the Ardor Blossom. I personally think it's a dud."

He rubs his chin with his fingers. "How come no one's ever discovered these before? I mean, they have to have come from somewhere."

I shrug. "Most are impossible to find, so they're just written off as legends. But truthfully, magical plants need magic to survive. Most of them come from sacred places imbued with magic. Specific ecosystems. Without those, they die within a few hours."

He nods and looks up at me, but his vision goes behind me. "And that building?"

I turn around and realize he's staring at the conservatory, glowing red and secured shut with steel vines locked together. "Uh…" I don't want to tell him, but I know Liam's smart enough to have figured it out on his own already.

"That's where the berries are," he says, standing. "The ones you made the potion out of."

I shake my head. I was hoping we wouldn't need to have this conversation, but there's no avoiding it now. "Yeah, but they're sealed away for a reason. My sister said something about it being the most dangerous plant we have in here."

Thankfully, he lets it go before it turns into something bigger. Liam nods and motions around and walks up to me, carefully choosing his words. "Quill, this is the most amazing thing I'll ever see in my life. Thank you for bringing me in here."

"You're welcome," I say, looking down. It's the most vulnerable I've ever felt with anyone, and as scary as that is, it's thrilling. "I really like you. And I really trust you." Simple words, but I mean them deeply.

As I'm looking down, his feet stop inches in front of mine. I look up, and his face and body are as close.

"Quill…" Liam's hand slowly wraps around my hip while his other palm presses gently on the side of my face. "I'll just come out and say it. You're the first thing I think of when I wake up in the morning and the last thing before I fall asleep. You're my favorite person in the world." His thumb gently grazes my cheekbone as a small smile breaks across his lips. His perfectly full lips.

I stare into his eyes as he slowly leans forward. He closes his eyes and tilts his head to the side—and I can't help but do the same. Suddenly our mouths meet, and electricity hits my veins. Both of his hands drop to my lower back, pulling me in to him as I link my hands behind his neck.

I can't tell if it's my heartbeat pounding or his, chest pressed against mine. The fruit is on his breath, but also the taste of…him. My new favorite flavor.

I didn't know a moment could feel like a split second and an eternity at the same time.

One of his hands goes up the back of my shirt, and I shiver at the feeling of his skin gently caressing mine. I'm aching to get closer to him, but I don't know how that would be possible. What started as something sweet melts into something with more urgency.

I want more of him. I can't get enough.

We pull each other closer, and I swear, if someone asked me how long we stayed like that, I wouldn't be able to answer. I could kiss him forever, but through my closed eyes, I feel his lips morph into a smile before he pulls away.

I open my eyes and see him looking back at me, beaming.

Holy shit, I can't believe this is happening. My first kiss, and it was…perfect. Liam is perfect. I wouldn't have wanted it with anyone else. I wish I could bottle this emotion here and now, tasting it and revisiting it for the rest of my life. I want more. I can't get enough.

"I hope that's the first time and not the last time," he says. I chuckle and pull him in close again, but he suddenly pauses. Bliss is replaced with what looks an awful lot like fear. "Do you smell that?"

I shake my head, wanting only to feel his lips on mine again. Something in his eyes, however, tells me this isn't the time. "No. What?"

He releases me and looks above the treetops. "Is that… smoke?"

Chapter Twenty-Eight

There's a thin black spiral floating in the air.

It's where the family trees are.

Fear grips my chest at the thought of my ancestors in danger. My grandmothers, my magic—everything is in danger. The damage would be irreparable, and they're helpless. And I can't shake the feeling that this is somehow all my fault. Something terrible is happening to the garden, and this is the worst possible scenario.

I gasp, run over to the well by the conservatory, and grab the bucket sitting there. "Stay here!" I shout.

"Let me help you!" he yells after me, but I'm already sprinting through the trees.

A flood of energy rushes through my body, my heart pounding. I sprint through the forest, taking the longest strides of my life to save the garden. How can this be happening? The happiest moment of my life, followed by my nightmare come true. This can't be happening.

I think back to my mom's story—her waking up with dread when my dad tried to burn the garden down.

Glimpses of my dream, the warped image of my father, bleed into the forefront of my thoughts.

I break into the clearing and immediately see where a small patch of flames sprouted—right in the center of the grove. I breathe a sigh of relief that it's luckily close to the stream running through the middle, blocked from reaching the ancestors. Fire and forests are never a good combination—but it's not that bad.

Still doesn't change the fact that the danger is real.

I dunk the bucket in the water and throw the liquid on top of the embers. After a half of a bucket, I see the source—a stray bush of Dragon's Hide. The heat from the leaves caused everything else around it to singe and burn wildly.

I shake my head, irritated that something smaller than a campfire had to sprout up out of nowhere. How the fuck did it even get over here?

First flowers becoming ash, then water turning toxic. Today fruit became mush, and now random plants are growing halfway across the garden. This is getting way out of hand. It may be time to get my mom involved if Laurel can't help.

But right now, it doesn't matter.

Because the last time a fire started in the garden, my mom came running.

Shit.

The biggest possible danger right now is her discovering Liam here. She may have met him and liked him, but there's no way she'd be okay with me bringing him to our sacred place.

There's a very real chance she's rushing this way right now, and I don't want to know what happens if she gets to him first. I need to get him out of here. I dash back through the woods to the courtyard, doing my best to suppress this brand-new shot of adrenaline coursing through my veins. I throw down the bucket and grab his hand.

"Let's go," I say urgently and pull him with me. It feels like my chest is going to burst.

"What's going on?" he asks as we race the mile back to the garden door.

I keep desperately pulling his arm, doing my best to explain while we sprint. "My mom might be coming. We need to get you out of here now!"

We run in silence for what feels like ages, lungs burning by the time we get back to the entrance. My stomach drops when we get there, though—the closet door is open.

Shit, I'm too late.

My mom is in here.

I freeze and hold out my hand for him to stop, waving him behind a nearby tree. I press my finger to my lips.

With the greatest care, I sneak into the hallway to check and see if the coast is clear.

With my luck, Laurel's probably on her way down. Except it's way worse than that.

Across the way, I peek inside my mom's room. Relief washes over me at the sight of her deep asleep, judging by her snoring. Thank nature—it's going to be okay. That is, until I realize something much worse. If it wasn't my mom, that means...

Someone broke into our home.

And into our garden.

Again.

There's no way it could have been Laurel. She would

have helped me stop the fire, or at least confronted me for bringing Liam inside.

The front door suddenly slams shut, and I jump, breath catching in my throat. Heartbeats ripping through my chest, I sprint to my room and grab my rose branch. Holding it above my shoulder, I creep into the living room.

All I find, however, is a dark room with nothing but empty furniture. The tension in my muscles loosens, but frustration quickly takes over.

Whoever it was is already gone, and I barely missed them. They must have gotten a head start, running back after they saw the smoke in the garden.

I march back into the garden and wave Liam out of hiding. I'm doing my best not to look pissed or overly anxious. He gives me a strange look and points at the bat, but I hold up my hand and shake my head. He gets the hint. No questions. I don't think I'm doing well at this overly anxious thing.

I guide him out into the hallway and back through my apartment, not saying a word. I don't want him to join in on the panic party. This thief isn't his problem—it's mine and Laurel's. I open the door for him as quietly as I can.

He walks out but stops on the mat outside. His hand slips to the back of my head, and he ducks in to kiss me on the cheek.

"Text me tomorrow?" he asks with a smile.

"Right when I wake up," I say with a grin, heart fluttering.

He nods once and walks down the hallway back home. I keep an eye on him until he shuts the door behind him. One last look around before I set my bat down and lock myself inside.

I pause, alone in the living room, and put my hands on my hips. For the love of nature, Laurel's gonna need to hear about this—minus the part about Liam being in there with me. She wouldn't be so pleased about that one.

I let my head fall backward, taking a huge breath in and blowing it out.

Liam, though… I… There are no words. Intruder aside, I'm just so fucking happy right now. I laugh out loud to myself and graze my fingers over my lips. I shake my head and walk back to my room, but as I turn into the hallway, something iridescent on the ground catches my eye. I bend down and pick it up—a used Rainbow Root. How did this get here?

My stomach drops. Maybe this is how they've been breaking in? Only a handful of these the first time they broke in would be all they need to get into the garden as much as they want. Whoever it is knows their way around rare and magical plants. Not a good sign.

I tear it up and bury it at the bottom of the trash can before going to my room. The last thing I need is for my mom to find out.

It's strange—the sky was so clear when I talked to my mom this morning. I guess I missed the change in the pressure, not even noticing that the clouds were churning before Liam came over. A storm's been blowing in all day, and at last, it's here.

The thunder outside rips the summer sky open while the rain drowns out everything else. It's the perfect lullaby—that moment the world resets itself. The scent of the storm creeps into my room, putting me at ease, except something feels…wrong. Out of place.

There's a presence out there, and it's one that doesn't

belong. I can't shake the feeling something terrible has already happened, yet somehow the worst is still to come. I do my best to block it out, but I can't.

Deep down, I know it's too late for me to stop whatever it is.

Chapter Twenty-Nine

Liam: Morning handsome :)

A grin spreads across my face as I open Liam's text. Any other time I'd be pretty pissed off at someone waking me up, but he's the only exception. I haven't seen Liam for a few days, since the night in the garden, but we've been texting almost nonstop.

Me: Hey you. What are you doing up so early?

Liam: Getting ready to go to the hospital. My dad is coming home today :)

My fingers pause as I reread Liam's message. I think about how awful his dad looked in the hospital when I saw him in the dream. How could he be well enough to come home? Then again, I know nothing about human medicine. Maybe they finally found something that worked for him. Or maybe Liam could have been imagining it in the dream to be worse than it was?

Either way, my heart fills with happiness for Liam.

Me: That's great news! How's he feeling?

Liam: Fine for the most part. Hoping he feels even

better once he's in his own bed

Me: That's pretty great news to wake up to, gotta say

Liam: So you're still in bed? Sounds fun… maybe I can stop by before I head to the hospital

My face flashes red hot. I close my eyes and I can still feel his hand on my back and his breath on my lips. *Play it cool, Quill. Play. It. Cool.*

Me: Don't tempt me haha

Liam: Good thing I'm already on my way

My eyes grow wide. Something tells me he's not joking. "Shit," I whisper to myself.

I throw the covers off and sprint to the front door, scooping up clothes on my way. I yank on a pair of gym shorts and my shirt, unlatch the door, and find Liam standing there with his fist in the air.

We both freeze, breathlessly staring at each other, but a slight frown forms on his lips as he looks me up and down. "I know for a fact you wear less than that when you sleep. You were practically naked when you tried to bludgeon me to death."

"Yeah, I left the deadly weapon behind, too," I say with a nervous chuckle. Please tell me he isn't here to try to get in bed with me. I'm pretty sure if he'd ask, my brain would melt and run out my ears and I'd forget how to use words. But I mean… Maybe I'd like it? *Fuck. Don't think about that right now. Keep it together.* "What are you doing here?" I ask.

"I couldn't wait to do this," he says, stepping forward. He slides his hand on the back of my neck and leans forward, pressing his mouth to mine.

My chest swells and I swear on everything in the world that's green, it takes everything in me not to melt underneath his kiss.

"Good morning to you, too," I say with a light breath. "And here I thought you were coming to do something more R-rated."

He leans in the doorway. "Maybe if you asked nicely."

The idea of pulling him into my room myself crosses my mind, but I put it to rest as quickly as it shows up. We're taking things slow. With clothes. And I need to focus on the Liam in front of me, not the one I felt pressing up against me in the water last night.

Luckily, before I can figure out how to respond, he flashes that gorgeous, crooked smile I love about him and changes the subject. "I actually only have a few more minutes before I have to head out, but I'm having a party tomorrow night, if you want to come. For my dad. He was pretty close with a lot of my friends before he got sick because they hung out at our house all the time, and I know he's missed seeing them."

"A party?" I ask, taken aback. "Doesn't your dad need to rest?"

Liam nods. "Turns out the last procedure at the hospital helped a ton. My dad is feeling way better. He's even the one who suggested it when I talked to him earlier."

"Wow, that's great." I'm happy to hear the good news, but then my heart picks up speed at the thought of a crowd. "Who's going?"

"Some kids from school. Part of the swim team. Max and James are gonna be there, too, so you'll at least know a few people."

Worries creep up on me. Me frozen in Times Square. Me making a fool of myself with all of these human customs. I barely learned how to use a seat belt last week, for fuck's sake. But this seems important to him, so I nod anyway. "Okay, I'll come."

Liam's face lights up, and I know I gave the right answer. "Amazing." He pauses, suddenly looking almost shy. "*You're* amazing, Quill. I'm so lucky to have you."

Then he heads out, leaving me swooning so hard I almost—almost—can ignore the giant pit in my stomach.

Chapter Thirty

The party started an hour ago, and I've been ready for way longer than that. Yet here I am, lying on my bed. Staring at the ceiling. Trying to hold off Liam for as long as I can because the thought of a crowd is driving my anxiety through the roof.

It was bad enough being in an imaginary Times Square in the middle of an imaginary mob, but this is real life. I can't imagine them away if it gets to be too much. I'm dreading what may happen if it's too much. The last thing I want to do is melt down in front of all his friends.

My phone buzzes yet again.

Liam: You almost ready?

Me: Yeah, sorry, long shower. Be there soon

Deep breath in. Deep breath out. I'd better not keep him waiting any longer.

I swing my legs off my bed, slip my feet into my shoes, and head to Liam's apartment. I crack my knuckles one by one, finish off with my neck, and do one more breathing exercise when I get there to settle my nerves.

In.

Out.

Knock, knock, knock.

The door opens, but it's not Liam staring back at me—it's some ripped blond guy with crooked teeth and eyes that are way too close together. He's wearing a letterman that looks exactly like Liam's.

The guy looks at me for less than a second and shakes his head. "Yeah dude," he says over the music inside. "Wrong house." He starts shutting the door, but I jam my foot inside.

"Liam invited me." Why is he guarding someone else's house?

He laughs and looks me up and down. "Not sure why."

Wow. I'm not even through the door and I'm already regretting this.

I narrow my eyes and look him up and down, disgust covering my face. *Who the fuck is this guy?* My sarcasm is my armor, sharp words poised to shred him apart, but a familiar voice cuts me off before they fly out of my mouth.

"Get out of the way, Trevor," Liam says and pulls the door open. The guy rolls his eyes and walks away, leaving Liam and me alone. "Hey," he says with a smile. "I was starting to worry."

"Sorry," I say as I walk in past him. The lights are dimmed inside. Hopefully they'll hide the bothered look on my face. "Who was that?"

Liam scoffs. "A guy on the swim team with me. Don't pay attention to him. He's been sneaking shots from his pocket since he got here."

"And your dad's cool with that?" I ask skeptically.

"No, but I don't think he's noticed. Trevor's behaved for the most part. Drink?" I side-eye him, but he laughs.

"Nonalcoholic. Not that kinda party."

I laugh gently to make it seem like I'm at ease, but I'm definitely not able to relax right now. "Oh good. Chlorine was bad enough. Let's not test anything new." My armor's already up, and sarcasm is easy.

Liam seems to buy it. He chuckles, grabs my hand, and leads me to the kitchen.

Right as we get in there, a man walks in from around the corner. I have to do a double-take—he's tall, bald, and has the same freckles as Liam. It's his dad, and even though Liam told me how much better he's doing, I'm beyond surprised to even see him standing.

"You must be Quill!" he says, shouting over the music. Before I can say anything, he walks up to me and pulls me into the tightest hug I've ever had. I swear he's about to break me in half.

He's nothing like the zombie who was in the hospital from Liam's dream.

In fact, he's way closer to the image of the man in Liam's InstaSnap than I was expecting—tall, well-built, and radiating strength. No wonder the hospital let him come home.

"Nice to meet you," I choke out awkwardly as he releases me. It's weird that he's basically a stranger and is touching me, but I do my best to not let it show that I'm getting overwhelmed.

He claps his hand on my shoulder and smiles. A familiar pair of blue eyes look into mine, only these are bloodshot. "Your mom's said nothing but great things about you. My son, too. I'm glad you could make it."

"Thanks for having me," I say, unsure of how I should respond. I think the obvious question may be the safest. "How are you feeling?"

"Fantastic." He regards me for a split second, but turns his head to Liam and nods in Trevor's direction. "Hey son, maybe your friend shouldn't be playing with your mom's knickknacks."

I snap my head around and see the guy from earlier tossing a golden picture frame from hand to hand. "Fuck," I hear Liam say as he rushes across the room.

"Drink?" Liam's dad says, pulling my attention back to him. He releases my shoulder, giving me that same crooked smile Liam gives me. It's weird to see someone else share his features. Those little quirks I love so much fit Liam so well, but they make me less trusting of his dad. It's like a warped reflection.

I think of how Liam met with my mom earlier. I need to at least try to be respectful and make a good impression. "Sure," I say politely, pulling up a seat at the bar.

"So Liam says you're homeschooled?" he asks, reaching down the counter and picking up a red cup from a stack.

I nod. "Sure am. Right next door." Short, sanitized answers are probably the best option.

"That's cool," he says, pouring a ladle full of red liquid. "And you work in your mom's garden, too?"

I would have thought Liam would have told him I worked in the flower shop instead. I still go with it. "Sure do," I say. This is so awkward.

He nods. "Sounds hard. Do you like it?"

I shrug. "It's okay. Mostly weeds and roses." Less is more, nothing offensive.

He laughs, still somehow amused by me, and hands me the cup. His fingernails are filthy, but I try to ignore it. The last thing I need to do is judge a guy with cancer.

"You don't sound so thrilled," he says. "Not into the family business?"

I don't want to lie, but I don't want it to get back to my mom about how I'm running my mouth to everyone about how unhappy I am. I take a quick sip of the stuff he poured, but I can't place the flavor. Fantastic, I'll talk about that. "Not particularly. What is this stuff?"

"Secret recipe," he says, nodding his head back and forth. "Fruit punch from my old college days, only without the vodka. I'm sure you'll get some recipes of your own when you go." He winks.

I raise my eyebrows with a forced laugh and take another sip. So fucking awkward. "Not sure if I'll go to college, honestly." I would like nothing more in the world for this to be over, please.

"Why's that?" he asks, crossing his arms.

"You already said it, family business." Another sip, mashing down my irritation. When did this turn into him grilling me about things that don't matter?

He chuckles. "What did you want to be when you were growing up?"

"Easy," I say with a laugh. "Not a gardener." *Shit.* There goes the same, classic Quill mouth—faster than my brain can move. I clench my jaw and force a smile, doing my best to not show how embarrassed I am that I bad-mouthed my family business to the man my mom is helping. I probably look so ungrateful right now.

Luckily he doesn't seem fazed by it. "That makes things easier," he says with another laugh. "Maybe you should—" His words are cut off by Trevor stumbling between us.

He dips his cup in the bowl and, scooping up another glass full, tips it to Liam's dad and stumbles out of the kitchen.

Liam hurries and turns to his dad. "Sorry, I honestly didn't think he'd be like this."

"It's all good. I'm gonna go pick up some more food for you guys. Pretty sure deliveries stopped a half hour ago." He claps me on the shoulder and nods. "Nice to meet you, Quill. See you soon."

"You too," I say, relieved that I've been released from this torture chamber of a conversation. I stand up and muster a friendly wave as he walks away.

Liam reaches down and grabs my hand. "Wanna go find Max and James?"

"Why not?" I say, forcing myself to seem as agreeable as possible.

So many people, so many sounds, and so many conversations I didn't brace myself to be a part of. It must be at least twenty people from his school, all complete strangers. I follow him to the couch across the room. I relax a bit when I see the two sitting there who were at my house last night. Long braids and purple hair.

"Hey guys," Liam says, leading me beside him.

Max's round face lights up as soon as she sees me. "Quill! So glad to see you!"

"Glad you could make it," James says with a wink.

I smile nervously. "Nice to see you guys again."

"Have a seat," she says, scooting away from James and leaving a space between them.

I'm beginning to wonder if all humans are born awkward or if it's just me. I sit down anyway.

"You okay?" Liam asks me, sitting on the arm of the couch.

"Yeah," I lie, pulling on my shirt to get some air on my skin. "It's kinda hot in here."

Liam cringes. "Sorry, our air conditioning broke this morning. I think my dad called your mom about it."

"It's all good," James says to me. "You could take your

shirt off. I won't mind."

Liam shakes his head at James and narrows his eyes. "Can you try to not hit on the guy I'm dating?"

I look at Liam, heart skipping a beat. "Dating? Is that what we're doing?"

"I thought that was obvious," he says sheepishly. "But if that's not what you want—"

"No," I say, pleasantly surprised and with a genuine grin. "Dating. Dating is great." It's the best thing that's happened all night, and this party just got a million times better.

"I think we witnessed a moment," James says to Max with a theatrical hand next to his mouth and a fake whisper.

"James, learn to be quiet for once," Max says as she reaches over me and punches him in the arm. I'm starting to like her more and more.

Liam sighs. "Are you guys gonna behave if I run to the bathroom?"

"Cross my heart and hope to die," James says, making a little *X* on his chest.

Max shakes her head at him but looks back at Liam. "He's safe with us. Go on." Liam shoots me one last smile and heads back through the kitchen.

"For what it's worth, you two make a cute couple," James says. "I still think we'd look cuter, but I'll accept it." He shoots me a wink.

Uh. Awkward. How do I respond? "Thanks, I think?"

"Oh shut up, James," Max says. "Weren't you just going on and on about how hot his sister is?"

"She is!" he says before looking back at me and shrugging. "Must run in the family."

"My sister?" I ask suspiciously. "How do you know my sister?"

James laughs and leans back. "Oh, Laurel? We go way back."

"Yeah, all the way back to this afternoon," Max says before looking at me. "We stopped by your flower shop before we came to see Liam and his dad. James could barely contain the drool as soon as he saw your sister."

"Come on, Max, have you *seen* her?" James asks, putting both hands over his heart.

I look at Max to see if this is normal, and I can't help but chuckle when she rolls her eyes.

"I've gotta say, I was pretty impressed at the stuff in your mom's shop," Max says, sipping on her drink. "I'm a little bit of a plant girl myself."

"Thanks," I say, suspicious of where this is going. "We all work hard to keep it up and running."

Max nods. "I mostly noticed your carnivorous plants. You have a few super-rare species in there on display. Was that really a *Nepenthes clipeata*?"

"The shield-leaved pitcher-plant?" I ask, growing a little proud. "Sure was."

"That's impressive, because they're basically extinct," she says, eyeing me carefully. Pride disintegrates as something tells me I may have fucked up. To my horror, she continues the thought pattern. "Barely fifteen left in the wild before we were born, but yours is so healthy. Where did you get it? What humidity do you keep it at? And what do you put in the soil to keep it doing so well?"

Damn it. Those are *actual* human gardening questions, and "magic" isn't an acceptable answer. So I shrug. "That's more of a question for my mom. We have a lot of rare things in the garden. I mostly just water and cut."

"I'd love to see it some time," she says. "Where is it?"

Shit. How do I respond to that without giving too much

away? I can't straight up lie to her—nature knows she'll find out eventually. And I can't say something to shut her up—this is one of Liam's best friends.

Besides, she's only making conversation, right? That's what humans do.

Just as my brain completely freezes up and neglects to spit out an acceptably vague answer, small droplets hit the back of my neck, getting sucked up by the time I turn to see Trevor flicking punch at us. Max scowls at him, but he and his friends start laughing.

Max sighs and turns back around. "We've been friends with Liam since elementary school. The jocks aren't huge fans of us, but they usually leave us alone. They need him on the team and don't wanna piss him off."

"I'm starting to think he's not a huge fan of me, either," I say and take a sip of my drink.

At this very second, I'm glad he's as obnoxious as he is. Excellent distraction.

What did my sister say about the thief? That they would know a lot about rare plants? I'm starting to wonder if she was onto something when she suspected Max and James.

"Just stick with us, buddy," James says, clapping me on my leg a couple of times. "We're the real VIPs here. We know where all the bodies are buried."

"God, James, you make Liam sound so impure," Max says. They both start laughing. Clearly an inside joke I don't get, but I stay quiet, dissociating from the conversation and weighing how likely it is that they have something to do with the garden malfunctioning.

"What's funny?" Liam asks as he walks up.

"Talking about your sainthood," Max says, holding back more laughter.

Liam groans as he walks over to me, grabbing my hand

and pulling me to standing. "While you guys do that, I'm stealing Quill for a minute."

"Have fun," James says. "We'll still be here."

The laughter picks up again as we walk away, through the kitchen and down the hallway into his room. He flicks the light on and shuts the door behind me. I shut my eyes and throw my head back.

I know my mom said no closed doors, but I'm so glad it is. I need some quiet—I was starting to get overwhelmed. My social anxiety is at its peak—asshole party guests, uncomfortable parent conversations, and the worry my new boyfriend's best friends are actually the bad guys.

It's all too much to handle.

In through the nose, out through the mouth. Liam's arms snake around my waist as he pulls my back into his chest, holding me close in the dim light.

"You doing okay?" he asks.

"Yeah," I say, holding his hands as they press into my stomach. My heart rate instantly descends and it feels like I can catch my breath again. "Just a lot of people."

"I know." He kisses the top of my head and rocks me back and forth. "I'm sorry. I didn't want to not invite you and have you feel left out."

"It's all right." I turn around to face him, draping my arms over his shoulders. "This makes it worth it."

"Definitely worth it," he says, pulling our hips closer. "Let's skip the party and cut straight to this next time."

"I could be down with that," I say with a grin. My eyes break away from his and scan the room. Nothing on the floor, bed tucked in tight, and not a speck of dust on the

TV. "I like your room. Suspiciously clean."

He shrugs and looks up innocently. "I was having company over."

"Oh yeah?" I laugh, completely amused at how he's trying to play this off. "Is there some human custom where everyone comes to hang out in the host's bedroom?"

"Nah, only the guests the host *really* likes," he says. His hand comes up and his thumb gently strokes my cheek. "I'm kinda bummed I got to kiss you only once today."

"Nothing's stopping you now," I say, leaning a little closer and tracing his strong jawline with my fingertips. We close our eyes, and right as our lips touch, I hear a voice.

"What the fuck is going on here!" Trevor yells.

I break the kiss off and snap my head to the door, mortified as he and his friends all start walking in.

"Come on Liam," Trevor continues as he walks up to me. "You can do better than this." He stops inches from my face. I'm assaulted by the alcoholic fumes on his breath and his rancid body odor.

All the tension I've felt the entire night bubbles to the surface, melting into straight up anger. I've had enough of this shit. "How about you get the fuck away from me?" I snap, gritting my teeth.

Trevor puts his hands up, backing away. "You're a little aggro, bro."

I keep walking toward him, losing all control of my impulses. "And you're so fuckin' drunk, you couldn't work a ziplock bag, *my dude.*"

Normally anyone else would back off, but Trevor laughs. "See, this is the problem," he says to his friends behind him before turning his words back to me. "Liam needs to stick to his own kind, not with freaks like you."

I don't waste any time. "The real problem is that he's

better than you and you know it."

"Quill, stop," Liam says, trying to get between us. "And Trevor, leave. Now."

"Say that again," Trevor says, coming face-to-face with me. I clearly struck a nerve.

My anger turns cold. I smile and go for the jugular. "Did you know no one actually wanted you here tonight?" I ask. Trevor's eyes widen and my mouth starts running. "Liam's too nice to say it, but I'm not. All you've been doing since I walked in the door is showing off what a fucking dick you are, but for some reason, no one wants to tell you. So here, let me do it. You're a sad excuse for a human and it's pathetic."

Trevor pauses and scoffs. He narrows his eyes. "*Human?* Then what the fuck does that make you? Inhuman?" he yells.

My stomach turns and my skin prickles. There's no possible way he could know, but it's still too close to home.

"You think you're special just because you walk in here with green hair?" he continues, twisting a finger along his own scalp. "All you are is some homeschooled freak and his flavor of the week until school starts again. Then he'll forget all about you, like those assholes on the couch."

Liam wastes no time shoving Trevor back. "Shut the fuck up."

The damage is already done. I know better than to listen to what Trevor has to say, but this whole thing with Liam seems so perfect.

The thing about perfect things, though? They're usually too good to be true.

Maybe Trevor is right. Flavor of the week, bound to fail as soon as Liam gets bored.

I think back to what James said on night one in the

movie theater, *How come you always get the cute ones?* Always? Liam's probably done this before, and it clearly didn't go well, since I'm standing here instead.

What we have may be a phase for him, expiration date set the second this all becomes less interesting. Doubt takes over and all the fight I had in me evaporates.

Trevor's eyebrows raise. "You're actually gonna take his side?"

"You're a guest, and now you're pissing me off," Liam shouts. "Get out of my house."

Trevor scoffs and freezes. It's either shock or alcohol slowing down his brain, but I have a feeling it wasn't all that fast to begin with.

"You know what? This party sucks anyway." Trevor chugs the rest of his drink, crumples the cup, and throws it on the bedroom floor. "Let's go, guys."

Liam herds the mob of them out and slams the front door behind them. He comes back over, standing by Max and James.

"So, where were we?" he says with a forced smile.

Trevor's a dick, but even wasted, he hit the nail on the head—I'm a freak. I'm a creature with a scalp the color of salad. Maybe my mom's been humoring me the last couple of days. Maybe she was waiting for me to see that I don't fit in.

I don't know how to blend in with humans, no matter how hard I try. Liam may be better off with his own kind. This night is a disaster. I don't have any fight left in me.

This is the last place I want to be.

"I should probably get going, too," I say, motioning to the door. I'm doing everything I can to bury my emotions. Become unreadable.

"Oh come on, don't let him get to you," Max says. "Only

the cool people are left now."

"Nah, it's getting late," I tell her and feign a small smile. "I'll see you guys again, though." I wave a halfhearted goodbye and turn toward the door, Liam following me. He grabs my arm on the way out.

He looks at me desperately and leans forward. "You know he's just jealous of you, right?"

"Sure, sure," I say, wanting nothing more than to escape. "Thanks for inviting me. I'll text you later." He goes in for a hug, but I turn away.

If I let myself get lost in the hug, I may feel the full weight of everything else. And I can't handle that right now.

Chapter Thirty-One

I shuffle into the kitchen, one eye closed to dull some of the sun coming through the windows. Of course, my sister's flitting around the room. I usually love it when she's around, but I'm extra testy and want to be alone today.

I'm pretty sure I would have had an easier time sleeping after an atomic bomb than after that party. Not only did my brain replay every painfully awkward second, but my phone was buzzing until the point I drifted off.

Then that same damn buzzing was the first thing I woke up to this morning.

I know it's all calls and texts from Liam, but I don't even bother flipping it over to look at the screen. I'm not ready to talk to him. It's bad enough that I regret going last night. All he'll do is pity me and reassure me and try to make me feel better, inevitably making me feel worse.

I don't understand why Liam would put me in a situation like that. He knows I'm bad with people—especially crowds—but that didn't stop him. Me going to a party was a disaster waiting to happen. I wasn't ready. I doubt I ever will be.

But then my brain turns, and it's not Liam's fault at all—it's Trevor's.

It's one thing to read about guys like him and see them on TV shows, but it's different when they're in your face.

I'm wondering if I'm even fit to be around humans at this point.

She turns around with a peppy smile when she hears me come in. "Good morning!" She extends her arm, handing me a cup of coffee.

"Too early. Too cheery," I say, stifling my irritation and taking it from her. I look her up and down. "Since when do you own anything black? And since when do you wear red lipstick?"

"Just trying out a new look," she says and pulls up a seat at the table. She looks me up and down and suppresses a laugh. "Do I even want to ask how the party went last night?"

I'll deflect her questions, let her say her piece, and then be rid of her. I sit across from her and shoot her a sarcastic smile. "It was fine."

She raises her eyebrows and looks at her fingernails. "Is the grass not as green as you thought it would be?"

"Oh good, a garden pun," I say, patiently sparring with her. "Hilarious."

"Don't be bitter because you don't like your boyfriend's friends," she says without looking up.

"He's not my boyfriend," I lie, taking a sip of the black liquid. It's not something I'm willing to share with her yet, but apparently I've become easier to read in the last couple weeks than I thought. I need more caffeine for this conversation.

"But you'd like him to be?" she asks with a smile.

I shake my head. "That's beside the point." I'm *not* getting into this with her. Not right now, not ever.

Laurel sighs. "Listen, people don't always make the best decisions. Sometimes they need a little help to make the right ones."

I shrug my shoulders in frustration. "I don't see how that helps me with his friends."

"Oh honey, they're probably hopeless," she says, tipping her head down. "Liam is different, but small-town boys are the worst. You need to see more of the world. The sooner you get out of here, the better."

"Laurel, I can barely handle being around ten people at a party," I snap. She's really pushing my buttons today. "How am I supposed to handle a city full of them?"

She cocks her head to the side. "What do you mean?"

The concern in her eyes stops me. I think, in her way, she's truly trying to help. I swirl my mug in my hand, doing my best to calm down while trying to find the right words. "I get awkward and nervous. I can't control it, and it's too much." I'm unbearably self-conscious confessing all of this newfound anxiety to her. It makes me feel like I'm weak.

"What's there to be nervous about?" She laughs.

She doesn't get it, but to be fair, I'm not explaining it well. "This thing happens to me when I go into crowds," I say, rubbing the grains of wood on the table with my thumb. "My heart starts racing and I get tunnel vision and I panic."

"That happened last night?"

"No, nothing that bad," I say, unsure if what happened last night is much better. "I kept it together for the most part. Except when I went off on a guy there."

She nods. "Did he deserve it?"

I tilt my head. "Maybe. I still shouldn't have done it. I was supposed to be blending in."

"You've been in this house your whole life," she says. "Blending in will be hard because there are things out there you don't understand yet. 'Yet' being the operative word. Sometimes I feel like that, too. Stay calm and adapt."

"I don't know, I…care what they think of me, I guess." It's something I've been resisting, but slowly coming to terms with. I can't believe I'm admitting it. "I don't fit with them. I don't know if I ever will."

She narrows her eyes. "You shouldn't fit with them. Bottom line is that what humans think of you doesn't matter. You're better than the best of them, even on your worst day."

I pull my chin back and look at her like she's grown an extra head and a half. Did she actually say that? "What's that supposed to mean?"

"I'll tell you a secret." She leans forward and tents her fingers, elbows propped on the table. "It means, that in the grand scheme of things, they are insignificant. They are cattle. They don't even live long enough to understand the world they borrow from creatures like us. You, on the other hand, are blessed. You're born from nature itself. Powers or not, they're beneath you, and don't you forget it."

My mouth hangs open. It's a disgusting, hateful thought and I can't believe my ears. "Why would you say something like that?"

"Like what?" she asks, unbothered. "The truth?"

I shake my head, looking her up and down suspiciously. "What's with you the last couple of days? You haven't been acting like yourself." I don't mean to sound accusatory, but there's no other way to put it.

"Maybe you're just seeing a new side of me." She shrugs, standing up and straightening her skirt. "Anyway, enough sisterly advice. I need to get packing for my next trip and make sure you don't have any other break-ins while I'm gone. You'd better get to work. Think about what I said."

She struts out the front door, closing it behind her and leaving me in stunned silence.

In the name of all that's green, what the hell came out of her mouth? That goes against everything our mom has ever taught us.

Sure, we were raised to be wary of humans, but never superior to them. We were taught to coexist. Sure, we have to hide what we are, but that's more for their protection than ours.

Our magic is too strong for them, so we keep a healthy distance. Boundaries.

My mom already skirts her own rule by giving out "natural remedies," but she doesn't give out anything that can't be done with normal medicine. No love potions or mischievous poisons. Not to mention that we collect and keep species that aren't safe in human hands.

We don't harm, we help.

It's a dark revelation, but I can't help wonder—is this who my sister's been the entire time? And now she's being honest once I can actually experience humans for myself?

If it's true, it seems cruel that she and my mom would teach me something false instead of preparing me for it. But even from my minimal experience, there's no way it could be true. Humans aren't animals. They're beings with thoughts and feelings and hopes and dreams. Even assholes like Trevor.

• • •

A little while later, I close the closet door behind me and start down the cobblestone path, same as any morning.

It's especially hot in here today, but I don't put much thought into it. I have too much to do. I flick through the list on my phone. Two orchids, three dozen roses, a bouquet of lilies…

A strange crunch catches my attention from beneath my feet.

I slow down, an unsettling feeling creeping into the depths of my chest.

Leaves from the trees above line the path, brown and almost sucked dry of moisture. It wouldn't mean anything on an autumn day, but autumn doesn't exist in here. Time doesn't exist. The garden makes its own laws of nature, immune to death and decay. Eternal health.

Even the smell in here is wrong—the sweet scent of rot wafting through the air.

I look into the canopy above. Dotted all throughout the limp, yellowing leaves are bulbs that don't look as they should.

I reach up, plucking an apple from a low-hanging branch. Crimson red flesh gives at the slightest squeeze, full of ripe juice. That's impossible. These were Granny Smiths yesterday, just like every day before that. *What the hell?*

My eyes scan the rest of the orchard, and it's not only this tree. The lemons? Fading into orange. The limes? A brown tinge. The peaches? The color of blood.

Everything in the treetops is either aging, stained with red, or a combination of the two. It's like I'm in some warped reality, a twisted version of my own life. My pulse quickens as phantom pins and needles prick my skin. *This can't be happening.*

Full-blown fear takes over as I jog farther into the garden, my feet pounding the stones beneath me. The flowers lining the path are taking on a ruby hue, exactly like the fruit in the orchard.

It gets only more corrupted the farther I go.

My skin runs cold at the sight of spiny black vines overtaking the trellises, strangling into submission whatever was there before. The woods are becoming a nightmare from a fairy tale, leading the way to the waterfall.

My feet come to an abrupt halt and I can barely catch my breath, not believing my eyes.

What was once liquid glass is now a pool of thick onyx. I approach slowly, bending down and letting my fingers graze the surface of the water.

I pull back and rub them together, but it's wrong—they're slick as oil. Toxic.

Everything in the garden is sick. And something is making it that way.

Chapter Thirty-Two

"Mystic Bloom, how can I help you?"

"Mom, it's me." I keep my voice level but serious, direct but not panicked. I try not to sound too worried, but she knows me better than that.

"Is everything okay?" she asks quickly. "Are you hurt?"

"I'm fine, but the garden is acting…strange." I don't mean to be vague, but she needs to see it herself. "You'd better come up here."

"Let me lock up. Give me five minutes." The phone clicks on her end.

I pace back and forth at the entrance while I wait for her.

I'm doing my best to keep my shit together, but I'm not doing a very good job. I have no idea what any of this means, but I'm sure she will.

I know I can't fix this, but she can. She can do anything.

Before I spiral out of control, the door flies open and she strides in.

"What's going on?" she asks.

I shrug, speechless, and point to the forest in front of us. Suddenly the words pour out of me, along with my nerves. "I don't know. There are leaves falling off trees. Fruit is turning weird colors and there are these spiky vines growing on the trellises. Even the water is slimy and darker than it should be. Mom, what's happening? What did I do?"

She freezes. "What color is the fruit?"

"Red," I say suspiciously. "Why?"

"And the vines?" she asks quickly, ignoring my question. "Are they black?" I nod solemnly and she sucks in a sharp breath. "Quill," she says direly, closing her eyes. "Did you go anywhere near the conservatory in the rare section?"

"No," I say quickly. A little too quickly. Her eyes fly to mine and she stares me down. I automatically cringe, embarrassed to be caught lying yet again. "Well, yes. Laurel showed it to me."

Her emerald eyes grow wide and her voice gets that much more strained. "Why would she… How close did you get?"

I sigh. I need to be completely honest with her if this is going to get better. "We went inside. She was teaching me about the flower and its berries. She made it sound all dangerous. She said the berries can heal or kill."

"For the love of nature," she says, pinching the bridge of her nose. "I never fully explained it to her. She wasn't ready."

"I'm so sorry," I say, regretting ever being curious about it. "I promise, we were super careful when she showed it to me."

"How did you even get in?" she asks, punctuating the words with her hand in the air. "Your sister can't wither vines, especially not ones that strong."

Here we go. The biggest thing I've been keeping from her for weeks, and the one thing I've been dreading the most. I didn't expect today to be the day, but time's run out and I need to confess.

I have to do this. She needs to know.

I gather up all of my courage and push the words out of my mouth, one by one. "The lock was sort of…broken when we found it."

She folds her hands at her waist and looks over the garden. I wish I could see into her head like she can see into mine. She takes a deep breath and nods once. "Then I hope it's not too late. Your grandmothers always passed down warnings about this day. At least it's only in here."

"We didn't want to worry you," I say, desperate to tell her my side of things. "We tried to figure out who broke in, but—"

"No one broke in, Quill," she says, strong-jawed but with fear swirling in her eyes.

My tongue gets caught in my throat. I've never seen her like this, and I don't understand why. Then suddenly it hits me.

"Something broke out," I whisper, cold terror squeezing my heart.

She nods gravely, but I shake my head. I don't fully understand.

"Was there something else in there? Some kind of animal? It must be in here somewhere." I look around the garden, wondering where it could be. The hiding places are almost infinite, but I'm sure I can find it. I have to. I've already fucked things up so much, I have to try to do something.

"No, Quill," she says quietly, taking a step toward me. "You saw the only thing in there. The thing the first dryad put in there. The plant."

"It... It can't be that bad, can it?" I ask, hoping that she'll say yes. "Laurel said you use it for healing potions." I leave out the part where I used it to make one for Liam.

All she does is shake her head firmly. "Its name is Azazel, and I use it only in emergencies. It's invasive. Highly invasive. Only humans can release it from the garden, so thank goodness it didn't get that far."

"Let me help clean it up," I say, desperate to help. The guilt is unbearable. "I'll go grab my shears. I'm sure I can—"

"No." She cuts me off. She walks over and kisses me on the forehead. "It has to be me. Go call Liam and get your mind off things. Get out of the house and see another movie or something. I'll handle it from here."

I look her in the eye, unsure of what to say.

Can it actually be that dangerous to the point of her wanting me to stay away?

It's so unsettling to see her so worried—but there's no way it can be that much of a threat. She's a dryad, and it's... just a plant. It doesn't stand a chance against her.

But I can't shake the feeling that she needs help.

I pull out my phone once I get inside my room and close the door behind me. It's strange. I've never seen my mom like that before. She wasn't furious at me like I thought she would be. She wasn't overly firm or curt with me, even like when she caught me sneaking out. I don't know how to describe it. Solemn? Determined?

She's probably gonna switch tactics and rip me a new one later. I'd better get out of here while I still can.

There's only one person I want to see.

I consider texting him, but something tells me breaking the silence would be better done with our voices. With a few swipes of my fingers, Liam's number appears on my screen right below the selfie he sent me of him in bed. Maybe not the most appropriate choice, but I like the way my heart jumps every time it shows up.

I take a breath, tap once, and hold the phone to my ear. It rings only once.

"Since when do you call me?" he says.

"Since I wanted to apologize for how I left last night," I say, kicking one foot with the other. "And not texting you back this morning. So… Sorry." If I can't fix the garden, at least I can fix this.

"Does this mean you aren't angry with me anymore?"

It makes me sad to hear him say that. I never meant to make him feel that way. "I was never angry at you," I say. "I just had a lot of thinking to do. But we're good."

"Oh thank God. I was worried you were gonna break up with me or something."

"Break up?" My breath gets caught in my throat, my skin prickling at the thought of us being together in the first place. "Last night I find out we're dating. Today I find out we're an item. What's tomorrow?"

He laughs. "How about we see how the rest of the day goes. What are you doing?"

"Calling to see if you want to go see another movie," I say, using every ounce of power within me to banish my feelings from my head. "I might even let you sit next to me."

"Scandalous," he says. "I'll meet you at the car in five."

Chapter Thirty-Three

Liam's car cruises down the side streets of our sleepy town.

I look out my window, trying to tamp down the guilt in my chest that I get to go on a date because my mom needs to clean up some hellscape I helped create. I grow more and more confused as we make our way through town—I may have never been out in the middle of the day, but it's oddly quiet, compared to what I was expecting. Barely any cars, and almost no people on the sidewalks. The sun is mild, clouds mingling to give plenty of shade. My hand hangs out the window, grasping the cool breeze as it rolls through the park Liam pointed out last time. Why is it still deserted? The only living things enjoying the sublime weather are the trees.

I'm doing my best to suppress all my worries, but my mind keeps traveling back to the garden, whether I like it or not. I'm still trying to figure out why my mom actually wanted me gone. She was acting so strange when I left—not remotely as angry as I thought she would be. Maybe she was suppressing it like I do. Or maybe she really doesn't have faith in me. She was either pissed at me or overprotective. The more I think about it, it's probably the first one.

If the plant were truly that big of a deal, she would have needed both Laurel and me there with her. She would have wanted all the help she could get. I'd bet she's at home right now throwing a fit to Laurel about how I can't be trusted with anything—and giving Laurel a verbal lashing of her own.

I'd better enjoy this while it lasts, because she may lock me up again. The more I think about it, the less my imagination can escape the worst-case scenarios.

If I knew what was good for me, I'd leave it alone. I shake myself back into the here and now with Liam.

"I'm sorry for how I acted at your party," I say after our second red light, making the conscious decision to focus on something I can actually control and understand. "I shouldn't have opened my mouth. I was out of line."

"No, you should've absolutely opened your mouth," Liam says as he flips his turn signal. "I'm the one who should be sorry. I pushed you to do something you didn't want to do. Besides, everything you said was true. Those guys are assholes."

That makes me feel way better, but I'm confused. "Wait… I thought they were your friends?"

He shrugs, leaning back in his seat. "Not really. And honestly, it took you to make me realize that. I haven't felt more like myself in a long time, and it's all been since we started hanging out."

I thought I understood his whole social dynamic, but now I understand that I don't get it at all. "That's your team, though. You swim with them, and you love swimming more than anything."

"No one said I have to be on a team with them to swim," Liam says, shaking his head with a smile. "I have options. Besides, that means I'll have more time for my real friends, like Max and James. And my dad. And you."

"So I'm not the flavor of the week?" I ask quietly.

He scoffs, looking over at me. "Definitely not. God, I don't even know where he got that from."

I feel cautiously lighter. "Maybe he has a secret crush on you," I try to joke as I shrug. "Stranger things have happened."

"He's not my type," Liam says through a grin. "I like my guys nerdy. And funny. Maybe even a little awkward. And if they have green hair? Whew, hold me back." He ruffles the top of my head, laughing.

I let out a small chuckle, pushing his hand away. It's amazing how he can wipe my cares away with a few sentences. "Okay, okay, I get it. Sorry. I let him get to me." If I'm embarrassed about anything, it's only how I blew this all out of proportion. I should have talked to him last night before I left.

"I'm not going anywhere. I promise." He reaches across and takes hold of my hand, entwining our fingers and giving a gentle squeeze.

"I'll hold you to that," I say, letting my head fall against the headrest and turning my face to get a better look at him.

"You know, the next round of showings aren't for another hour or so," he says, making another turn. "Did you want something to eat besides popcorn?"

"Might be nice. What did you have in mind?"

Liam bites his lip and thinks for a moment. I love that he's putting so much thought into this. "Edamame? Tangerines?"

I nod with a small smirk. Good choices. "That actually sounds perfect. Where should we go to get it?"

"You've never been to a grocery store, have you?" he asks

with narrowed eyes.

I shake my head, trying not to laugh at his question. "What do you think?"

I take a few deep breaths as Liam pulls into the parking lot, telling myself I can handle a building full of people, but to my surprise there are only a couple of other cars already there. Maybe today won't be so bad after all.

"Lucky us," he says, reading my mind as he unbuckles his seat belt. "Must be a slow shopping day."

We walk inside the gigantic building, greeted by a pitiful little cluster of buckets holding small bouquets. The selection isn't great to begin with, but I shake my head with pursed lips.

Those poor flowers—manhandled and starved, and I feel so awful for them. It's a grisly sight. The color from their blossoms is already fading, leaves wilting as their stems desperately try to suck up the stagnant water they're in. If only I had a little magic, I could spruce them up.

But there they sit, waiting patiently for the end and missing that spark of life my family's shop specializes in. These were things that were once living. They deserve more respect.

"Not quite what you're used to seeing, is it?" Liam asks.

Trying to silence how displeased I am, I shake my head and walk around the display. Aisles and aisles of cans and boxes catch my attention instead, plastered with every color of the rainbow.

"How do humans know what's what?" I ask Liam. "I'm pretty sure that box doesn't have tiger meat in it. And I don't even know what a leprechaun would taste like."

He laughs, picking one up and flipping it over, pointing to

a picture of a textured pile of rubble on the back. "It's cereal. This is what it looks like inside."

"Pellets?" I say, unimpressed. "With suns and moons and red balloons? That doesn't look anything like the cereal I've seen in movies." I don't want to try to make sense of how bizarre this stuff is. It's basically candy.

"You might actually like it if you tried it," he says, putting it back. "Might be too sweet for you, though."

"I'll stick to stuff that comes out of the ground, thanks," I say, half-joking. "Speaking of?"

He nods his head to the far end of the store. The closer we get, the better I can see it—rows and rows of sickly fruits and vegetables. I'm starting to think this place is a cemetery for anything green.

"What do you think?"

"It's…a decent selection." But the quality? It's all sitting here, a matter of time before it's thrown in the trash. I feel like I'm grave robbing. I pick up a box of soybeans from a large cooler and a bag of clementines from a nearby shelf. "This'll tide me over. What about you?"

"Junk food, duh." He puts his hand on my lower back, guiding me to the back of the store. It sends a silent shiver up my spine. However, the quick hit of bliss doesn't last as long as I hoped it would.

"What is that awful smell?" I ask, but before he has time to answer, we turn the corner and I almost run into a small cooking stand manned by an elderly woman.

A whole two heads shorter than me, she's dressed in a sweater that's far too warm for this weather and an obnoxiously bright neon orange vest. I don't think Laurel would dare let that color near her closet.

"Free sample, dear?" she asks with a sweet smile, kind eyes glimmering from behind her glasses. She pushes a tray of greasy paper cups toward me. I look inside and my stomach turns—it's some collection of beige cow parts staring back at me.

"Vegan," I say, taking a step back and covering my nose and mouth. I'm doing everything I can to keep my coffee down, stomach churning from the intense disgust. The last thing I expected to see in here was an adorable old woman hawking chunks of sizzling meat.

"That's okay, dear, we're giving it away for free today and it goes well with anything," she says. She lifts up a homemade bottle of herbs and spices, shaking it joyfully with a giggle. "Not just beef. There's fish, turkey, chicken..."

I narrow my eyes, not sure if she's unaware or if she's a bad salesman. "Do you not know what vegan means—" I start asking, but Liam interrupts me.

"Sorry, no thanks, bad heartburn," he tells her as he gently pushes me down the aisle.

She waves after us as we walk away, still beaming. "Enjoy your day, dears!"

"Sometimes it's better to just say 'no thank you' and walk away," Liam tells me quietly, kindly making sure we're out of her earshot.

"But shouldn't someone correct her?" I ask, honestly confused. "My mom is always honest with me, and I'm always direct with my sister."

"Most humans don't like that at all," he says patiently.

I shrug and keep walking. "Just trying to be nice, but if you say so." Maybe I should consider the possibility that humans are even more sensitive than I've been lately.

Liam slows to a stop, his eyes traveling along a wall of empty coolers and refrigerators.

"What's wrong?" I ask, worried by the strange seriousness on his face.

"All the meat's gone," he says. "And the dairy."

I let out a pent-up breath, relieved to hear that it's nothing important. "Fine by me," I say. "You know I think that's all disgusting anyway."

"No, but..." He pauses, carefully considering the apparent phenomenon. "I've never seen it cleared out like this. It's weird."

I shrug, ready to keep moving. "Don't ask me. I wouldn't know the difference."

Liam nabs a few bags of snacks before we make our way back to the front. I promise to pay him back as we check out on our own with some fancy scanner machine. No conversation necessary. What a brilliant invention.

"So what did you think?" he asks, starting the car.

"Our garden is better, but I wouldn't mind coming back," I tell him, doing my best to keep looking on the bright side. "I could count the number of people in there on one hand. That's my kind of social outing."

"Yeah, that wasn't normal," he says, running his hands through his dark red hair as he drives away. "You got lucky. This place is usually packed, but I'm glad we could start you slow."

I watch Liam out of the corner of my eye as he opens his gummy worms. He glances down as he grabs them two at a time, matching their colors. It's kind of adorable.

I like watching his little quirks when he doesn't think I'm looking—the way he pulls his ear when he's thinking, how he mouths along with the lyrics but never sings, and even how he chews on his straws although it makes them almost unusable. This time he catches me staring at him and smirks.

"Want one?" he asks with his mouth full, holding the bag out to me.

I'm curious, seeing as how he's chomping down without

a care in the world. They must be good. I reach inside and pinch the squishy thing, powder getting all over my fingers.

I pop it in my mouth and start chewing, but a sharp pain goes through my teeth and I gag. I lean out the window and spit it out.

"Not a fan?" He laughs.

"That's appalling," I say, wiping my tongue. "I think I have a cavity already."

"Try a potato chip," he says as he tears open the bag. He holds it out to me and smiles. "They're buffalo."

"I don't know if you knew this, but buffaloes are animals," I say, staring him dead in the eye. "Four legs and everything. Pretty sure they moo, too."

"No," he chuckles and shakes his head. "It's a flavor. Salty and spicy. Nothing living."

I narrow my eyes, suspicious after that little gummy demon I was just chewing. Still, I reach into the bag, pull out a bright orange chip, and examine it.

I stick out my tongue and touch the chip and it's…not bad. I pop it in my mouth and crunch, nodding after a few seconds.

"This is good," I say wholeheartedly. He looks about as surprised as I feel. "Can I have another?"

"Go for it," he says, happily handing me the bag. I munch in silence for the next few minutes, chip after chip, staring out the window. Mindless peace at last, only me and these buffaloes.

"You gonna save me some of those?" He chuckles.

I look down and most of the bag is already gone. "Sorry." I grimace as I hand it back to him and lick my fingers. "It was mostly air, I promise."

He laughs. "Everyone knows that."

Chapter Thirty-Four

We get to the theater, hand in hand, and make our way to the window. This morning feels like a distant memory, and I feel like I can actually get through the day without feeling as awful as I did before Liam and I left.

We get closer to the ticket booth, and exactly like she was last time, Max is inside. She's propped up on her chair, stoic, arms by her sides. Her eyes are staring straight at her screen without a hint of friendliness on her face.

"Hey Max, how are you?" I ask brightly, folding my arms on the counter.

She doesn't bother to look up. "Fine."

I look to Liam and he seems as confused as I am. "Oh, uh, that's good," I manage, self-consciousness flooding me again. "Could we get two for the one o'clock?"

"Sorry, that's sold out," she says, still not looking at me.

She's being incredibly cold, and honestly, it's starting to confuse me. "Really?" I ask. "In the middle of the day?"

She shrugs. I look back at Liam and he shakes his head.

"Okay, well…got any good horror movies?" I ask,

thinking back to our conversation at my house. Maybe that'll loosen her up.

She looks at me flatly. "That theater's closed down."

I nod. I'm trying as hard as I can right now, and I don't think I'm doing anything to make her so hostile. "Then I guess we'll see anything that's playing."

"Whatever you say." She starts tapping her screen.

"Max, it's ninety degrees out," Liam says from behind me. "Why are you wearing a sweater? And why are your eyes so red?"

She shrugs again but still won't look at either of us. "I think I'm getting sick. I've been cold all day." She slides the tickets underneath the glass, gets up, and goes out of the booth without another word.

I look at Liam. "What the hell was that? She didn't even ask me to pay."

"I honestly have no idea," he says, putting his arm around my waist and walking me inside. "She must feel pretty gross if she's getting sick. But hey, free movie. Looks like the friends and family discount still works."

We walk into the lobby, stride across the tile, and head straight to the counter.

It's much darker in here than it was last time, yet I can still see James's silhouette sitting behind the counter. Like Max, he's plainly standing there and watching us walk up.

No hi. No hello. No movement. Nothing.

It's pretty fucking creepy and I don't trust it, but Liam ignores it.

"Hey James," Liam says. "Think you could sneak us some popcorn?"

James stares him straight in the eye with a cold expression. "Machine's broken."

"Oh, uh… Okay," Liam says. "Two drinks, then."

"Those are broken, too." They stare at each other for a long and awkward moment.

"You all right?" Liam asks, a slight edge in his voice.

James's gaze shifts to just over our shoulders. I spin around to see Max right behind us, staring at us with a flat expression. "Time to go," she says.

James vaults over the counter at her words and, before I know it, they close in on either side of us.

"Guys, seriously, what the hell?" Liam demands.

But they don't answer. Instead, in one swift motion, James wraps his arms around Liam and scoops him up while Max grabs my collar and arm, dragging us out of the theater.

"What the fuck!" I yell, frantically trying to pull away from her, but her grip is solid.

Liam isn't having any luck, either—he's flailing, but James is completely overpowering him. We struggle and hit and push against them, but it's no use. It doesn't stop or slow their pace in the slightest. In under a minute, they've dragged us to the front door. James kicks it open and throws Liam on the pavement, Max shoving me out on top of him.

"What the hell is wrong with you?" I shout at her.

She stops and stares down at me. "I have a better question you should be asking. Maybe, how did Liam's dad recover so quickly?" She slams the door shut and locks it behind her.

What the actual fuck *just happened?*

I push to my feet and look down at Liam, who's still flat on his ass. "What was she talking about?" My voice is soft and shaking.

I already know the answer, but I'm praying that I'm wrong. I'm already fighting back my rage and my tears, knowing what he's done. I think part of me knew ever since I got the text from him that his dad was coming home.

That night I took him into the garden.

The conservatory.

Leaving Liam when the fire started by my ancestors' trees.

I don't want to believe it, but I can't explain it away. This is all his fault.

"I—I don't know." He struggles as he stands but avoids eye contact.

I clench my jaw, tempering my rising anger. "You're a worse liar than I am," I say, my voice sharp like ice.

He clenches his jaw and closes his eyes. He doesn't want to say it, but I'm not giving him a choice. I wait for him to give up. "Please don't be upset," he finally says, softly. "My dad was getting worse."

I take a step toward him, grounding myself on the concrete. It's taking everything in me not to yell at him. I'm so angry, I'm seeing him through tunnel vision. But what's worse? The disappointment is tearing straight through me. He betrayed me. He used me. It's unbearable.

"What did you do?" I push, but he remains silent. Finally, my anger gets the better of me. "Just fucking say it!"

His face snaps to mine, shocked. He bites his bottom lip, looking like he's about to cry—and I don't blame him. I haven't spoken to him like that since the night he showed up on my fire escape, and we've shared so much since then. But none of that matters anymore.

"The night you showed me the garden..." he says quietly. "I... I took something."

Hearing it out loud is awful. It confirms my greatest fear. I had the tiniest sliver of hope that I was wrong—overreacting, thinking the worst. Maybe I was wrong. Maybe I wasn't giving him the benefit of the doubt.

My eyes grow wide and I take a step back, shock overtaking my system. A cold, hard ache blooms in my chest as I cover my mouth, and all I can do is shake my head. Liam's voice calls from a parking space thirty feet away.

"No. This can't be happening." I hope he doesn't keep going, because he doesn't even need to explain further. He doesn't need to spell it out like I'm a child, because I know exactly what he stole.

"You ran away and I used one of those clover things to enter the conservatory," he says anyway. "I took a berry that looked like the one from our dream and locked the door with the clover when I was done."

It's all coming back to me now. "That's what I found in the hallway when you left," I say to myself, doing everything I can to steady my breath. I thought the used Rainbow Root belonged to the thief, and it turns out I had a second one in front of me all along. I look around at the empty street around us, but the image of the twisted leaves on the key are still so clear in my mind.

"Quill, it was the only way I could save him," he says softly, holding his hands out to calm me down.

He betrayed me. He was the one person in this world I trusted completely, and he took advantage of me the first chance he got. "I can't believe this," I say, turning away from him. My chest feels empty and dread prickles my neck. I feel physically fucking ill. I didn't know a feeling like this was even possible.

And on top of it, Liam told Max and James about my secret. He told them about how he healed his dad with our magic. Why else would she have said that? How else could she have known? No wonder they were both so weird just now. They were probably up all night talking about me, and now they know I'm a freak. My mom is going to be furious. We'll need to move and hide and it's all my fault. All because I trusted some conniving human boy. This is all my fault.

"Please. I'm so sorry. I wanted to tell you so badly, I just didn't know how." He puts his hands on my shoulders, but I throw them off and spin around.

"But you didn't," I snap at him. "You lied to me. You were using me, ever since the night I healed you. None of it was real." My heart feels empty as I look at him, but my vision tunnels as I see his face. Rage. Fury. Is this what hate feels like?

He looks like I stabbed him in the chest. His face is twisted in pain, and all I keep thinking is that it's good. He deserves it. Still, it doesn't stop him from speaking like I hoped it would. "All of it was real," he says, eyes wetter than they were a second ago. "Everything I said was real. Quill, you're my favorite person in the world—"

"Stop!" I shout at the top of my lungs, holding my hand up to cut him off. I'm so glad no one's around to see this humiliation. "Fuck you! You don't get to say that to me, not after what you did!"

"Please," he pleads, tears rolling down his face. "Please don't do this. It was only a berry. One tiny berry. It wasn't a big deal."

I shake my head, disgusted with him. Disgusted with myself. "It's a huge deal, Liam. It was magic. Dangerous magic. You have no idea what you've done. I need to get home."

He bites his lip and nods. "Okay, let's go. We can fix this. The car is right across the street. We—we can talk on the way." His voice is so desperately hopeful, and all it does is make me hate him even more.

I'm hurt and I'm mad. Mad that my sister was right, no matter how much I didn't want her to be. Mad that I let myself get wrapped up in this *human*, just like my mom warned me against. Mad that this is all his fault. Everything that's gone wrong—it's all on him.

He's a traitor.

I back away from him, shutting down and going back to that same cold place I was in when I ripped Trevor apart. The next words leave my mouth with more venom than I thought possible.

I want to hurt him. I want to crush him.

I want him to feel everything he's made me feel.

"Thanks for showing me that your kind truly are horrible," I say. "And out of all of them, you might be the worst. Stay the fuck away from me."

I take off sprinting down the street, not bothering to look back where I left him. I want to run. To escape. To stay numb.

Chapter Thirty-Five

It takes me over an hour to run home.

My lungs and legs are on fire from the running. I'm pissed and crushed and devastated, not only by Liam's betrayal, but by my own foolishness. I shouldn't have trusted him.

My mom was right all along—I wasn't ready.

My family is the most important thing in my life, and I know that now. I was reckless and let my feelings get the best of me. And what do I have to show for it? An infected garden and exposure to the human world. Hopefully my mom's solved the first problem so we can get started on some memory potions. I honestly wouldn't mind taking one myself, but I'll never let myself forget everything. I'll never let myself go through this again.

I enter our building and climb the stairs, keeping my eyes straight ahead when I pass his apartment. Behind that door is where he sat when he planned this entire theft. Where he was when he lured me in and sent me every text message to trick me.

It's all meaningless, now that I know he was just going

to backstab me. I stop in front of my door and close my eyes, breathing deep and gathering the courage to tell my mom how badly I fucked up.

Three.

Two.

One.

I turn the doorknob and step inside. "Mom, I need to talk to you." I wait for a moment to hear her voice, but she doesn't respond. Damn it, she's probably still clearing out the garden. Yet another consequence from the boy next door.

I walk through the silent apartment, inching toward her inevitable fury. How can I blame her? I feel the same thing right now. I take a left at the end of the kitchen, but I freeze when the closet door to the garden catches my eye. Black vines encase it and seal it shut.

"No," I say, rushing toward it.

There's no way in, and my mom's worst fear came true. Liam released the plant from the garden and it's grown out of control. How much further can it possibly go? I run my hands through my hair, breathing deeply and desperately thinking of any possible way to get through.

Fuck, fuck, fuck.

There has to be a way. This growth is completely out of control, and I'm terrified. What do I do? What can I do?

My heart pounds as I try to pry the vines off, but with each one I rip, another grows in its place. *Shit*. This is so much worse than I thought. This can't get any worse. I need something to break through.

The first night Liam came to my window comes to mind, and I have an idea.

I run to my room and grab my rose branch, hoping I can brute force it, but terror takes over as I come back out into the hallway. My mom's room is covered in the same plant, and I have the worst feeling in my bones that she's trapped inside.

My poor mother. Captive in the one place we're supposed to be the safest, and there's nothing I can do. I'm powerless. Is she okay in there? What if the worst has happened? What if it took her over, too, and she didn't make it…?

No. That can't be real. There's no way. She's too strong, she must have found a way to put up a fight. I'm sure there's something she could have done to protect herself.

I still need to get to her, one way or another. I put the bat on my shoulder, wind up, and swing. It lands with a thud and the vines jump away from it. Okay, fine. At least it makes them scatter.

I swing again and again, clearing the vines section by section. Doing my best to contain my panic, I take a deep breath, close my eyes, and give the hardest swing yet. Pulp flies through the air as the vines shrivel, life sucking out from where my blow landed.

Holy shit. The bat's been magic this whole time.

My mom must have enchanted it and never told me. Gee, would have been nice to know when she locked me in my room.

Confidence growing with each tendril I kill, I desperately hack away again and again, killing a new layer of vines with each swing. *I can do this. I can fix this.* But as I reach the last layer, a sound from the living room distracts me—the front door opening and slamming shut.

"Hello?" I yell.

No answer.

"Who's there?" I call again, but still nothing. That had better not be Liam. He knows damn well what he did and he'll stay away if he knows what's good for him. I stomp to the living room, reinforced with my anger. My sister is standing in front of the door with her hand on her hip.

"What are you doing here?" I ask her urgently, walking forward. "Did Mom tell you what's going on?"

But Laurel doesn't answer me.

With a flick of her wrist, the vines in the living room begin writhing. They shoot toward me, wrapping around my legs and arms and chest and lifting me in the air.

Chapter Thirty-Six

"What the fuck are you doing?" I shout, my brain not processing fast enough to fight back. My bat falls to the ground before I go flying through the room, tendrils pinning me to the armchair and binding me in place. My breath gets caught in my throat as I struggle to get loose, but the vines have already hardened. Did she finally snap?

She walks over and sits on the couch opposite me, crossing her ankles and smoothing her dress. She looks at me with bloodred eyes. My gaze widens at the sight of them as a cold chill runs down my spine. I couldn't imagine a worse situation. A creature with the unlimited gifts of my sister.

My breath catches as I lose the ability to blink. I'm stuck staring at what looks like my sister, but wrong. "You're not Laurel," I say quietly as the realization hits me. This can't be happening.

"No… No. Not Laurel, I'm afraid." It smiles politely and shakes its head. "My name is Azazel."

Azazel. The conservatory plant. My mom's words in

the garden earlier come back to me:

Its name is Azazel, and I only use it in emergencies.

It's invasive.

Highly invasive.

I gape at my sister-turned-deadly-plant in shock. My worst fear come to fruition. And here I am, bound in place, trapped with nothing to do but watch it happen.

I try to stay as still as possible, doing everything in my power to keep my shit together. Show no fear. But quite honestly, I'm not too sure how well I'm keeping up the act. "What do you want from me?"

"Just to talk to you, of course." It laughs and it sets its face on its palm. "Have another one of our little heart-to-hearts."

The fact that it's being so pleasant makes it that much more terrifying. "I've never talked to you a day in my life," I say, shaking my head defiantly. It keeps smiling knowingly and looking at me like we're old friends. The pit in my stomach grows the longer I look.

"Oh you sweet boy, we've spoken before. Yesterday in the shop, while your mom was meeting Liam." It points below us. "Then again at the party last night when I poured you punch." It points next door. "And even at the kitchen table this morning." It motions behind it.

A chill runs through my veins as the realization hits me. I can't believe I missed it. I knew something was wrong with Laurel—she'd never say such hateful things like she did earlier. The more terrifying thing is that she wasn't the only one. "Liam's dad, too?"

"Um-hum," it says, nodding its head matter-of-factly. "And Max and James. Shared consciousness is handy like that. Everywhere all at once." It has this singsong voice that should make it seem kind and personable, but it's making it seem only more dangerous. Like it's capable of anything worse than I can imagine.

This thing is unbelievable. I try to take a closer look at my sister's face and see traces of black roots beneath her skin on the edge of her face. I swear I see one of them squirm under the surface, and I can't help but shudder. It's disgusting, but I hold down my bile.

"I wasn't so kind to you at the movie theater, though," Azazel continues. "Sorry about that—I hope the pavement didn't scrape you." My sister's features contort into a wince as Azazel tries to get a better look at my exposed skin from where it's sitting. I instinctively turn away from it as much as the vines will allow.

It's surreal—a look I've never seen on her face before. Is she still in there somewhere? Does she know what's happening? I imagine her screaming for help somewhere deep inside.

I can't decide what's worse—being fully asleep when something steals your body or feeling every twitch against your will. Either way, my heart aches for her.

My mom wasn't kidding when she said the plant was invasive, but I never imagined anything like this. This is monstrous.

"You made them attack me?" I ask, careful not to upset it. The last thing I want to do is to set it off into a rage.

I knew they weren't acting like themselves. It's even more terrifying how completely it was able to control them—moving their limbs against their wills. Are all of them in there somewhere? Everyone it's taken over? Trapped? In pain? Conscious at all?

It tilts its head, humming to itself. "Less of an attack, more of a wake-up call," it says, looking up at the ceiling. It's pissing me off at how lightly it's taking all of this.

"I needed to get another little one-on-one with you," it continues. "Your mom mentioned a movie in the garden, so I waited for you there." Azazel pauses, but as soon as it sees the shock on my face, it gasps and holds its hand up. "I was never going to actually hurt you if that's what you were thinking. I hope you don't think that."

I'm beginning to lose my temper. This disgusting attempt to reason with me is having the opposite effect. It doesn't care about me at all, and I wish it would stop pretending. "Where's my mom?" I ask through gritted teeth, ignoring all of these false niceties. "What did you do with her?"

"Don't worry, I didn't harm her," it says consolingly. "She's just napping for as long as I need her to be. I took over the family trees as soon as you left. Full-blooded dryads are sensitive like that. Your mother's full-grown, though, so I couldn't control her even if I tried. But your sister…" It leans back, extending its arms along the back of the couch. "Easy enough once I got out into the real world."

I scoff and narrow my eyes. "And how long have you been driving my sister around?" I immediately regret letting my mouth run faster than my brain again, but luckily Azazel doesn't seem insulted.

"One of my roots got into her the same night I broke that ridiculous lock," it says, rolling its eyes. "Do you know how hard it was to lift that glass case with my leaves? How long it took my vines to grow to reach the door? How hard I had to push on it before it snapped? She caught me at the wrong time and we've been together ever since. Luckily I had her clean most of it up before you came along."

My stomach turns and I feel nauseous at the idea that I've been talking to a stranger for weeks and didn't even realize it. I'm a horrible brother.

This has been going on for way longer than I thought. "So you've been my sister this whole time?"

"No, not the *whole* time." It pauses and holds up its index finger. "I *did* have access to her thoughts, though. What she knows, I know. Don't get me wrong, she wasn't aware of me once I got in." It leans back again and shrugs. "Small gaps in her memory—just long enough to make her forget, in case she saw anything out of the ordinary. Tiny suggestions she'd write off as intuition—like bringing you into the conservatory or helping you get closer to a human."

"But you were—I mean, Laurel was—helping me find the thief."

Azazel narrows its eyes and its mouth spreads into a sly smile. "Is that what I've been doing? Or was I distracting you a little longer to let you think it was handled?"

Fear is overtaking me the longer I'm bound in front of this monster. How the fuck am I gonna get out of this one? Keep it talking? It obviously wants something. I shake my head and do my best to find out. "I don't understand. What do I have to do with this? Or Liam?"

"Only a human could release me. I couldn't leave on my own. I was jailed in that cell and magically sealed inside the garden. I needed someone to bring me over the threshold, and you two were my only shot."

Unbelievable. It was no accident—this was a jailbreak, and I was an accomplice. "How did you do all of this with one berry?"

"It's pretty fascinating," it says, giggling and leaning forward. "The berries are the easiest way, since the juice heals my hosts to perfect health. Plus they're delicious. The real secret is inside." It lifts up its hand and flares its fingers, turning them over and flexing them in the air. "I know you noticed my nails at the party last night. I saw you staring at them. Polite of you to not say anything, by the way—they *are* a little gross. But those were seeds sprouting from my nail beds, and all it takes is for something to swallow one for me to spread. Then I show up within hours, rinse, and repeat. The free sample station at the grocery store made things pretty handy."

For nature's sake, I've literally been seeing this monster all over for days. All I can do is close my eyes and try not to dwell on how oblivious I've been. "So I'm guessing the missing meat and dairy were you, too?"

"What can I say?" it says, still examining my sister's manicure. "My hosts need their protein. I'm a carnivore at heart, but I'm an equal opportunist. I mean, the garden kept me going fine all this time, but it was never quite enough."

I need to try to distract it. Maybe I can pull free and get out of here. "So how come you aren't controlling Liam and me?" I gently strain against the vines again, but it's in vain. There goes that brief hope. "We both had those seeds last night."

It takes a deep, exhausted breath. "Honestly? That potion you both drank. The damn Phantom Root your sister added mixed with my berry and made you immune. I've always hated that stuff. So frustrating."

An immediate relief floods my body knowing that Liam is all right. It gives me strength knowing that he's not about to be possessed next. "At least he's safe from you," I snap, my temper rearing its head.

"Ugh," it says in exasperation. "I don't understand what you see in that boy. That little fire with the Dragon's Hide was the exact opportunity for him to do what all humans do—serve their own interests. He may be different, but not *that* different."

That was the last thing I expected it to say. "*You* started the fire?"

"Technically I had your sister do it, but yeah," it says indifferently with a small nod. "It was a little sloppy, since you almost caught her leaving, but it paid off. I had to get out of the conservatory, and you needed to see the error you made with Liam. Win-win."

Suddenly I'm realizing Liam got used worse than I did. I shouldn't have blamed him as much as I did.

What he did was terrible, but it wasn't completely his fault. Azazel made him a pawn. It's been lying in wait for who knows how long, looking for the best opportunity to break free. It was only a matter of time before it coaxed someone into smuggling part of it out of the garden.

At least Liam was tempted by its healing properties—as much as I hate to admit it, a noble reason. It was awful, but he meant well. He was desperate.

As angry as I am at Liam, I feel sorry for him. The hate I held for him mixes with pity and regret for everything I said to him. It's replaced, however, with uncontrollable hatred for Azazel. White hot anger inside me bubbles over and I can't keep my mouth shut anymore. "Go fuck yourself, you parasite."

With a sharp thwack, a vine smacks me across the mouth and knocks my head back. The sharp pain mingles with a copper taste on my tongue. I clench my jaw as I find Azazel's eyes again.

It shakes its head with an exaggerated pout. "Oh Quill, there's no need for name-calling. I like you," it says with a coddling tone and a concerned expression. But within a split second, its eyes and voice become frigid and threatening. "Let's not change that."

It has me where it wants me. I'm trapped and it can keep me here for hours if it wants—maybe days—torturing me. My mind is racing for a way to escape. I need to get away from here and find a way to stop it.

"Why are you doing this?" I say, shaking my head and pulling at the vines again.

It gets up and starts pacing back and forth. "History lesson. Your bloodline's kept me trapped for eons. I don't blame you, though," it says, stopping to point at me. "You didn't do anything wrong. You don't even have powers. But I'm older than all of your ancestors combined. I had already crawled out of the primordial soup and built a kingdom by the time the first of your kind emerged from a twig. But my, how this world has changed, and boy, it suits me better than the pre-human era. These little meat sacks make it so easy to...put down roots, for lack of a better term."

"You literally got out fewer than two days ago," I say, shaking my head and narrowing my eyes. It doesn't make any sense. "There's no way you could have done all of this."

"Oh, the town will be mine by sundown," it says as it puts its hands on its hips. "The farther I spread, the faster I spread."

"Well, congratulations," I say, my voice dripping in sarcasm. "You'll be the new mayor. Then what?"

"Oh sweetheart." It chuckles. "There are seven whole continents to worry about. I have my work cut out for me."

"The world?" I ask, letting out a bark of a laugh. This really couldn't get more supervillain-y. "Are you kidding me? What's your endgame here?"

It walks to me and hunches toward me, hands on its thighs and face-to-face with me. "Humans are the world's first and only plague. I've seen their minds and learned their history. The world used to be a beautiful place, but they've outnumbered the creatures. Hunted us. Driven our kind into hiding. They aren't even safe from each other. All the blood and crime and pain… It's time the herd was culled, and if I'm the one to do it, so be it."

I clench my jaw, staring daggers into the face that used to be my sister. It hurts so much to see her like this. Maybe she can still see me, and maybe she can do something.

I mentally will her to give me a sign—anything—but the longer I stare, the more I realize there is none.

Azazel sighs, gently patting the side of my cheek. "Your mother disagreed, too. You don't understand yet, but one day you will."

I stay as still as possible, but its touch makes my blood boil with fury. I jerk away from the light graze, my stomach turning. "I still don't know why you care what I think," I spit.

"I've been trying to get to know you," it says as it stands and backs away. "You may be young, but you're complex. Full of wants and needs, starved of free will. I want to help you. I'm not evil, Quill. I just want to live. Be free. Is that so bad? Isn't that what you've always wanted, too?"

I'm stunned for a second. It's talking to me almost like a mentor.

Yes, I want those things, more than anything. But more than my mom? My sister? At the cost of others? Never. I would do anything to protect them.

It assuming that I'd put myself above them makes my blood pound in my ears. I can barely hear myself think.

But then a thought strikes me—maybe Azazel isn't evil, only warped. And all these years as a prisoner clearly haven't helped. But for it to assume that we think the same way? Absolutely not.

"You've got it all wrong," I say, my voice icy. "You know nothing about me."

"Your mother and sister did nothing but stifle you your entire life," it says, crossing its arms. "I've seen inside their minds, and they have no faith in you. But I do. You're more than ready."

Lie. This is a lie…isn't it?

That's the worst part about all of this.

Azazel is the most dangerous liar, right down to mastering someone else's face. Everything it's said has had some truth to it, and it's made it so hard to tell what's real and what's not. It's the same thing I did to my mom for weeks. Half-truths are almost worse than flat-out lies. My mother and sister have always kept me confined, but they supported me and loved me and cared for me.

They may have always reminded me that I don't have the power of a dryad, but they've never made me feel less than or pushed me aside. I've always done my best to do my part, even if that means working in the garden. In my core, I hope with everything inside me that what Azazel is saying is untrue.

I know it's untrue.

Azazel lifts its hand, coaxing a vine to stroke the side of my cheek. "You're free now, to go and do whatever you want. No overbearing mother or insufferably *perfect* sister or some human weighing you down. A God ready to walk on his own. There's nothing to be afraid of."

I know it's wrong about my mom and my sister, but what's hitting a nerve is Liam. I'm disgusted by how it used him—preyed on him. "So he was your key the entire time? You knew what he would do?"

Azazel scoffs. "You need to get past him. I told you

humans are beneath you. Trust me, I didn't mean to lead you on about him being different, but you needed to see what he is for yourself. Just like the rest of the humans. And now you can go. No one holding you back. Isn't that what you wanted?"

I shake my head. "No. I didn't want this. Any of this. This is absurd." I've never been more truthful in my entire life.

It shrugs and lets its arms fall to its sides. "I'm sorry you feel that way, but I'll make you an offer anyway—your freedom. You can walk out of here and go anywhere in the world. I'll never bother you again."

"And if I refuse?"

It sighs and folds its hands politely with a kind smile. "I'm not sure if you belong here anymore. I can't guarantee how long you would survive."

My stomach drops. The message may seem like a warning, but is a clear threat: run or die.

"I could go in there and cut you down in that conservatory." I shouldn't be so blunt, but I don't have much to lose right now.

Azazel laughs. "Like you'd actually do that. Here's the brutal truth, kiddo. I'm part of every last plant inside that garden, and we both know you won't sacrifice your precious ancestors to get rid of me. And after everything your poor mother's been through, we both know that would devastate her."

And there it is.

If I want to kill Azazel, I need to get rid of a square mile of magical forest. Impossible. Not only that, but I'd be killing the family trees. My family's magic. I'd be condemning my mother and sister to human lives with human deaths.

This isn't real. This can't be happening. "I—I can't leave them here. Not like this."

"I'll tell you what," Azazel says as it shakes its head. "Give me a few years to grow and make some backup plans. If you're feeling lonely, then I can release them. Fair?"

Rage builds up in my chest, but I hold my tongue. What it's asking is impossible. Let it completely take over? With some vague promise that it might let them go? It's not enough to go on, but it has me cornered. I don't have another choice right now.

It taps its foot. "I need an answer, Quill. Yes or no?"

I nod my head firmly, choking down my bile. I already hate myself for my answer.

"Beautiful," it says with my sister's glorious smile. It waves her arm and the vines unwind from around me, releasing my restraints. "I wanted to do this with a face you knew well so the message would sink in, and now that it has, you're free to go."

I solemnly pick up my bat, but on my way out the front door, Azazel speaks one last time.

"Don't forget, Quill—this was your only warning. Don't come back. Stay out of my way."

Tears fill my eyes as I walk out and close the door behind me.

Chapter Thirty-Seven

I stumble down the stairs of my building, dragging my bat behind me.

I feel nothing, but it's not a comfortable kind of numb. It's empty.

Azazel says I'm free. It says to give it time, and that it'll let my mom and sister go…eventually. I know it doesn't mean that. My sister and mom are gone. I'm alone.

I'll never get to talk to them again.

The thought gets bigger and bigger as the ache carves a spot in my chest, one gaping raw chunk a time.

I see my sister's face in my mind, beautiful and shining, immediately replaced by the sick version that kidnapped me. That's her now. That's reality.

It crashes over me and sucks me down, sobs bursting through my lips. I bring my hand to my mouth to stop them—maybe that'll help me get myself together—but clenching my teeth doesn't help. The sobs sit in my throat, muffled, but still captured and thrashing.

How is any of this happening?

I step into the stairwell and press my back against the cool wall, sliding to the ground. When's the last time I told my mom that I love her? What's the last thing I said to her? Nothing meaningful or important.

She was trying to shield me from this thing—a monster I helped set free—and I spent the afternoon irritated that she didn't trust me. I was being an ungrateful fucking brat.

And not even just then, but for weeks.

I pull at my hair, pounding the ground with my fist. The world is spinning through my blurred eyes, but it doesn't matter. I couldn't process any of this, and that was before my sight and hearing lost control.

My mom was nothing but kind and patient and protective and I went behind her back and broke her rules every chance I got. She was doing her best while I kept spitting in her face.

I'll never hear her stories or advice or voice again.

I'm finally on my own—something I was so desperate for—but now I'm helpless. I should have listened to her. None of this would have happened. I should have been the one to keep her safe all along.

I don't know how long I'm out there for, but the sobbing eventually slows.

My fingers wipe my face as the last traces of moisture are getting sucked back into my skin. Are those tears? When did I start crying? I didn't even feel them roll down my cheeks. The skin around my eyes feels tight and sore, lids stinging. Sweet Eden, I don't remember the last time I cried.

But now I'm empty again, which is slightly better.

I focus on the emptiness and do everything I can to keep it that way. Feeling nothing is better than whatever hurricane of emotion that was.

What does shock feel like? Is it when nothing feels real? Like I know this is actually happening, yet I can't help but hope this is all some elaborate daydream that's taken over my senses. No…this is real.

Stay numb. Stay numb, damn it. But as my sister crosses my mind…I can't.

Laurel is trapped while that thing inhabits her body. It's been using her this whole time and I've been too fucking self-centered to even see it. My sweet sister is being defiled by that thing. I should have known something was wrong.

I may not get to see my mom again, but seeing Laurel like this is worse.

It's some unholy doppelgänger of the person who knows me better than my mom—with full access to my sister's thoughts and hopes and fears, stealing them and using whatever it needs to its advantage.

Sobs and gloppy hiccups cut through my chest again, coated in toxic anger. At Azazel. At myself. If only I'd been paying better attention, maybe I could have done something. I would have done anything to stop this.

I need to save my mom and sister.

I need to kill Azazel.

I need to do whatever it takes.

Chapter Thirty-Eight

He's not my favorite person in the world right now, but I can't do this by myself. Trotting down the stairs, my fingers flit over the screen and send Liam a quick text.

Me: Where are you?

I'm barely watching where I'm going by the time I push the door open with my shoulder, staring at the screen and praying to the forest that those three dots pop up.

"I'm right here," he says.

My head shoots up, and I see him sitting on the trunk of his car. "What are you doing here?"

He shrugs and looks at me with a tiny smile. "I'm not going anywhere. I promised."

My heart swells, but he gives me a strange look. Concern fills his eyes. "Are you okay?" he asks quietly.

I must look as awful as I feel, but I don't want to break down in front of him. Not to mention—it isn't safe for us to talk in an open alley.

Azazel could be listening through any neighbor around us. I point to the car, walking around to the side. I hop into the passenger seat and toss my rose branch in the back seat. He follows on the other side and shuts the door behind him.

"Did you go inside the building?" I ask him with a sniffle. I hope he didn't.

Liam's kind enough to not point out how obviously upset I am. Against my highest hopes, he nods. "I went to check on my dad. Except…he's not my dad anymore. He's like the rest of them. It told me that it doesn't want me, only you. That I'm irrelevant and that it'll let me go if I give up on you."

I sigh, shaking my head. Damn it, it must have been so awful for Liam to see him like that. Emotions swell again, but I ignore them and focus on the fact that Liam's safe right now.

Deep breath. Numb. Clarity.

"Its name is Azazel, and it released itself weeks ago," I say. "It orchestrated this whole thing. Took over my sister, overran the garden, and led you straight to it. It knew I'd sneak you in eventually. It was waiting for the right time to lure you in so you'd bring it into the normal world."

He squints. "So…it's not my fault?"

"Oh no, you still fucked up," I say, my mouth working before my brain again. "Except you had something helping you fuck up." I could have probably been more sensitive, but there's no use sugarcoating any of this right now.

Liam looks down at his lap, twisting his fingertips absentmindedly. "I truly am sorry. I didn't mean for any of this to happen."

"Don't feel so bad," I say as I put my head back and look at the roof of the car. "It's been in there for thousands of years, biding its time. It was bound to happen sooner or later. You happened to be the tool it needed." I can't be too hard on him. It was more my fault than it was his.

We sit in silence, but Liam keeps fiddling with his knuckles. I reach over without looking, put my hand on his, and give it a gentle squeeze.

"Does this mean you forgive me?" he asks quietly.

I turn my head and look him in the eye. "Can I forgive you and be still pissed at the same time?" The last thing I want is to fight with him anymore. We have bigger things to worry about.

"I can live with that," he says with a nod and a small smirk. "So what do we do?"

I shrug. There's only one real option. "I've gotta kill it," I say decisively. "To do that, I need to destroy the garden."

"Great," Liam says. "Burn that asshole down. Good choice."

I nod and look away, thinking of everything we'll be losing once that happens. It's an impossible, heart-wrenching decision, but there's no other way.

I need to be logical right now, not emotional.

"Quill," Liam says. My face snaps back to his, and he looks so worried all of a sudden. Knitted eyebrows and those lips turned down. I know why. I realize that I didn't try to keep the devastation off my face. "What aren't you telling me?" he asks.

I bite my tongue for a second, but there's no avoiding the brutal truth. "The garden is the source of my family's magic. If it gets destroyed, we'll be…human."

"You can't do that. Not if that's the cost. There has to be another way."

I shake my head, letting a sarcastic laugh escape at the irony. To save my family, I need to let go of our legacy. I shrug. "Liam, what good is magic if it hurts more than heals? What good is magic if I don't have my mom? My sister? There's no other way."

He pauses. "You're willing to do that?"

"There isn't another choice," I say firmly. "I just don't know how to get it burning so quickly."

He's silent again for a moment. "Use an accelerant."

I should have thought of that. "Great. Gas station? Hardware store?"

"Probably not the best idea," Liam says. "Azazel most likely has puppets watching in town."

I nod. He has a good point. We need somewhere that's deserted. Suddenly, a lightbulb the size of a redwood goes off. I grin at him. "What about the high school? Paint thinner from the art classes?"

Liam nods, eyebrows raising. "I couldn't have thought of a better idea."

"I wish I knew how we could get in." It took magic to get us in the last time, and that's not something I have handy.

"With this." Liam releases my hand and digs through his pocket, producing an iridescent clover with four leaves. A Rainbow Root. "I took an extra that night, just in case. I've been keeping it with me for an emergency."

I'm royally pissed that he couldn't help but steal just about everything he could from my garden, but I chuckle because it actually paid off. Things are starting to look up. Well, as up as total chaos can look. "It's pretty safe to say that this is the best time. And starting the fire?"

Liam furrows his brow for a moment, then his face clears. "I have Trevor's lighter in my car. He left it at my house the night of the party, and I kept it with me so my dad wouldn't find it and think I smoke. And if that doesn't work, my dad keeps a camping kit in the trunk."

"At least no one can accuse you of not cleaning up

your messes." His eyes drop down, and he turns his head away as my words sink in. "Shit," I say. "Sorry. That came out harsh."

"Harsh but true." He looks down at his hands, his words coming out quiet and somber. "I'll help however I can."

Liam shoves the keys into the ignition, and the engine roars to life.

With a quick reverse and turn of the wheel, we're on our way to the school.

I keep my head held high, on a mission, but the bizarreness of Azazel's hold on the town pulls me back down. If I thought it was empty earlier, now it's positively deserted. Not a soul remains to be seen anywhere.

Probably because all the souls belong to Azazel now.

Every last man, woman, and child in the city limits is gonna be under its control within a matter of hours. It's not only my mom and sister. Every family. Every loved one. Gone.

The familiar ache creeps back in, and I'm unable to shake it.

"It was awful seeing my sister like that," I confess to Liam. "It was like some sick copy of her. It was using her voice and her face and I wanted to rip it out of her." My stomach turns at the image of those vines twisting and turning beneath her skin.

"That's how I felt about my dad," Liam says, his voice full of shame. "After what I did to you to save him…I can't help but wonder if I should have just let him go. He wouldn't have wanted this. It's not even my dad anymore."

I look over at this boy I've grown so close to and see a bit of myself. He's clenching his jaw and trying not to feel what he said. It's horrible to think about everything he's already been through, but worse now that he thinks he gave his dad a fate worse than death. "I promise, I'll try to find a way to save him," I say in the most convincing voice I have. "But we need to get rid of Azazel first."

He squeezes my hand and nods as he speeds through town. "It's so weird that it's not going after us. It makes no sense."

Now that he says it, the way Azazel was treating me doesn't add up. Even if drinking the berry with the Phantom Root protected us from Azazel to this point, the plant has enough people under its influence to come after us if it wanted to. "I don't know. It said it didn't want to hurt me. It only wants me out of the picture."

"Maybe it's so you won't fight back?" he asks, blowing through red light after red light.

I shake my head, staring out the window. "Then the easiest thing to do would be to kill me."

Black vines are starting to creep up a few of the trees on the sidewalk. Not a good sign, but I can't afford to get distracted.

"It would have done that already if it could," he says, making a sharp left.

It's true. It's had every opportunity for days now, but here I am. "What if it still needs me for something?"

"Either that or it's scared of you."

I shrug and rub the back of my neck. I haven't had more doubt in a single statement in a long time. "I don't know why. There's nothing special about me. There's nothing about me to be afraid of. My mom's the one who was the real threat, and it removed her from the equation immediately. Which makes me wonder, if she didn't stand a chance, do we even have one?"

Liam doesn't answer or speak much for the rest of the drive. I'm starting to get the feeling he thinks this plan is more of a gamble than I do. There's so much at stake, but realistically, the odds are probably one in a billion.

Azazel is as ancient as it is dangerous—not to mention, as much as I hate to admit it, pretty brilliant. There were so many moving parts to its plan and it executed them all with surgical precision. Who knows how many scenarios it's prepared for? How many defense systems it has set in place?

We pull up to the school, the parking lot as empty as it was the night we snuck in. It's a good sign—Azazel probably has no idea what's coming. We need to keep it that way.

After grabbing an empty duffel bag from the back seat and walking up to the door, Liam pulls out the Rainbow Root. It stings to know this is exactly what he did the night he kissed me, the moment he got the chance. The moment he broke my trust.

"You okay?" he asks me.

I nod, cautiously hopeful, but still struggling to hold together the pieces. "Yeah," I lie. "We've gotta move fast. I don't want anyone seeing us." *I need to give him more credit. He's trying to make this right.* Even though I'm worried this plan will fail worse than we can imagine.

"Here," he says, holding the sprig out to me. "You do it. We have only one and I don't wanna mess it up."

I take the clover between my fingertips, but the second I do, it shrivels into a black stem.

Chapter Thirty-Nine

"What the hell?" I drop the shriveled root in shock.

"What happened?" Liam asks, eyes going wide.

I shake my head, gritting my teeth. "Fucking Azazel. It's still controlling the garden. It's probably absorbing any magic that's come out of there." I close my eyes and count back from ten so I can center my anger. "What do we do?"

Liam bends down near the edge of the sidewalk and picks up one of the large rocks lining it. "Old-fashioned way, I guess."

I back up as he uses every ounce of his strength to bash a hole in the glass on the door. Reaching around the sharp edges, he presses the lever inside and lets us in.

"Let's just get this over with," I say under my breath. I'm not about to give Azazel the opportunity to keep fucking us over.

Down the halls and into the art room, Liam goes straight for the cabinets.

He throws them open and starts pulling out can after can of paint thinner—at least ten. I'm not sure if that'll be enough to start the size of fire we need, but it's definitely enough to weaken Azazel.

All that needs to happen is to get the blaze to the point where it's uncontrollable. Then we need to run as fast as we can while it spreads on its own and consumes the magic. A pang jolts through my stomach at the idea of actually destroying my family's legacy.

"I wish we had something to distract it with," I say, thinking out loud. "Especially since it's using my sister's body and powers."

I'm focusing as hard as I can, running every play I can imagine. I can't send Liam in as a decoy, and it would see right through me if I came barging in. It would take Liam and me out in no time. I don't know of any other dryads. And for all I know, it's only Liam and me left in this entire town who aren't possessed. Nothing seems doable.

Liam pauses, his eyes suddenly lighting up. "I've actually got the perfect thing." He walks over to a nearby drawer and digs through, pulling out a plastic bag filled with little rubber tubes of every color. "Throw that stuff in the trunk. I'll be right back." He grabs a small basket from the teacher's desk and bolts out the door.

The amber sunlight streaks through the blinds in the dark art room, and I stand there watching the specks of dust float in and out of the rays' reach. The quiet invites the demons out of my heart.

What if this doesn't work? What if I'm playing right into Azazel's hand?

The doubt is awful, at least until a worse thought crosses my mind: what if Liam gets caught in the crossfire? Yet another casualty caused by my recklessness.

I choke back another sob, hugging my arms across my chest.

No. I can't think like this. I need to have faith and focus on the plan.

It has to work.

I wipe my face and pile the cans into the duffel, one by one. I sling the heavy bag over my shoulder, walking back out the front of the school, leaving those dark thoughts behind. With a quick pop of the trunk, I set the bag against the side. Liam comes out holding his basket as I finish.

He lifts the basket, incredibly proud of himself. "Water balloons filled with pool chemicals. I'm assuming she soaks up liquid like you do. If the water made you sick the night we came here, I figure it should at least slow her body down."

A smile spreads across my face. "You're a genius," I tell him, but that same worry about him putting himself in danger creeps back in. I pretend like it's not there.

"I try." He sets the basket inside the car and closes the trunk. "Now we only need somewhere to hide for a while so it thinks we left. Any ideas?"

"We need somewhere private. Hard to get to." Only one place comes to mind. "How about the cave? There are definitely no people over there. No way it can spy on us." And maybe I can think of a way to keep him safe while we're there.

He nods. "Great. Let's go."

We don't have much to say on the way down the highway and up the mountain. The anxiety is palpable, but it's like we made an silent agreement not to speak about the plan. Just to be together.

His hand clasps mine while I look out the window,

wondering what'll become of the town by tomorrow.

Everyone will be possessed.

Azazel will have full control, waiting for others to pass through and get infected. It'll be in the nearby towns before we know it.

Liam remembers which tree to turn at without my help, to my surprise. I guess he was paying closer attention than I had thought. It shouldn't surprise me, though—he's been so observant of everything since the very beginning. Nothing gets past him. I didn't give him enough credit.

My heart fills with admiration for him.

Car bumping all the way through the overgrown path, we reach the gravel clearing and shut the car off.

He takes a deep breath. "We should probably talk about a game plan. I'm thinking we do this tomorrow morning. Let Azazel think it's gotten away with its plan and then we jump."

I nod. "Sounds good to me. When we get there, I'll clear the vines and go inside. I'll distract Azazel while you burn it down."

"And how are you planning on getting through the vines? I saw how quickly they were growing while we drove to the school. I'm assuming it's even worse inside your house."

"Actually, I have just the thing." I get out of the car and pull my bat out of the back seat. He opens the driver's side door and stands up, leaning on the car.

"Watch this." I walk up to a nearby tree, gripping the bat on my shoulder, and swing.

The second the thorns make contact with the trunk, the entire tree shrivels, and its dead leaves rain on the ground. I literally knock the life out of it.

I place my hand on the tree, feeling the death within

it. It pains me that I did this to a living thing, but an actual spark of hope ignites in my chest. For the first time since meeting Azazel, I have a feeling that we might have an actual chance at stopping the parasite.

"Good God," he says, eyes wide. "Thanks for not hitting me with that the first night."

"I think it works only on plants," I say, still processing what I saw it do. "Must be something my mom did to it when she gave it to me. Wish she had told me."

"Can I try?" he asks, walking over and holding out his hand.

I hesitate for a moment, not wanting to harm another tree, but I hold out the handle. I'd feel better knowing Liam is safe, too. "Mind the thorns."

Liam throttles the branch as he aims at another tree. Adjusting his fingers and stance, he winds up and uses every muscle in his body to demolish the trunk in front of him.

Right as it makes contact, it bounces off with a loud thunk. His shoulders sink as he turns to give it back to me.

"Must be a dryad thing," he says, disappointed.

Strange, but I'm thankful the tree is unharmed. Usually enchanted plants work for whoever's holding them. "Guess so." I take it and gently swing it into a shrub next to me, withering it. At least it works for me.

"Now all we have to do is wait. Wanna go inside?"

I nod, walking up to him and taking his hand.

Chapter Forty

"Think we could get some sparks again?" Liam asks as we reach the heart of the cave, the coolness of its walls and shadows surrounding us. Liam takes my hand, and I squeeze it tight in response, not wanting to let go even for a minute. Part of me wants to kiss him right now and never stop. I think I'm losing my mind. It literally feels like the end of the world, yet right now, all I can think of is holding him close. This can't be normal. I'm getting carried away, and I need to keep it together.

I release his fingers, bending down to pick up a Light Cap. With a simple flick, I illuminate the room with brilliant sparks. He shuts off his phone and eases himself down to the ground against the wall. With a couple of pats on the ground, he invites me to sit beside him. I'm more than happy to.

Liam pulls me close. The earthy smell of the rocks and the woodsy smell of him mix, almost creating a bubble of safety. It's only us. We sit in silence for a few minutes, doing nothing but being. Existing.

"What if we just ran?" he asks quietly. "Gave it what it wants?"

"And go where?" I look at the lights dancing in the air.

I feel his shoulders shrug. "Anywhere. Up north, down south. A city, a beach, the mountains. Get as far away from here as possible. We'd be safe and we'd be together."

A life with him. It sounds like Eden, and I want it more than anything, but I shake my head.

"I can't. I know its plans and I can't let that happen." I have a duty to fix this. I may not be as strong as my mom or sister, but it was the first dryad who imprisoned this thing. The oldest of my grandmothers passed this danger down, and now this is my responsibility.

He takes a deep breath before turning his head and kissing my temple. "You're right. I know you're right. Then it's decided."

It isn't fair of me to let him do this. He's human. He's fragile. This isn't his fight—this is mine. I take a deep breath and try to convince him as earnestly and delicately as possible.

"Liam, I know you're probably scared. I get it. You don't need to do this."

He squints like I spoke a foreign language. "What are you talking about?"

I sit up to look in those gorgeous blue eyes. "I promise I'll do everything I can to save your dad, but please don't put yourself in danger. Time is running out. You can still go. I'll be happy as long as I know you're safe."

I'm expecting him to argue, but all he does is smile. "Remember what I told you the night we came here?"

I shake my head and meet his eyes. "What?"

"I told you I would protect you. I won't let anything bad happen to you."

My heart feels so full, but a tragic feeling sits at the center of my chest.

A lot of people have told me that they would protect me. My mom. My dad. Liam. But it may not work this time—at all. This could be the end of everything.

"Liam… If I don't make it out of this…"

He presses his palm against my mouth. "Don't say things like that."

I pull away and look into his eyes, tears brimming in my own. My fucking emotions are boiling over again, and I can't escape them.

"Then I'll say this. When we were fighting earlier today, I cut you off, but I heard you. I don't know what love feels like, but I do know you're the only person I'd want to be here with. And I can't imagine a world without you."

A gigantic smile spreads across Liam's face—a look of pure joy.

I meant what I said. Liam's become so important to me—a crucial part of my life—that I could never imagine letting him go. He saved me in so many ways, and even though he may have stumbled, he's stayed true. Kind. Reliable. He's accepted me for everything I am, and more.

And if love feels stronger than this? He's the one I want to feel it with.

He pulls me in for a kiss, passionate and deep and endless. All around us, the glittering lights deepen, brighter than they ever had been before, and flood the cave with a warm golden light.

We break apart as he lies on the ground and pulls me toward him.

I lay my head on his chest, hearing the light thumps of his heart. I close my eyes, remembering the way he tastes—my new favorite flavor. All around me, his breathing echoes off the rocky walls, and his warmth soothes me against the cold earth.

They're the last things I sense before I drift away.

Images pass in my mind.

I'm standing in the garden on the path in front of my family trees, but everything is dark. I could have sworn I was alone, but the closer I walk to the grove, I see that another figure is much closer—it's my dad.

I sigh with relief, knowing he's here to help, but suddenly he lifts a stick in the air and a black flame explodes from the end. His head twists toward me with bright red eyes and a wicked smile. My blood runs cold as my breath catches in my throat.

"I'll protect you," he says with wild laughter.

He throws the torch toward my grandmother's tree, twisting and warping it as the onyx fire travels upward. Hundreds of screams burst from the canopy above, warping into wild, ear-splitting laughter.

Pure terror possesses me to a depth I've never felt—urging me to run, fight, do *something*—but I'm frozen in place watching everything burn. I'm helpless.

My body flails in the dirt of the cave, my hand scraping on the rocky wall as my eyes shoot open. It's pitch-black and I'm freezing.

"Liam?" I call, reaching out around me.

He doesn't answer, and a pool of dread grows in my chest. I scoop up another few mushrooms and throw them into the air, showering the room in starry spores.

He's nowhere to be seen.

Chapter Forty-One

It's fitting that the new moon leaves the sky in the same state as my heart: empty.

I knew it would be a long way back to town, but at least I've been pushed to the point of being numb. I honestly don't know if I'd make it if I had to bear the full weight of the last day.

He left me.

He left me in the middle of the woods and saved himself.

He lied to me again, but this time I'm glad he did.

My heart is broken, but this means he'll survive. And that's something.

All through the night, I stumble down the mountainside, over fallen trees and craggy ground. I focus on my feet, commanding my legs to walk.

It doesn't matter that it hurts to feel. Or think. Or breathe.

I have somewhere I need to be and people relying on me to get there.

I feel like a calf walking into a wolf den. My chances weren't great when Liam and I were working together, but they're slim to none now. I know I can't fight Azazel and torch everything down at the same time.

My only hope is that I can kick the snowball down the hill and let gravity take care of the rest. The fire will do most of the work for me depending on how long I can keep fighting. Still, it's a kamikaze mission with no alternatives.

I switch the duffel from shoulder to shoulder as I get to the highway, over and over every quarter of a mile or so to ease the weariness of my muscles. The bat weighs almost nothing compared to the paint thinner.

About halfway back to town, I realize he didn't bother leaving me any of the balloons to ward off anti-Laurel. Oh well, probably better that way. With my luck, they would have burst all over me and left me helpless on the side of the road.

Not one car leaves town during my journey. It's a small highway to begin with, but it makes it all that much eerier. Azazel's plan must have worked by now, controlling everyone in the city limits.

It's obvious by the time I walk into the first suburb as the sun peeks over the horizon. No people—too early for that anyway—but each and every tree, bush, and shrub are knotted full of spiny black vines.

Azazel wasn't kidding when it said it works fast. I stay as far away from any plant I see on my way back home to avoid tipping it off that I've returned. Most likely for the last time.

I didn't think any of this could get worse, but right now, it's beyond bleak.

My heart aches that Liam betrayed me not only once,

but twice. He promised he would be there with me. Protect me. On the other hand, wherever he is, I'm glad he'll be safe. But I'd be lying if I said that him being with me didn't give me the smallest bit of strength I had left.

I left my phone in his car, so I can't even try to say goodbye one last time.

I'll need to settle for last night—it's all I have. Hopefully he survives and lives a long and happy human life. The truth is that no matter what he's done to me, no matter how hurt I am, I can't bring myself to wish him harm. He made the smart decision by saving himself.

I get to my building and the sight makes my pulse and fear rise to dangerous heights.

This is it—now or never.

I sneak around back, on the off chance Azazel has spies on the lookout, and open the back door of my building.

I walk quietly up the stairs, listening for any puppets that may be around. I get lucky—it's empty. I would have thought protecting the garden would be priority number one for Azazel, but it seems I was wrong. Maybe it thinks the threat to the garden has been sufficiently neutralized and is focusing its efforts elsewhere. Better for me.

I go down the hallway and silently open the front door.

It's still unlocked from the last time I was here. Mass-murdering forces of evil don't need to worry about home security.

I look around, and thank nature it didn't leave my sister's shell here to guard it. It did, however, take over the inside of the apartment.

Black vines and spines are everywhere, on every piece of furniture and inside every houseplant, strangling each thread and tendril. Everything I know and love, warped, wrong, and endangered.

This needs to end. I tiptoe around them like they are a web of lasers, careful to not alert Azazel. At last, I get to the hallway.

I'm as focused as I've ever been. I have no room for error. The second I bust through the garden door, I need to run in and douse as much as I can with the accelerant. How long do I have? One minute? Maybe two before it comes running down from Laurel's apartment to stop me? After that, it's me and my rose branch versus Azazel and my sister's powers.

I set down the duffel and stare at the closet door to the garden writhing in vines. I can't imagine the horrors I'm about to see inside. And what I'm about to do? I'd rather beat a thousand hornet nests than go forward with this plan. So much safer. But there's no other option.

I grip my bat and steady it on my shoulder.

Three deep breaths later, I swing at the door as hard as I can, the vines falling to the ground as dust at first contact.

I suck in another gasp of air, shocked that it took only a single blow, but I don't have time to think about it.

As fast as I can, I snatch up the bag and throw the door open.

Chapter Forty-Two

Pins and needles assault my skin—it's worse than I imagined. Not only are the trees gnarled and twisted and coated in spines, but red prevails over all. The leaves, the fruits, the grass—even the soft starry sky that was once so deep and dark burns ruby.

The heat in here is sweltering, hotter than any summer day.

Azazel's taken over, and danger closes in all around me. The garden belongs to it now. I'm in the belly of the beast.

Grabbing the cans and ripping off the tops, I frantically soak the tall grass and crimson blossoms in the foul-smelling paint thinner.

"I knew you would be back," the voice of Azazel whispers from inside the flowers all around me. Azazel is possessing them and using them as speakers for its own voice. So it is in the garden, after all. Probably waiting for me, knowing I would be foolish enough to come back.

I ignore it, digging into my rage, and keep dousing. Can

after can, I go until every last drop is on the earth and tree trunks around me. I'm terrified, but it's almost over.

"We can work this out," the flowers try to sway me. "Why don't you come and meet me by your family trees?"

"Fuck you," I snarl. The fumes from the paint thinner strip me of my sense of smell and remind me there's only one way this can end.

I pull the lighter out of my pocket and flick the wheel with my thumb. I take a deep breath and look as the small orange flame ignites. *I did it.* But right as I'm about to drop the lighter, the flowers speak once more.

"Do what you must," they say from every different direction. "If you want to burn the ones you love, go ahead. They're already here. We've been waiting for you. Otherwise, I'd get to walking."

I freeze, a sharp pain shooting through my chest.

My mom and sister are in here. It knew I would come back. For the love of everything fucking good in the world, it planned this, too.

I'm soaked in sweat and doing everything I can to not start hyperventilating, but then it dawns on me—there's nothing I can do. I close my eyes. Didn't I see this coming? I close the lighter and shove it in my pocket before grabbing my bat.

I'm terrified, but I'll be damned if I go down easy. I walk down the cobblestone path under the bloodred sky.

Gnarled and twisted, the corrupted garden surrounds me the farther I go—vines writhing and slithering, a soft creaking coming from all around. It feels as though it's closing in, but that must be my imagination. I hope it is, at least, until I turn around—my path back out is completely blocked by a wall of thorns. I was holding out one last hope to escape, but I've just about given up.

It has me. It's over.

I walk to the tallest trees in the garden, now in full bloom with crimson leaves. It's as breathtaking a sight as it is earth-shattering. My ancestors stand strong but are perverted in this warped world. My entire history is before my eyes and taken over by something dark and hungry.

I walk closer to the largest trunk as something emerges from the treetops.

Vines lift Laurel's form down from above, followed by my mother's sleeping body—wrapped from neck to knee and dangling right above the ground. My gut wrenches at the sight, but I'm powerless. I want nothing more in the world than to reach out and rip them down, but Azazel would tear me to pieces before I could even take two steps.

Tears well in my eyes, but I refuse to let Azazel see me break. I won't give it the satisfaction.

Azazel lithely steps down into the grass, vines unwinding around it as it rights itself up and smooths its clothes.

Black tendrils have sprouted out of my sister's skin on the sides of her face, twisting upward into a thorny black crown. A jolt shoots through my stomach seeing Laurel trapped inside, stuck as part being and part plant.

Its mouth contorts into a small smile.

"It took you long enough." Its voice continues to echo from the blossoms all around me. I think Azazel's gotten exponentially stronger, and it hasn't even been a day.

I stop in the middle of the meadow. "Sorry. I was a little far from home."

Azazel shrugs. "Liam's been waiting here with me all day long." With a wave of its hand, vines rotate around the trunk of the tree and pull him front and center.

Like my mother, he's completely bound. My heart feels as strangled as he looks.

"At least since he tried to burn the whole building down."

I know I'm breathing, but it feels like I can't get enough air. Liam didn't leave me—he came ahead of me. He was trying to save me. Suddenly I notice Azazel, doing its best to suppress it, but is shivering uncontrollably in my sister's body.

And there it is—the thing I needed the most. Hope.

"Not looking so hot," I say with a smirk, confidence growing as I remember Liam's water balloons. "What's the matter? Chlorine not agreeing with you?"

"Minor inconvenience," it says with narrowed eyes. "Trust me, though. Liam paid for it." Out of the corner of my eye I see the vines hug him tighter to the tree. "I truly was hoping you'd accept my offer. I clearly underestimated how much he means to you. My mistake."

"He's not the kind of human you think he is," I say defiantly as I grip my bat.

Azazel looks down at my hand and smiles. With a flick of its fingers, vines shoot out from behind me and snatch the bat from my hand. "Doesn't matter. New plan and last chance. Leave or I squeeze the life out of him and feast on his flesh in front of you. Try that one on for size."

I stand there in the meadow, helpless.

That brief chance I had—gone.

Azazel finally stripped me down and found a pressure point. No more options and no more game plans. It's over.

There's nothing I can do to save my sister. Or my mom. Or Liam. How did this all happen? How could I have been so happy for such a short time, finally getting everything I ever wanted, only for it to be ripped away?

I don't think I'll ever see them again. I know Azazel will never free them. They're going to die here, sucked dry by this parasite. This is all my fault for not seeing the signs sooner. And I'm lost.

My life has no meaning without the people I love. I'll be truly alone. I think of all the times my sister gave me a hard time, the times my mom ruffled my hair, and the sweetest moments I shared with Liam. They're all gone. There won't be any more. Just a life of true loneliness.

I could have had a future, and for just the smallest amount of time, I believed it. But Azazel took that from me. I was careless with forces I didn't understand. I had one job—protect the garden—and I ruined all of their lives. Not just Liam's and my family's but everyone in this town. I would give anything to undo it, to go back and try again. There are so many things I could fix. But it's too late.

My emotions well up, and it takes everything in my power to choke down a sob. "One last kiss. Please. I'm begging you."

"Disgusting," Azazel says as it rolls its eyes. "If that's what it takes to convince you, fine, if you must."

I walk past Azazel, eyes locked on Liam. *This is it. This may be the last time I see him.* As quickly as the thought appears, I banish it. I can't accept that.

"I'm so sorry," I tell him, cupping his cheek in my palm. "I'm going to find a way to save you. I swear."

"Save yourself," Liam chokes out, struggling to breathe against the constricting ropes. It's agony to see him like this—it would almost be better if he were unconscious like my mom. "Please, for me," he continues. "It'll let your family out eventually. Just let me go."

I squeeze my eyes shut and rest my forehead on his. I failed.

I'm losing everyone I've ever loved.

Tears sting my eyes, overflowing as they roll down my cheeks and drip from my chin. Then, I hear a sizzle.

Chapter Forty-Three

I open my eyes to see a vine withering by my feet, life being sucked clean out of it.

There's no way. That shouldn't be happening. It's impossible. I wipe a still-fresh tear from my face and drop the moisture down toward the garden floor.

Another sizzle, and I watch in shock as the vine where my tear landed shrivels into nothing.

This is the power she was trying to teach Laurel in the shop the day she met Liam. I've seen this happen only with my mother's touch. It's the same magic she enchanted inside the bat. The darkest of our gifts, ones Laurel thought were unnatural.

Only it wasn't the bat. It wasn't my mom.

It was me.

Every strange thing that's happened to me—rotting the fruit, the rosebush turning to dust, the Rainbow Root shriveling... Azazel doesn't kill plants; it only takes them over.

It was me all along. That's what Azazel was afraid of.

My sister could always grow things without even trying, but I can do the opposite.

Kill.

Hope. Anger. Strength.

It all flows through me, awakening something inside.

I embrace all my emotions, feeling them as deeply as I can as I focus on every bit and method of magic I've ever seen my mom and sister do.

I'm so grateful for the miracles my family's shown me—they may not have been teaching me, but I still learned from the best.

Suddenly it all makes sense, as an energy swells inside my chest.

It's raw power.

I press my hands to Liam's vines, drawing the power out of the void growing inside me. "Embody the decay," I whisper. "Winter incarnate."

My fingers buzz with energy that bursts out and seeps into the vines. Like a row of dominoes, the plants dissolve, starting with the vines holding Liam, up the tree, and ending at the ones holding my mother. Their bodies fall to the ground.

"No," Azazel says, eyes wide.

Instant relief floods my heart. Hope springs through my chest as I see them released, only Laurel still cradled in the spiny black vines.

I stare Azazel straight in the eyes, resolute and channeling all my fury. "Nice try."

"It's too late, dryad," it says through gritted teeth.

Raising both of its hands causes the grass in the meadow to sharpen as vines erupt from the soil.

They whip toward me, trying to pull me down onto the spikes, but each one disintegrates as it touches my skin.

Azazel can't touch me.

I smile, knowing with every inch of my being that I can do this. I lift my knee and stomp the ground, the blades the creature created shattering throughout the field.

A pulse of energy travels down my body and ripples from my foot, washing over the entire area. The grass twists and warps into black wisps, flecks of dead sprigs releasing into the still air.

Azazel steps back, its eyes frantically looking around until they settle on Liam. "You might be able to save yourself, but he's not getting out of here alive," it says with a wicked smile. "I'll take him down with me, and you can live with that for a thousand years."

Clenching both fists, Azazel points every leaf from every tree toward Liam—millions of razors poised to shoot.

A calm knowing takes over me from the depth of my soul as I hold my palm out in front of my mouth. The razor-sharp leaves hurtle forward, but as I blow, a black fog rolls toward them.

Every blade in its path goes up in powder, deadly air creating a wall between Azazel and us. Laurel's body chokes as the piece of Azazel inside her is poisoned by the cloud.

I know Azazel won't give up. It's time to end this.

I turn and press my hands to our most ancient tree, right at the base of the trunk. This is the moment—I have no other choice, but that doesn't make it any easier.

"Please forgive me," I whisper as I close my eyes, already grieving my family line. "The magic of life, back to its source."

I swear, for that one moment, every one of my ancestors is standing beside me.

I feel them pressing their hands into me.

I feel their power, their love, and it's flowing into me. A howling wind begins to blow, fanned by the thousands of trees as they flail and are ripped apart cell by cell. The vortex picks up speed and closes in on the monster, mixing with its shrieks as it whips around faster and faster, until it's nothing but a blur. And then until it's nothing at all.

Laurel's body falls to the ground, the wind slows, and I release the tree.

Chapter Forty-Four

As the last tree in front of me fades into smoke, my power fades as well.

I run to Laurel's side and drop down next to her. Her skin and eyes are back to normal, but she's shivering and sobbing.

"Laurel, are you okay?" I say, grabbing her hand, worried.

"I w-was so afraid," she wails as she sits up and clings to me. "P-please f-f-forgive me."

"Shh, it's okay," I tell her, smoothing her hair. "It's over now. It's not your fault. You're safe."

I hold her and let her cry. I can feel her pain—the helplessness, the trauma, and the despair. I want to reach inside and take it all away, but I'm powerless. There's nothing I can do but be there for her. At least I can do that.

I know her.

She's going to blame herself for this for who knows how long. Her breathing returns to normal and I pull away to look her in the eye. I smile as I wipe one of her tears away, returning a polite grin and nodding to help her get up. I pull her to her feet.

"Are you okay to stand?" I ask her.

She nods, doing her best to stop her teeth from chattering. It hurts me to my core to see her like this. Without the hot spring, she'll need to be in the bathtub for days to soak out the chemicals.

"How are my kids?" my mom's voice asks from behind me. I turn and find her hobbling over, clinging to Liam's arm. Her bright red curls are mixed with white, her skin not nearly as bright as it always was.

"Mom, your hair," I say, my gut wrenching as I reach out, grab hold of a lock between my fingers. "And you have wrinkles. Are you okay?"

"I'm fine," she says. "The garden is gone. Half the lifespan of a dryad means more than half the lifespan of a human. I'm only starting to look my age."

My heart breaks to think of losing her sooner than I ever wanted to. I've hurt her so much by doing what I did.

"Mom, I'm so sorry," I say.

"It's okay, sweetheart," she says, rubbing my shoulder. "It's the price you had to pay. Our power means nothing compared to saving everyone." I look her over again—taking in each detail—and she means the words she says. She stands strong, wise, and beautiful.

"But Quill, your hair, too…" Liam breathes, reaching forward and running his fingers through it.

I grab a chunk of it, but it feels the same. I pluck a strand and examine it. As black as can be, almost absorbing the light around it—as dark as death itself. "What… How?"

"It's your magic," my mom says. Her voice shakes a little as she speaks. "I've never seen pure force like that… You did things that even I can't do, and you made them up on the spot."

"Mom..." I say, at a loss for words. "Did you know?"

"Not at all," she says, shaking her head. "But Azazel did. I could see what it was thinking when it had me under. It was terrified of you. It sensed you use your powers a couple of times without you realizing you were doing it. As long as it made you think you were powerless and as long as you went away, it was safe."

My mom looks at Liam and pats his arm, releasing it to embrace Laurel.

I hold back tears as I wrap my arms around Liam and pull him close.

"I thought you left me," I murmur.

He shakes his head against my shoulder, clinging tighter. "I was trying to save you."

"But the supplies?" I ask, pulling back to see his face.

He chuckles and runs his thumb across my cheek. "That was in case I didn't make it. Looks like you didn't even need them."

Something clicks in my mind that dims the overwhelming sense of relief in this moment. I turn and look at my mom, catching her eye. "What...what about Liam's dad?"

My mom gives Liam a kind smile. "Azazel already healed him, sweetheart. He'll be fine."

Liam's eyes go glassy. I grab his hand and give it a squeeze, doing my best to reassure him. "It's going to be okay now," I tell him as he buries his head against my shoulder again. "Everything is going to be okay."

Chapter Forty-Five

The four of us trek through the garden, which is littered with remnants of trellises and flowerpots and the cobblestone path. We're all on our way to the conservatory to make certain every trace of Azazel is gone.

I don't really know how to feel. The streams have dried up, exactly like the soil—cracked and arid. Nothing green remains. Everything in the garden appears to be dead, which means we're human now. We have nothing left except our normalcy. Life is about to change as soon as we leave this place. I don't even know if the garden will exist once we walk through that door. It wouldn't surprise me if it went up in smoke like our ancestors.

It's a dismal day for my family, but at the same time, we're alive. We have each other. I have Liam.

We get to the rare section, and the conservatory's been blown to bits. The only things that remain are a bare floor and an empty pedestal surrounded by broken glass.

"Does this mean we're safe?" I ask my mom. I'm hoping more than anything it does.

She looks at me and nods, but something catches her eye behind me. I turn to see what it is, and my heart skips a beat. Not twenty feet from us, in the now-uninhabitable soil, lies a lime-green, matte, sickly-looking fern. I close in on it carefully, staring.

It makes no sense. How did it survive?

Liam steps up beside me and wraps his hand around my waist, pulling me close. The leaves tremble the moment he does, and a bloom opens—producing the most hypnotic, heartbreakingly beautiful white light flowing from its curled petals.

As the bright light beams from it, I'm shocked, but something about it seems…right. It makes total sense, and although I didn't need it, it is concrete proof that what's between us is real. I sneak a glance at my sister and mom.

Laurel's eyes are wide. "The A-ardor B-b-blossom," my sister says. "But h-how?"

"Easy," my mom says, completely unsurprised as she smiles at me and tips her head at Liam and me. "True love."

Liam blushes and goes speechless, but I squeeze his hand to reassure him. I, however, still can't help worrying.

"But how do we know Azazel isn't part of it right now?" I ask.

My mom shakes her head. "Azazel was toxic and fueled by hate. The Ardor Blossom, on the other hand, is pure, and fueled by love. It must have been immune to Azazel."

"So what does this mean?" I ask.

My mom flourishes her hand, and the flower grows larger, but only by an inch. She smiles. "It means that things always work out, just not always in the way you expect them to."

Epilogue

It's been a week since I killed Azazel. The town is back to normal. A lot of people woke up in strange places with no memory of the few days beforehand. News stations are blaming rancid meat, and the industry is recalling every product. Nothing like a little collective denial.

For our family, as much as some things are different, one thing remains the same—the love among all of us.

My mom is moving slower than usual, but somehow I think it's made her even more patient than she used to be. Still, I know now she won't be around forever, and I feel a pang of loss whenever it crosses my mind, but I'm getting closer to accepting it.

A week of hydrotherapy fixed Laurel right up physically. But she's still pretty jarred from getting possessed. She's been staying at our house most nights. After what happened, she's not ready to be alone. I don't blame her in the slightest, and honestly, I'm happy to have her around.

My time's been spent solely with my mom and sister,

coming up with a plan of how to move forward—not only with the business but as a family. The Ardor Blossom saved us from turning fully human and saved the garden from being completely destroyed. Things might go back closer to the way they were, except not completely. The garden will get bigger, but it'll never reach where it was, at least not in our lifetime. My mom's and sister's powers don't work as well as they used to.

Nonetheless, my mother and sister are both so excited I finally got powers of my own, even if those powers aren't exactly what we pictured. My mom says it makes total sense, though. Laurel and I are two sides of the same coin, prodigies in our own ways. We each represent a cycle of life—the start and the end. Neither is good nor evil, only nature working as it's intended.

My powers haven't shown up since Azazel, but my mom says they'll come back eventually, just maybe weaker than before.

Let's be honest, though—I'm not sure how much help I'll be once the garden is up and running again. There are no more plans to capture and jail bloodthirsty specimens, so the only goal will be to keep things *alive* this time, and apparently that's not my specialty. What I can do isn't something that comes naturally to dryads—it's kind of the opposite.

The best rebuilding we've done, however, is literal rebuilding. The company my mom hired to reattach our fire escape finally came by and got the job done within a day.

Sure, I can go out into the human world whenever I want now, but there's something about my own private bubble that's special.

Well, mostly private.

• • •

"I have a surprise," I tell Liam that night as we sit outside on the fire escape in the warm night air. It's become like a ritual for us, meeting here and watching the stars every night. I push my shoulder into his, excited to break the news I've been waiting to tell him all day. "My mom signed enrollment papers this morning. Never thought I'd see the day."

Liam's eyes light up. "No *way*," he says. "This year's gonna be awesome. Max and James are gonna be so excited, too."

"Me too. I'll have to get a handle on the social anxiety thing, but…I just killed an ancient evil that was about to wipe out the human race. High school can't be that hard, right?"

Liam pulls me closer, wrapping an arm around my shoulders. "Not when I've got you," he says to me, and a shiver runs through me. I wonder if my body will ever stop reacting to him like this. I'm not sure I want it to.

"I have a surprise, too," Liam says, turning his hand palm-up on his thigh. I reach down and press my hand on his, feeling his skin on mine. "Your mom offered me a job."

I chuckle. "Doing what?"

"Stocking the flower shop now that she needs to start outsourcing. She said you're gonna be busier now that she'll be giving you lessons and sending you on trips with Laurel."

"Wow, I'm surprised she trusts you that much." I instantly cringe at how that sounded out loud. There goes my mouth again, working faster than it should.

Liam, however, laughs. "That's exactly why she offered

it. She said she needs to keep a closer eye on me, at least until she knows I've learned my lesson."

"My boyfriend the thief," I muse, looking up at the sky.

"Thief, not so much. But boyfriend? Is that what I am?"

I freeze, blushing with a twinge of embarrassment. "Uh…"

He pulls me in for a kiss. "Sounds good to me. Does this mean my dad and I are invited to family dinners?"

"Ugh, only if you promise to let me pick the produce at the grocery store," I say, exasperated that sickly vegetables have become our only option. "But sure. Are you planning on becoming a vegan?"

"If by 'vegan,' you mean, 'eat cheeseburgers in secret,' then yes."

I laugh and nudge him. "I can live with that."

"I don't know, it was pretty impressive," he says, scooting back against the brick. "It's a gift."

I scoff. "Death is not a gift." After everything I saw, I'm not sure there's much that's gonna change my mind.

Liam shrugs, folding his hands on his stomach. "Depends on what you do with it. I'm glad you have it."

"Let's see how useful it is next week," I say skeptically, crawling back to sit next to him. "First family trip."

"Oh yeah? Where you flying to?"

"Absolutely no airplanes," I say, holding my hands up. "I like my feet on solid ground, thanks. I'll stick to cars for now." I've been scared a lot in the last month, but heights are at least a normal fear. I don't even want to think about being stuck that high in the air.

"Where are you going?"

I laugh, amused at how ridiculous it is. "New Jersey."

We sit there in silence, watching the clouds roll across the black sky and the starlight fight its way down to earth.

The sweet summer wind swirls around us, but beyond that, there's not one sound coming from the night beyond.

"So, before you go on your trip," Liam says, his voice hesitant. "I wanted to ask you something."

My heart catches. I'm already not thrilled at being away from Liam for a week, but Mom and Laurel are insisting on our first family road trip to none other than Paramus, New Jersey. We need another Midas Vine, and apparently there's one being used as decoration in some outlet mall.

"What is it?" I ask, trying to keep my tone casual.

"Well…is this a good time to talk about the Ardor Blossom?"

I turn my face up to his, caught by surprise. "What about it?"

"Well, true love…" He shrugs. "Sounds kind of intense."

"Are you wanting me to say three little words right now?"

Liam chuckles, looking up at the sky. "Not necessarily. It's been only two weeks. Kind of weird for a plant to tell you something before you've even figured it out."

I gently press my fingers to his cheek and turn it to me. "Then let's settle for me telling you that you're my favorite person in the world, and I never want that to change."

"At least we'll get a discount on flowers for the wedding," he says, raising his eyebrows twice.

"I hate you."

He perks up and his voice goes higher. "Catering too! Organic, high fiber, seven courses. Homemade champagne. Watermelon for a cake."

"You are the literal worst."

He lets out a goofy laugh, leans in, and kisses me. "You're my favorite person in the world, too," he says softly.

I let out a small laugh and relax back into him, feeling his breathing and his warmth. It's bliss.

"So what's next?" I ask quietly, almost to myself.

He chuckles lightly. "It's been a pretty eventful few weeks. What more do you want?"

The question isn't lost on me. I look back into my room, the home that was lovingly built by my mother from the ground up. All the sacrifices she made to give me the life I have.

I look into the alley that I've always watched from above, and then out onto the street at its mouth. I think of how much my life has changed and the human world I was aching to be part of.

"You know what, you've got a point," I say, laying my head on his shoulder and entwining our fingers, feeling his pulse in my hand. "This is all I need."

ACKNOWLEDGMENTS

Once upon a time, I wrote a book during the pandemic. It was a hard period for everyone, and I wasn't a writer by trade, but the fact that I wasn't creating anything made it relatively unbearable. With the coaching of G.A. Johnson and Janet Walden-West, I kept going day and night to make something out of nothing. To say I literally had no idea what I was doing is an understatement.

Then the query trenches started. That was an entire war, but The Query Shark herself helped brace me. Janet Reid hacked and slashed my pages and query, teaching me so much about the dos and do-nots. I highly recommend her if you need any help whatsoever. She's fierce and unyielding and brilliant. Her reputation is well-earned.

The book itself was gritty and unpolished and…got over two hundred rejections. But I kept sending it out to anyone who might want to take it on. I'm shameless like that.

I was about to give up, but that's when I sent it to Entangled and heard immediately from my editor, Jen Bouvier. It was a dream come true. The original book died on the vine, but we collaborated on a new project instead—the very one you just read. It's been a hell of a ride, but Jen's been with me every step of the way. I owe Entangled so much for making this happen. Eternally grateful doesn't even begin to cover it.

It was at that point that I found my rock star of an agent, Ramona Pina. She got my vision from day one and has been my champion for all things, literary or otherwise. She's gone to bat for me, shielded me, and read my mind more times than I can count. I'm so fortunate to have her in my corner and wouldn't choose another human being in the world.

But my true Swiss Army knife? My critique partner, Jenny Lane. She's been a listening ear, a warm shoulder, and her mind works in ways that I'll never stop marveling at. Jenny's been with me from the very beginning, rejections and all, and I couldn't ask for a better friend in the world of words. She's talked me out of so many self-imposed corners and brought new life to *Evergreen* in more ways than I can count. I honestly wouldn't have gotten this far without her constant support. (I'm needy. She won't tell you that. But I will.)

I want to thank my alpha and beta readers: Emily Fowler, Amethyst Johannes, Carla Gutiérrez, Kenneth Creech, and Aya Maguire. Their perspectives helped give the story a depth it needed and kept me on track when I wasn't sure what the hell I was doing.

My family, friends, and agent siblings have been constant supporters as well. Writing a book is hard, but when you have a community of people around you who love and support you, the process only gets easier. I wasn't sure I could write a book, much less two. But they made me believe I could.

I also want to thank all the brilliant people at Entangled. Thank you to everyone who's helped with the contracts, PR, marketing, and especially the cover art and copy edits. Elana Cohen, thank you for your expert perspective. I appreciate the heart you put into this. LJ Anderson, you're a genius artist, and I feel so lucky to have your talent on this project. Nancy Cantor, you're a gem. Your attention to detail astounds me.

And most of all, thank you, dear reader, for picking this up off the shelf. I'm so grateful for you, and I hope you fell in love with Quill and Liam the way I did.

Evergreen is a fast-paced exciting paranormal romance with a happy ending. However, the story includes elements that might not be suitable for all readers. Mentions of past assault, blood, illness, past loss of a loved one, cancer, anxiety, panic attacks, swears or curses, fire, nightmares of traumatic events, hospitalization, terminal illness, and mind control are shown in the novel. Readers who may be sensitive to these elements, please take note.

Let's be friends!

@EntangledTeen

@EntangledTeen

@EntangledTeen

@EntangledTeen

bit.ly/TeenNewsletter

entangled teen

an imprint of Entangled Publishing LLC